FOUR WAYS OF BEING HUMAN

Also by Gene Lisitzky

THOMAS JEFFERSON

4/9/65

FOUR WAYS OF

An Introduction to Anthropology

What is man, that thou shouldest magnify him? and that thou shouldest set thine heart upon him? —JOB 7:17

BEING HUMAN

by GENE LISITZKY

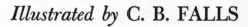

Illustrated by C. B. FALLS

PUBLISHED BY THE VIKING PRESS

To
Wanda

CONTENTS

AUTHOR'S NOTE   9

INTRODUCTION   13

I. SEMANG: PEOPLE OF THE RAIN FOREST   27

    1. The Jungle   29

    2. The Kinship Band   33

    3. Life in the Bamboo Age   40

    4. Family Life   49

    5. The Invisible World   56

II. POLAR ESKIMOS: PEOPLE OF THE ICECAP   65

    1. Discovery of the Northernmost People   67

    2. The Innuit   70

    3. The Igloo   73

    4. Clothes   80

    5. Hunters of the North   84

    6. The Dog Sledge   94

    7. The Odyssey of Kridlarssuark   100

    8. Fear   109

    9. The Brighter Side   114

    10. The Family   118

    11. The Year's Cycle   123

III. MAORIS: People of the Pacific   129

    1. Long White Cloud   131

    2. *Mana* and *Tapu*   140

    3. The Warriors   151

    4. The Artists   167

    5. Making a Living   181

    6. Making a Maori   192

    7. The Rediscovery of Long White Cloud   203

IV. HOPIS: People of the Desert   211

    1. A Short History of the Pueblo Culture   214

    2. The Peaceful People   228

    3. Mother Corn   240

    4. Clan Mothers and Priest-Chiefs   247

    5. The Dancers of Tusayan   255

    6. Kachinas and Snakes   263

    7. The Road of Life   273

    8. A Day of Peace   284

INDEX   299

The masks appearing as chapter decorations in this book were used in religious ceremonies by the Eskimos and Hopis. The Maori masks were purely decorative.

AUTHOR'S NOTE

When I first thought of this book, more than twenty years ago, it was not only because I felt sure that the exotic materials of primitive societies must be naturally attractive to young readers. I was also thinking of anthropology as the perfect educational tool it is—a mind stretcher, prejudice dissolver, and taste widener. I could conceive of no better road by which to lead young students into the other social sciences. In anthropology they would find geography and history, economics and sociology, clothed in their most meaningful as well as most colorful terms, easy to assimilate and, above all, not artificially separated or abstrusely generalized as they apparently must be in their own textbooks. Art and technology, language and law, could all be seen in their mutual interrelations because they were shown to be only different ways of looking at the same single whole called culture. I confidently expected that someday elementary anthropology must become part of the standard high-school curriculum.

As far as I know, this has not yet happened, in spite of the fact that, meanwhile, a world war, the United Nations, and America's new role in world affairs have enormously quickened our awareness of other peoples and other cultures. Perhaps my small daughter, who is being taught something called "social studies" in place of the geography and history of my own public school days, is thus being prepared for that next step into anthropology proper. I hope so, and if hope must be deferred again, she may at least have this book.

9

When such a book is undertaken by one who is by profession neither an anthropologist nor an educator, it is all the more seemly that it make due acknowledgment of the debts it owes to the writings of others. Unfortunately, this is easier said than done. After a quarter-century of reading by fits and starts, and of even more fitful note-taking and writing, I cannot possibly hope to remember all my debts. Most of the writers from whom I have learned all I know or believe about man and his cultures have, by a process they would themselves understand best, become anonymous parts of my own culture. My thanks to them, and my plea for indulgence for having interpreted them as I have, are none the less sincere for having to take this comprehensive and broadcast form.

It is only by the merest haphazard of my personal history that certain names have not been lost against the background of my general education. These I am glad to mention, not only out of a gratitude which I owe equally to the others, but because they should also be of some interest to readers who can be persuaded to go on to the original sources in the subject.

I owe my own first undergraduate enthusiasm for anthropology to the lectures and numerous writings of Franz Boas, acknowledged father of the American school. His famous student Ruth Benedict, whom I was privileged to know personally, kept that interest alive and warm until after I had begun the first preparations for this book. While still on the subject of general anthropology I must mention, as a work I have kept close at hand for many years, C. Daryll Forde's *Habitat, Economy and Society*. It is a mine of succinct information on the actual living techniques of many primitive peoples, as well as a valuable point of departure for further reading.

The writers on whom I have chiefly drawn for the chapter on the Semang are W. W. Skeat and C. O. Blagden, Ivor H. N. Evans, and Paul Schebesta, whose works are, of course, standard sources.

It is not so easy to sort out of the much greater mass of Eskimo literature the writers on whom I most depended. But first I must thank Vilhjalmur Stefansson for once having given me a quick sketch-map for guidance through this vast terrain, a kindness he must long ago have forgotten. It is an exciting literature, whether written by daring explorers or professional anthropologists, and includes such names as Sir John Ross, Fridtjof Nansen, Knud Rasmussen, Charles Francis Hall, Julian Bilby, Kaj Birket-Smith, and Peter Freuchen. Stefansson's own works are, of course, indispensable, and I would especially recommend even for young readers his *My Life with Eskimos* and *The Friendly Arctic*. A fascinating history of the whole drama of Arctic exploration is Jeannette Mirsky's *To the North!*

Two exciting early works on the white man's first contacts with the Maoris are *The Journals and Voyages of Captain Cook* and Frederick E. Maning's *Old New Zealand*. Among other writers on the native New Zealanders I have read with profit are Edward Tregear, Felix Keesing, Elsdon Best, Raymond Firth, and J. C. Beaglehole. I feel I should reserve a special sentence of indebtedness for *The Coming of the Maori* and the older *Vikings of the Sunrise* by Sir Peter Buck (Te Rangi Hiroa), anthropologist and Maori.

The number of works on the small Hopi nation still bewilders me. Of classic sources I will mention only J. W. Fewkes, Elsie Clewes Parsons, G. A. Dorsey, H. R. Voth, Victor Mendeleff, Walter Hough (*Mesa Folk of Hopi Land*), Wayne Dennis (*The Hopi Child*), Edgar L. Hewett (*Ancient Life in the American Southwest*), and Ruth Underhill (*First Penthouse Dwellers of America*). The Federal Writers' Project booklet *The Hopi* is an excellent brief summary of Hopi life and customs.

Among more recent publications to which I owe a sharper insight are: on Pueblo archaeology, the articles by Erik K. Reed and

Dale S. King to which the whole May 1951 issue of *Arizona High-ways* was devoted; on early Hopi history, the articles by K. Bart-lett, E. Nequatewa, L. L. Hargrave, H. S. Colton, J. O. Brew, and J. T. Hack reprinted by the Museum of Northern Arizona in a booklet entitled *Hopi History;* on the psychology and outlook of the modern Hopis, Walter C. O'Kane's *The Hopis: Portrait of a Desert People* and Laura Thompson's *Culture in Crisis,* as well as her and Alice Joseph's earlier *The Hopi Way.*

Myself an Arizonan, with a brother who is still a "neighbor" to the Hopi reservation, I have had the opportunity of visiting Walpi myself, and even of witnessing a Snake Dance, but only as a tour-ist with an inside track, so to speak. I repeat that this book is not an account of my own scientific observations. I will have done all I am possibly capable of if I have convinced some readers that further study in this direction will bring them a clearer under-standing of their own human nature and of the society and world they live in.

GENE LISITZKY

New York City, 1956

INTRODUCTION

Four ways of being human? When people say you can't change human nature, they would seem to mean that there is only one way of being human. Yet anthropology—and the word means the science (*logos*) of man (*anthropos*)—denies this. It does not deny that it is pretty hard (though by no means impossible) to *change* human ways once they are set. But, say the anthropologists, it seems to be fairly easy to *make* different kinds of human nature if you start early enough. There are therefore many, and not just four, different ways of being human.

Anthropology is the scientific study of these differences. Since some of them can be seen in the human body itself, there is a branch of this science called physical anthropology. It measures the skin colors of men, their head shapes, blood types, body proportions, and all such inherited, unchangeable physical features. These are the traits by which we try to separate men into different "races," and their study is simply just another branch of zoology, the general science of animal life. It does not tell us much, if anything, about what we call human nature.

But regardless of their races, all men can also be separated into different nations, tribes, or other more or less organized groups that we call "societies." For membership in these societies, it does not so much matter whether people look alike as whether they talk and act and think alike. A grown creature that did not belong to one of these human societies would be not really a human being at all, but only an animal shaped like a man.

For the zoologist there is so little difference among the *races* of man that he is obliged to class them all in a single species— only one out of the million species that share the earth. But there is no end to the *social* varieties of this single species, and the differences among them can be as startling as anything to be found among the hundreds of thousands of insect species. None of these human social differences is inherited in the same way in which bodily or racial traits are. They have almost nothing to do with zoology. They are man-made, pure inventions or conventions. It is with these differences that anthropology is chiefly concerned, for it is these that make up most of what we mean by human nature.

Every animal other than man is born into the world with special "built-in" ways of handling it, called instincts. If you moved an ant egg into a beehive, you would not expect it to grow up to flit among the flowers for honey. But if you smuggled a Japanese baby into a Hopi cradleboard, you know that he would grow up a Hopi, who is a vastly different sort of human being from a Japanese, with altogether different tastes, attitudes, and beliefs.

The human baby does not have his future way of life spelled out for him by instincts. Only after he is born can he learn the customs by which his society expects him to live. But he can be taught these customs so well that in time they will seem as natural to him as it is for an ant to live as an ant and not as a bee or a grasshopper. In a way, therefore, human beings are made, not born. Man makes himself. That is why there can be so many different ways of being human.

Now all the customs—the different ways of behaving and believing—that each society teaches its members are what the anthropologist calls its "culture." A culture is an enormously complex thing, for it includes not only the society's ways of using material things, such as tools and weapons and shelter and clothing and food, but also its language, morals and manners, religion and science, economics and art, government and family relationships, and even its ways of sitting down and making love and committing suicide and whittling sticks. Cultures are what anthropology is chiefly concerned with.

In theory, the anthropologist is just as much interested in big, complicated societies like those of modern Japan or ancient Rome as he is in the small, simple cultures of the Hopis and Hottentots. But, as a matter of fact, what the science of man has most carefully studied are the tribal societies that we call "primitive" or "uncivilized," by which we mean that they have not built cities, invented writing, or discovered the use of metals.

One reason for this partiality is the desire for scientific detachment. The anthropologist knows that he is himself a member of a particular society whose subtle prejudices he may not be able altogether to avoid. He therefore prefers to study cultures as unlike his own as possible. Another reason is simply convenience. It is certainly easier for a few students to get a quick over-all view of how a whole society works if it is smaller and less complicated. Besides, the less crowded and confusing the setting, the more likely the anthropologists are to uncover any fundamental principles by which *all* cultures work.

Finally, these primitive cultures seem insignificant today only because we see them as tiny remnants struggling hopelessly to survive in the nooks and crannies of a world rapidly being taken over by our own more powerful civilization. But against the background of the history of mankind, they are vastly more representative of human culture than we are. What we call "civilization"— the culture of cities, of writing and metals, of advanced agriculture—is only a few thousand years old. For many hundreds of thousands of years before that, for practically its whole lifetime, mankind lived only in small wandering groups by gathering wild plants and hunting animals. Even the simple cultivation of the soil is fairly recent, by these time standards. It is we who are the exceptions in the ways of mankind. For all we know, civilization may yet turn out to be only a "flash in the pan." Primitive culture —the life of plant-gatherers, hunters, and simple cultivators— has amply proved its ability to support a human way of life indefinitely.

Make no mistake—it was and is a fully human way. These primitive men made tools, used fire, spoke languages, and lived in societies regulated by custom, not instinct. Nothing less than human can do any of these things. Their tools were of stone and wood, but it was with these—and not today's atomic energy and jet planes, or even yesterday's railroads and steamships—that man conquered the earth. Man's dominance over his million fellow-species, his invasion of every continent and every climate, was the accomplishment of primitive men. The tribes who still live as they did are our last, fast-disappearing chance to find out how they lived and felt and perhaps even how they got started on the road to civilization.

So it is that the science of anthropology sends its students of human nature into the remotest corners of the world, to live under the most rugged conditions in the sole company of "savages." One happy result of this practice is that the scientific reports of these anthropologists have some of the flavor of adventure stories and travelers' tales. The earliest writings that can be called anthropological were in fact the accounts of adventurers and explorers, missionaries and traders, who took time to observe the customs of the tribes they visited.

The reports of the trained anthropologists are less naïve than most of these, less eager to amaze the reader with outlandish practices and heathen beliefs, less full of the personal exploits and beliefs of the writer. Nevertheless, they often contain revelations of human nature no less hair-raising than those brought back from his imaginary voyages by that prince of imaginary anthropologists, Lemuel Gulliver, Esq.

Unfortunately, most scientific studies of primitive life are not written with the general reader or beginning student in mind. They are often filled with highly technical and elaborately detailed discussions of tools, customs, languages, myths, head measurements, and family relationships. An anthropologist must know something about a great many sciences, to say nothing of professions and trades.

I have therefore tried in this book to pick out only the highlights from many such studies of four primitive tribes, and to work these into broad pictures of their normal lives. By comparing a number of different cultures in a single book, I hoped to bring out more strongly how various are the ways of being human. I feared, however, that if I touched on too many cultures, or spent time on comparing them custom for custom, the reader might lose the sense of how *human* they all are. I wanted not only to describe strange beliefs and practices, but also to show how natural they must seem to the people holding them. So I have treated each of these four cultures separately and as fully as I thought necessary to prove that each one allows for a completely rounded human life.

Almost any other group of tribes selected at random might have served this purpose. These four, taken together, do, however, point up one very important fact about cultures in general. At bottom, cultures are man's own peculiar way of adapting himself to the special conditions of his environment—in short, of meeting the challenge of survival. They do for man what natural selection does for all other creatures by having them evolve special instincts or specialized organs, like the horse's hoof or the camel's hump. Now each of these four cultures, like those bodily organs, has successfully solved the problems of a different extreme of natural conditions. The four together are a living demonstration of primitive man's ability to make a home anywhere at all in the world simply by inventing a suitable way of being human.

It was once believed that all things could be described in terms of four fundamental properties: heat, cold, wetness, and dryness. Their presence or absence or differing proportions was supposed to explain the nature of everything. How the ancient philosophers would have loved to illustrate this theory with the four worlds of our tribes—the Semang on the hot equator, the Eskimos near the cold North Pole, the Maoris in the wet Pacific, and the Hopis in their sun-dried desert!

Moreover, these four peoples represent what used to be considered all the "races" (or colors) of man, except the white—the black, yellow, brown, and red. (Nowadays it is more fashionable to consider the last three of these as making up a single race called "Mongoloid.") They are separated by whole quadrants of the globe, equally divided between its eastern and western hemispheres and distributed over four of the earth's five zones, all except the uninhabited Antarctic.

Two of them—the Maoris and Eskimos—live on the sea, but how strangely different are their oceans! The Semang and Hopis are landlocked, but as if on different planets. Two are simple food-gatherers—the Semang passive root-diggers, the Eskimos aggressive hunters. The other two have learned the beginnings of agriculture, the peaceful Hopis much more wholeheartedly than the war-loving Maoris. Two have practiced cannibalism, but only one of the four is warlike.

The four together cover the whole range of nomadism, from the restless Semang forever turning in their small jungle circles to the immovable Hopis, and from the Eskimos' seasonal house-movings to the great sea voyages of the Maoris. Finally, their languages and ways of thinking are completely alien to one another.

Is there, then, anything they have in common—aside from their all being primitive? Yes, there is, though it is likely to be blurred by all the dazzling differences. Things we take for granted often become invisible. For what all these cultures have in common they also share with us; it goes to the heart of what makes us all human.

Consider, for instance, the variety of tools and their diverse materials—the Semang's bamboo, the Eskimos' skin and bone, the Maoris' wood, the Hopis' stone, and our metals. If we become too much taken up with these dissimilarities, and their doubtlessly important consequences for daily living, we may let escape the much more basic fact that *we are all tool-makers*. The variety of materials, and even the different purposes of the tools, are by comparison mere accidents of what the particular environment has to offer. What is really important and truly striking is the unfailing ingenuity and inventiveness by which men respond to the environment's challenges and opportunities.

What is true of men's physical devices is just as true of their arts, religions, and other customs whose only "practical" utility is to make human beings feel more human. Maori carving, Hopi dances, Semang music, Eskimo legends—all have this in common: they show the same surplus of creative energy that every culture manages somehow to generate.

A culture is man's answer to the problems of survival, as a shell is the oyster's. But though the environment sets the problem, and limits the means for its solution, it never dictates the whole answer. The culture always adds something more than the problem calls for, something unpredictable because unnecessary, a little something extra for its own sake, a surprise. If people learn to make pots for holding water, eventually they learn to make them beautiful. There is no language without its poetry. Every useful skill becomes the germ of an art or science pursued for its own sake. In human cultures, every shell has its pearl. In fact, when we use the word "culture" in ordinary speech, we mean these pearls. The anthropologist, however, knowing that both shell and pearl arise from the same human qualities, uses the word in its wider meaning to include both the harp *and* the hoe.

Any acquaintance with anthropology is therefore bound to awaken a feeling of pride in the human race, in the inexhaustible fertility of its power to create cultures. With that comes tolerance. We may not care to adopt the customs of another culture for ourselves, but they are never again so likely to strike us as "wrong" or "ugly" or "immoral." We see that they were come by precisely as we came by ours, that it is only a matter of how one is brought up. What may possibly seem wrong is the act of needlessly imposing by force the customs of one culture on another.

Sympathy and tolerance are no doubt the marks of a civilized mind, but—you may ask—is there any practical use for all this bewildering information about cultures other than our own? Knowing about these curious customs may be entertaining; they may even teach us something about human nature in general. But if we are not professional anthropologists ourselves, what difference can it make to us whether these simple cultures vanish before the onslaughts of our conquering civilization without leaving a record of what they were like, as so many have done before them?

The practical importance of any young science is almost never obvious. It is usually considered irrelevant by the scientists themselves. Yet any scientific knowledge about the nature of the world eventually brings us some useful power. Who could have guessed a hundred years ago that oil would bring about a new industrial revolution and that the finding of oil would depend on the new science of geology? Now we must be grateful to the founders of that science for searching out their "useless" information, sustained only by the passion for pure knowledge.

Anthropology may never bring benefits as obviously practical as oil or uranium. (It has some value even now for government administrators of native tribes in reservations and colonies, but this does not affect very many of us.) But some day it may just possibly save all our lives, or at least the human way of life. Consider this small illustration of how learning alien customs can become important.

For hundreds of years white men explored the Arctic, first to find a northwest passage to Asia, later to reach the North Pole. Each generation went into battle against this inhuman environment better equipped than the last had been. They came with their very latest scientific inventions—ships, wagons, stoves, fuel, canned foods, thick woolen blankets. Yet they all left behind a tragic trail of brave men lost and killed. And the mapping of the top of the world remained heartbreakingly slow.

It was only when they realized that the "primitive" Eskimos had already invented the perfect clothing, shelters, vehicles, and weapons for the climate that the white men became better explorers. Once they stopped being ashamed to throw away their civilized prejudices, white exploration began to advance at great speed. Only when they were willing to imitate and learn from the "backward" Eskimos were they able to improve on Eskimo ways.

Now consider that all over the world, and for ages past, little groups of men living in similarly primitive cultures have been inventing and testing out countless different kinds of tools and techniques for handling every possible sort of environment. Think of the numberless discoveries about the secrets of nature that may have been lost. While I am writing this, the papers are carrying reports about a wonderful new drug for the treatment of mental diseases that used to require dangerous brain operations. Who discovered it? It has been used for centuries by medicine men in the peasant villages of India. In the same way there have been discovered many secrets of *human* nature, especially about how people can get along together and enjoy life under very different conditions and customs. Each of these tools and customs was embedded in a culture, a successful way of being human, a workable scheme for a good life.

The fact that someone else invented or discovered them is no argument against their usefulness or value to us. In this vast outpouring of the creative human mind, we are not surprised to find contrivances of great ingenuity or exquisite works of art that we have never happened to dream of ourselves. We find no difficulty nowadays in taking over Eskimo kayaks or African sculpture to enrich our own culture. Why should it not also be possible to borrow from other primitive cultures customs and even ideas of the good life? That, as a matter of fact, is how most cultures, including our own, have come by most of their ideas—by borrowing.

For us this is no longer a matter of mere tolerance. Our civilization, as it steadily covers the globe, is rapidly becoming the world culture. As more and more peoples adopt it more and more completely, this one culture becomes increasingly responsible for the survival and happiness of the whole human race. But it would be risky to put all humanity's eggs in one basket—even one without a hydrogen bomb in it.

We have seen too many other great civilizations fail in the end, from either external or internal causes. Some have been overwhelmed by an outraged nature's revenge—by soil erosion, pollution of streams, exhaustion of natural resources, or new diseases. Others have succumbed to their own "irrepressible conflicts"—civil wars and wars of conquest—for man is his own most hostile natural force. In history we have always seen some more primitive or barbarian people pick up the torch from these fallen civilizations. But what if any of these latter had contained all of mankind? All humanity might have gone down together in its crash. That possibility exists now for the first time.

So it behooves our civilization not to drive us all into the same dead end. It must be as flexible and adaptable as the sum of all the little cultures it replaces. It must make room for every worthwhile human trait, for every vision of the good life that would not itself destroy a world culture. (We obviously could not welcome cannibalism, for instance, but cannibals may have other ideas worth considering.) A truly human world culture could not afford to dismiss the possible contributions of its weakest rival. If any primitive tribe has achieved some marked success along a path untrod by the rest of us, then we must at least learn all about it. Some day we may need it.

Such contributions cannot, however, be the mere fancies of writers of utopias or of science fiction. They should be values and ideas that have come into being, and been tested, in actual living cultures. They should therefore be studied on the spot and in action. And that is the "practical" function of anthropology. It is the "practical" reason why all civilized persons should share with the anthropologist his tender regard for the fast-vanishing cultures of primitive men.

S E M A N G

"We must have trees around us."

I. SEMANG:
People of the Rain Forest

*If human beings are pretty good at climbing, it is no wonder:
their bodily make-up betrays their tree-dwelling ancestry. Even
long after our ancestors had come permanently down to the
ground, they must have clung to the forests. A million years
ago, before they had made an ally of fire, or invented clothing
and shelters, they must have been confined to a climate that
was warm the year round. Before they had tools and weapons,
they must have had to live on what they could gather and catch
with bare hands and eat raw. Like his cousins the great apes,
man had to start his career in a world that was always warm and
green.*

Such a natural hothouse still exists. It is the tropical rain forest that girdles the globe at the equator. Here the earliest natural conditions of human life remain the least changed, and men still live in them. This world has always had its own terrors; it is not a bed of roses for human beings—otherwise men might never have left it of their own free wills to take over the rest of the earth. But at least it does not pose the novel challenge of cold winters, barren deserts, or treeless seas. Here there is less reason for men to change and adapt themselves by inventing new cultures.

So if we wished to find people leading lives most nearly like our remote ancestors', this would be one of the places to look. In fact, some of the most primitive cultures in the world are still flourishing deep in the same jungles where, as on the tropical island of Java, there have also been found the fossil bones of early ape men.

But never forget that these modern jungle dwellers, no matter how primitive their lives may seem, are, like ourselves, removed by a million years of evolution from those ape men. Not a whit less than ourselves, they are modern men. Biologically, we all belong to the same single human species. Culturally, they too have everything that makes us human—fire and tools, languages and customs. When we call them "primitive," we mean only that their societies—their way of life as a whole—are organized on much simpler lines than our own.

Not very far from that same Java where an ape man first stood erect lives a tribe called Semang, whose way of life is about as simple as any that exists today. This tribe's visitors have not been many and have not stayed long enough to bring back very full reports. But the Semang are a good people to start with, even if only for a short visit.

Their very nakedness brings home one important lesson: how much ingenuity it takes to make any environment humanly liv-

*able—even our original rain-forest home. They can also teach us
that there is no human society so primitive that it is satisfied
merely with surviving; it must have its art and religion and all the
other pearls of culture. Finally, we may learn from them why
the people who live the simplest lives are the slowest to change
them.*

1. THE JUNGLE

The Malay Peninsula, or Malaya, is a long slim tongue of land
forming the most southern extension of the mainland of Asia.
Shaped like an Indian club, it juts down from Burma and Siam
a thousand miles into the South China Sea. Its bulbous southern
end is thrust, like a poorly fitted stopper, into the narrow bottle-
neck between the great islands of Sumatra and Borneo, where
the Pacific and Indian Oceans meet. The great British naval base
of Singapore, at the extreme southern tip of the peninsula, is
almost directly on the equator.

The backbone of Malaya is a series of mountain ranges, which
reach heights of seven to eight thousand feet, but there is no
timber line on their slopes and there are no snow-covered peaks.
Despite the altitude of the interior, Malaya is almost one vast
tropical forest, a gigantic carpet of lush vegetation with a pile
a hundred feet thick.

It may seem strange that here, in the very middle of the Torrid
Zone, the sun should be a rare thing to see. Yet the competition
for sunlight among the enormous varieties of plant life is so intense that the trees must shoot up a hundred feet or more before
they can usefully put out a single branch. High in the air the
woody giants interlace their lofty crowns to form one enormous
parasol over the ground beneath. For the little sunlight that filters
through, the hosts of climbing, creeping, and parasitic plants—
ferns, mosses, fungi, and orchids—compete with equal vigor on

the trunks and branches of the trees, while the space between the trees is interwoven with rattans and thick ropes of lianas.

Beneath this thick canopy is a hot, steaming, dim twilight even at high noon. It is natural to imagine a tropical jungle as a riot of gorgeous colors, of brilliant flowers, dazzling butterflies, and flashing birds. But since every blossom, butterfly, and bird strives to reach the sunlight on the topmost branches of the great trees, the floor of the rain forest is more like the bottom of a lake, a green dusk occasionally lit up by a ray of sunlight that has pierced the roof of foliage.

To support their great heights and to withstand the frequent tempests, the huge trees burrow their big roots deep into the soft, wet soil, spread them writhing in all directions on the surface, and sometimes send them arching out from high up on the trunks, like the flying buttresses of Gothic cathedrals. These tangled roots, and the dense layers of shrubs, bushes, and creepers covering the ground between the trees, make a matted jungle so impenetrable that to this day the greater part of the peninsula has probably never been trodden by human foot. Through much of it one cannot take a single step forward without hacking one's way with a bush knife, and a fair rate of progress might be a mile a day.

As if the sheer quantity of the vegetation were not enough to impede the jungle traveler, it often takes the most dangerous forms. Every other plant seems to be armed with some protective weapon for strangling, cutting, stabbing, or poisoning. Trees, shrubs, and grasses are provided with prickles, thorns, or sawtoothed edges that can give the most painful wounds. Many have poisonous saps besides, and the sting of the giant nettle is the terror of man and beast.

It is therefore fortunate for the inhabitants of the jungle, both beasts and men, that Malaya is lavishly supplied with rivers and small streams. Along these, if one faithfully follows their meander-

ings, one may move a few miles a day even on foot. These water-
ways, like the jungle itself, are formed by the immense amount
of rainfall. Some parts of the peninsula average more than one
hundred fifty inches a year—thirteen feet of rainfall! Most days
are rainy days, if one counts the almost daily sudden, violent,
though brief downpours of equatorial showers, and more than
half the days of the year are wet clear through. The resulting
humidity is more than most Europeans can bear. The land is
soggy, the plant life always green and quick-growing. A forest
fire is all but impossible; a man-made clearing is overgrown and
obliterated in days.

It is not only the plant life that is so luxuriant on the Malay
Peninsula. All the well-known jungle beasts of Asia are to be
found here—the elephant, the rhinoceros, and the tapir; the
tiger, the leopard, the panther, and other jungle cats; the wild boar
and the wild dog; pythons, cobras, and many other dangerous

snakes; crocodiles and lizards; tropical deer of many sorts; a great many varieties of monkeys and apes; to say nothing of countless kinds of birds, squirrels, forest rats, and many other small species.

To cope with the density of the underbrush some of our more familiar animals have taken on strange shapes. Most are tree climbers and tree dwellers, and many have made a try at developing wings, or at least parachutes. Besides the "flying foxes" (which are really bats), there are flying squirrels, flying lemurs, flying lizards, and flying frogs. With the aid of flaps of skin growing between forelimbs and hind legs these small beasts glide through the air from one tree trunk to the next, skimming above the matted jungle floor.

Finally, there are the uncountable hosts of insects, scorpions, centipedes, and worms—biting, stinging, flying, climbing, burrowing, wood-boring, and man-eating. One of these manages to make life worse for the forest-dweller than even the tiger or the elephant. This is the tiny land leech, which is everywhere along the paths, clinging to shrubs, dropping from trees, creeping on the ground, waiting to fasten itself on the traveler, pierce his skin, and suck his blood. These slimy gray little monsters, no longer or thicker than a matchstick, will in certain places cover a man's legs in five minutes. Clothing rather helps than hinders them, for it makes them harder to find and brush off. The natives will take off their loincloths before going through the thorny undergrowth.

Where nature has been so generous with the forms of wild life and with the vegetable means for their existence, it would be surprising not to find man living on both. The coasts have for centuries been occupied by civilized Mohammedan Malays, to whom in more recent times have been added Chinese and Europeans; and thinly scattered along the mountain slopes there live, as they have lived since long ago, three races of savage tribes. First, there are the Savage Malays, of the same race as the brown people of the coast except that they have remained untouched by the coast civilization. Older inhabitants than these are the people called Sakai, a light-yellow folk who build their houses in trees and are most famous for their poison blowpipes. Oldest inhabitants of all are the little people known as the Semang.

2. THE KINSHIP BAND

The Semang are Negritos, literally "little Negroes," related to the better-known Pygmies of far-off Central Africa. They have black or dark brown skins, hair that grows close to the skull in tight little kinky curls, no beards, broad noses, and very full lips. The average height of their men is only four feet ten inches, while their women are usually three or four inches shorter.

The Negritos must be among the oldest inhabitants of Southeast Asia—no one knows how old. Tribes of them are widely scattered in the most inaccessible parts of the islands along these shores. There is a tribe in the Philippine Islands called Aeta, another larger one native to the isolated Andaman Islands in the Bay of Bengal, south of Burma, and still others in the interiors of the Indonesian islands of Sumatra and Celebes. It is quite impossible that they should have fought their way to these least favored corners past the present coast dwellers. More likely, the Negritos have been gradually driven there by their bigger fellow men, who were later arrivals on these shores.

Like all the other Negritos, the Semang of Malaya live on such a low, "savage" level of culture that they are despised—and superstitiously feared—by the civilized Coast Malay. He has not made up his mind whether to regard them as little better than the forest apes, in fact just another orangutan (the word means "man of the forest"), or as mischievous wood demons. But the few white travelers who have made the acquaintance of the shy Semang, and have lived among them, always speak of their intelligence and native kindliness. Their smooth round faces, wool-capped heads, round bright eyes, and small, well-proportioned bodies give them the attractive appearance of very bright children. "The cheery little hunters" they have been called, and, in view of the conditions of their life, this description does them great credit.

For, surrounded as they are on every hand by more trees, plants, and animal life than an Eskimo shaman or Hopi priest could possibly imagine in a lifetime of extravagant visions of heaven, the Semang yet live a life as poor and insecure as any led by primitive men on the face of the earth. For them this unbelievable wealth of growing things is no horn of plenty, but rather a hardship and a menace.

It is a curious fact about tropical forests that few trees or plants of the same kind will grow together in the same place to form large groves or beds. Conditions that are ideal for one plant are usually also ideal for a hundred competitors, and every valuable growth is soon buried among others—some of them harmful—like a needle in a haystack. Only where men have learned the art of cultivation in fields or patches, fighting back the jungle with constant weeding, can they bring together enough plants of the same kind to feed a large number of people fixed in one place.

But this art of cultivation, which may seem to go as naturally with being human as the use of fire or speech, is only a very recent discovery, made within the last ten thousand years. It was made independently in only a few favored places—the Near East, China, Central America—and from these gradually spread outward to the rest of us.

Agriculture has made the greatest revolution in human life since fire and speech, tools and customs, made human beings.

It has made it possible for people to settle down in stable communities. It has produced a surplus of food for those communities to grow on and even to support cities of craftsmen and kings and other specialists. These specialists, freed from having to find or produce their own food, have in turn been able to push the invention of tools and customs at an ever faster rate. They have found ever more complicated ways of being human. They have given us our idea of, and fondness for, progress.

The Semang are, however, among the many peoples whom the art of cultivation has not yet reached either by discovery or by teaching. They still live in the earlier manner of all mankind, as wild-food gatherers and hunters. They still pass their lives in little roving bands that must be forever on the move, from one wild fruit tree to the next a mile away, from one bed of wild yams to another a day's journey through the jungle. Rarely can they stay more than three or four days at any one camp site before even their little bands have exhausted all the food around it.

Of course, the food grows all year round somewhere else, and there is no real need to store up surpluses. But that also means there is not much leisure for doing anything else; everyone must keep a constant sharp lookout for the day's supplies. Among food-gathering peoples like this, everyone (except infants, the very old, and the sick) is always busy earning a living in exactly the same way. There are no specialists and there is no progress.

These nomadic bands of the Semang are really only large families, so-called kinship bands. A couple of grandparents at the head, their grown children, and their children's children will make up a typical band of six to a dozen households. Twenty or thirty persons, including children, are considered a large band. It cannot be much smaller without danger of being wiped out by the hosts of its enemies. Nor can it be much larger, for then it would have to cover even more ground to find enough food.

Forever on the move

It would have to move even more frequently, and traveling through this jungle would become much too unwieldy for such a large group.

You must not imagine that, because the Semang are constantly on the go, they get to see much of the world. In the first place, they would not know how to live outside the rain forest they were born in. They would not be happy anywhere but in this familiar jungle. "We must have trees around us," they say; "then all is well."

In the second place, the whole extent of a Semang's lifetime of ceaseless travel may be no more than a rough circle five miles in diameter, an area smaller than that of some cities. But before you put him down as less nomadic than a modern suburbanite who commutes several times that distance every day, remember that he does not return every night to a fixed abode.

Remember, too, the snail's pace at which he must hack his way through the plant life of this eternal midsummer, which can in a few days obliterate every trace of his last passage. The only made paths he can follow are the tracks worn by elephants or other big beasts, the sole road-builders of the jungle. Men and women on these trails wear a hunted expression, from constantly watching out for snakes or other dangerous animals taking the same road. Even here they walk slowly, and deliberately raise each foot high in the air before setting it carefully on the ground. This gives them a sort of "clodhopper" gait, like that of farmers used to walking through plowed fields.

So the tract of twenty square miles that the Semang spends his whole life circling and crossing is both his "home" (since he lives all over it) and his "world" (since he never leaves it). He is a nomad within very narrow boundaries. Each band is recognized by all its neighbors as owner of its territory. Perhaps "own" is not the proper word, except in the sense that a tiger owns its regular hunting grounds. There is no ownership of land as we understand it, as something that can be bought and sold, but here the band feels at home and knows it has special rights and interests. Any other band may wander through at will, and even camp overnight to hunt or dig up roots, but it is only in passing. It will leave all fruit trees strictly alone until it gets back to its own territory.

Wandering thus, one Semang band may occasionally run into a neighboring one and be able to exchange some news or views. But if a Semang were transported twenty miles from his own tract, he would be in a foreign country. Though he is likely to meet only other Semang, he may even have some difficulty with their different dialect. Even among us, small isolated groups soon develop a special vocabulary and intonation of their own. And the away-from-home Semang would have very little gossip of common interest with his hosts, for they are used to discussing only family matters. The Semang have no sense of being a nation or a tribe. Their whole social world is the tiny kinship band.

The head of the band is the grandfather. He usually chooses the camp site for the night and decides when and where to move. The others normally defer to his judgment for, aside from his authority as their father, his age has given him the most experience. But that is as far as government goes among them. There is no chief who is owed unquestioning obedience or who can enforce his authority.

The leadership of old age is the rule among many primitive peoples, and naturally so. In a civilized nation, whose past experience and wisdom are accumulated in books, a young man may acquire considerable knowledge. In simpler societies, experience is the only teacher, and the old naturally have more of that. So if a Semang only lives long enough to marry and have children and to have his sons marry and have children, then he may hope to rise as high as possible—to the leadership of a kinship band.

Along the way he will have garnered the necessary experience for coping with the jungle; otherwise he would not have survived. But his whole life will have been passed in the exclusive company of relatives—first, his grandparents, parents, aunts and uncles, brothers and sisters, cousins; later, his wife, sons and daughters, nephews and nieces, grandchildren. Occasionally he will have had some slight contact with a few other families, not very different from his own, to which he is also related by the marriages of his kinfolk. All his social relationships will have something warm and strongly felt about them since they are all actually family relationships. There will be a sense of security from everyone's definitely "belonging." But there will be none of that invigorating variety that comes from having all kinds of special relationships with people, on the basis of mere business, or play, or just friendship.

To this isolated, tightly closed family circle, new ideas will have a hard time penetrating from the outside. Inside the family the emphasis must be on learning the old wisdom from one's elders and teaching it to one's young. Every child in the band has only the same models to imitate, for all the adults practice the same techniques of gaining a livelihood and follow exactly the same social customs. All the children in the camp have the same grandparents, those aged and respected repositories of the wisdom of the family who have all the answers to the problems of life because they have lived long enough to meet them all. So for generations and centuries, as long as the rain forest remains the same, there need be no change in the life of the people.

For it is variety that breeds variety, as it takes a little yeast to make a lot. The most usual cause for a primitive people's changing its ways is its dealing with a different people with different ways. Meeting others in war—conquering them or being conquered—is one unfortunately common means for the exchange of ideas and inventions that gets a wave of progress started. Another is the peaceful way of trade, the meeting in the market place of tribes with different skills and hence different products to barter.

Until recently the Semang have had nothing to tempt either the conqueror or the trader into their impenetrable jungle. Their immediate forest neighbors of other races live more or less the same lives as themselves. Anyway, they have long ago exchanged with one another whatever ideas and inventions they came here with that were mutually acceptable. Their little bands are too small to support full-time craftsmen. Everyone must hunt and dig—and make his own arrows and digging sticks. Without full-time specialists there is no time or incentive for creating the variety that breeds variety. It is therefore no reflection on the intelligence of the Semang that for a thousand years they have not pulled themselves into a higher level of culture by their own bootstraps.

3. LIFE IN THE BAMBOO AGE

Not so many thousands of years ago, the ancestors of the present Europeans lived the same sort of primitive hunting and gathering life, in narrow little family groups, as do the Semang. They too had not yet learned the art of cultivation, or of writing, and did not know the use of copper or iron. Of course, their environment was vastly different. It was a northern forest, with no plant food during the winter; these people had to depend more on the hunting of big game. They laboriously made their weapons of chipped, and later of polished, stone, the strongest and most durable material they could find readily available. Hence this period in European history—it lasted for tens of thousands of years—is known as the Stone Age.

When Europe became civilized and sent its explorers into other continents, they usually found that the newly discovered primitive peoples also made their weapons and tools principally out of stone. This was true of the Eskimos, most Indians, the South Sea islanders, and many others. Later the anthropologists fell into the habit of referring to these peoples as being "still" in the Stone Age and as "not yet" having reached the Iron Age. It was as if they believed these to be inevitable stages in the evolution of all human tribes, much as every individual, if he lives, must pass through childhood, adolescence, and maturity. It was forgotten that even the Europeans learned the use of metals from others, that there was nothing inevitable about it, or even about their previous use of stone. In fact, there is nothing inevitable about any human practice, whether it is part of metallurgy or tennis.

The Semang, for instance, have never had a stone age in the sense of working chiefly in stone. It is not only that good workable stone may not be so easy to find in the fertile jungle, with its floor of decayed vegetation several feet thick. It is also that this same jungle gives the Semang a material for tool-making that the Stone Age Europeans and the modern Eskimos might well have envied them.

Their chief material for tools is bamboo—a woody grass. It is extremely hard and durable, with a naturally polished surface. Its many varieties come in all thicknesses, from that of thin reeds to diameters of six inches or more. It grows in segments, making a connected series of hollow tubes. Cut off a single segment to include only one knot, and you have a ready-to-use cooking vessel capable of withstanding fire—or a drum, or a chair, depending on the diameter of the bamboo. Take a piece several segments long and bore a hole down through all the knots except the last, and you have a tube, of any size or length you desire, for carrying liquids. Narrower lengths can be made into arrow quivers, tinder boxes, tobacco jars.

Thin, flexible rods of bamboo can be woven into an ideal bedspring or a latticework shelter. Split lengthwise into long strips, they can be woven into fine baskets. Splinters of bamboo make knives sharp and hard enough to cut designs into other bamboo. The tender shoots can be eaten. The Semang have done not at all badly in the age of bamboo.

Nor has the skipping of a stone age prevented the dawning of an iron age. In faraway Europe and America, certain commonplace products of the Malayan jungle have come to be considered treasures, and high prices are paid for gutta-percha, damar resin, camphor, fragrant eaglewood, and even rattan. This has encouraged Coast Malay traders to brave the rain forest and offer barter to the jungle dwellers. They have brought brass fish-hooks, iron bush knives and choppers, and even lumps of crude iron and scraps of tool steel. Their husked rice and cured tobacco have become much-sought-after delicacies among the Semang.

The jungle treasures eagerly bought by the Malays and white men are things the Semang can find and pick up on his normal food-gathering rounds. He has, for instance, always collected damar resin to keep his fire alive on the trail; now he has only to put some aside for the occasional trader. Thus the white man's need for the resin to put in his varnishes has given the Semang iron rattan-splitters. Because of it they have learned to make fire by striking steel on flint. They have even learned by themselves to shape iron into arrowheads by heating it and battering it be-tween two stones. (So that stonework *is* after all introducing an iron age, or is it that ironwork is introducing an age of stone?)

The new metals have not, however, made any striking dif-ference in the way the Semang live. We may continue to call them a people of the Old Stone Age if by this we mean only that they are still food-gatherers, earning their living by catching or digging up or knocking down their food where they find it.

This ceaseless searching for food has sharpened their forest senses to a very fine pitch. In the densest foliage they instantly recognize a bird or animal hidden in the branches. In what seems only a tangle of weeds they at once make out some edible plant buried among them. The forest, for all its gloomy terrors, and no matter how reluctantly, gives them not only all the food they need, but also their shelter, clothing and ornaments, tools and weapons, medicines, and art materials.

The diet of the Semang is mostly vegetarian. They are not full-time hunters and fishers, like those primitive tribes among whom it is the regular duty of the men to forage daily for animal food. But they will not pass up the chance to hunt when it presents itself, and they are very good at it—keen, clever, and patient.

In case of need they will, with their simple weapons, stand up to tigers and elephants, but then it is in self-defense; it is they who are the game. They prefer to hunt squirrels, forest rats, birds, lizards, monkeys, and wild pigs. They show a remarkable keenness of sight, hearing, and even smell in tracking these down. They seem to find by intuition the favorite watering places and salt licks, the clearings where the pheasants dance, the trees where monkeys look for grubs, the pools deep in the forest where the birds drink. They are careful and accurate shots with bows and arrows or with fire-hardened palmwood spears tipped with slivers of bamboo.

The Semang bow, five or six feet long, is considerably taller than the hunter and seems unnecessarily large for the small size of his usual game. This one alone of his more important tools is made not of bamboo but of an even more supple wood. A branch of the langsat tree is scraped down with rough stones and sharp slivers of bamboo until it is about an inch thick in the middle and tapers down to a point at either end. It is wound round with bamboo basketry for greater resiliency. The bowstring is sometimes of sinew but more usually of twisted bark fiber.

The arrows, too, seem outsize. They are a yard long and have rather clumsy-looking, heavy wooden points. The range of these arrows is some hundred and fifty yards, but the Semang usually do their shooting at thirty or forty paces, at which distance they are very accurate marksmen. Certainly there are better-made bows and arrows to be found among primitive peoples elsewhere, but not more interesting ones. For these arrows are tipped with poison.

Ipoh poison comes from the milky sap of the great upas tree, which grows, forty to sixty feet tall, in rare places throughout the jungle. These trees are owned by individual tribesmen, as are the fruit trees. The owner with a few friends will go out to collect the sap very much as we tap sugar maples, by chopping V-shaped gashes in the bark and letting the juice drip down into a bamboo receptacle. The sap is then poured over both sides of a broad wooden spatula, which is constantly kept turning over a fire until the juice becomes a thick brown sticky gum. While it is still soft, the arrow points are stirred into it and then laid aside to dry.

Three ounces of sap are enough to poison a hundred points, but they must be used while the poison is still fairly fresh, else it loses its potency. Arrowheads are often poisoned again and again, since a hunter may use as many as thirty arrows a week and always tries to retrieve them.

Fresh ipoh can kill birds and small animals almost instantly, but the Semang prefer to half-paralyze their game rather than kill it. A small bird that drops dead in the thick jungle is almost impossible to find, whereas, if it can still struggle a little after falling to the ground, the hunter can follow the noise it makes. When hit by a poisoned arrow, an animal the size of a monkey will fall from the tree within two minutes, and its attempts to rub off the arrow will only break the point off under its skin.

Though care must be taken lest it spurt into the eyes, handling the poison while collecting or cooking it is not very dangerous, since to have a lethal effect it must enter directly into the blood. In any case, the Semang believe that they have an antidote for it. They say that if a man sickened by this poison eats earth of any kind he will at once get well, and that they learned of this remedy by observing a crow recover from the poison after pecking at the earth.

The bow and poisoned arrow are the ancient weapon of the Semang, but gradually they have adopted an even more interesting one from those other forest inhabitants of Malaya, the tree-dwelling Sakai. This is the poison blowpipe, which operates on the same principle as a pea-shooter. The blowpipe is a slender tube from eight to twelve feet long made from a rare bamboo in which the knots come some five or six feet apart and of which the hollow center is very narrow. A two-section length is split in two and, after the knots are bored through, is carefully fitted together again and held in place, as well as kept from warping, by an outer tube of ordinary thicker bamboo. Finally there is a mouthpiece and, just above it in the tube, a wad of the downy fluff that collects around the leaf bases of certain palms. This wad prevents the leakage of air when the hunter blows, and also keeps the poison dart from falling back into his mouth.

The very light dart, only a few inches long, is made from the midrib of a palm leaf scraped down to the thinness of a knitting needle. It is notched near the poisoned point so that it will break off in the wound. The poison used is the same ipoh of the upas tree. It is amazing how accurate the hunter's aim can be at thirty to fifty yards. He holds the long tube steadily with both fists clasped near the mouthpiece and without any other support to keep it from trembling. He gives a strong puff that makes his lips pop, the dart whirrs, and almost instantly the prey drops from its tree.

These uses of poison certainly add to the terror, though not to the contempt, with which the Coast Malay regards the Semang. It must indeed be a chilling thought on the somber jungle trail to imagine being spied on from behind every huge tree trunk by a grinning little black demon who can send you silently to your death with a mysterious poison. On the other hand, how is it possible not to admire a primitive folk who "have not yet reached the Stone Age" but who have already invented chemical warfare or, even better, chemical hunting?

Besides the fire-hardened lance, the bow and arrow, and the blowpipe, the Semang also catch some small game with pitfalls, simple nooses of fiber, and spring traps of basketry. Birds are also ensnared by the ancient European device of "liming," that is, by smearing the sticky sap of the wild fig or gutta-percha tree on splints of bamboo so that the birds' feet are caught and held in the gluey stuff.

Semang women never hunt with bows, but they do trap with the baskets they themselves have made, and they always join the men in fishing when the band comes to a river. Small fry are taken in plaited bamboo scoops, while the larger fish are speared with the long sharpened midrib of a palm leaf. Simple weirs or fish traps are also made, and there is some angling with bamboo poles.

The Semang do not know how to make canoes, though they will lash together lengths of bamboo to make a crude raft when they wish to cross rivers or to travel down them for short distances. Those of the Semang whose territory does not happen to include a deep enough bit of river or lake usually do not even know how to swim.

Hunting and fishing are, however, not the major occupations of the Semang. The greater part of their food they get by gathering wild fruits, berries, nuts, the pith of certain edible palms, tender leaves, bamboo shoots, young roots, and tubers—those starchy underground vegetables that are like our potato. The women go out regularly every day in search of plants, and it is therefore they who contribute most to supporting the family. What they chiefly look for are tubers, especially the big wild yams, which often grow three feet underground. The women dig for these, the men often helping, with a long digging stick that has had its point hardened in fire.

The Semang overlook nothing in the way of edible plants and have even learned to depend upon many that in their natural state are quite poisonous. To eliminate these poisons often requires very complicated operations lasting several days, and it is a mystery how these people without chemical laboratories learned, in the first place, that the food was good if the poisons were driven out, and, second, how to remove the poisons. Where most other primitive peoples voluntarily deprive themselves of many good foods by placing taboos upon them and convincing themselves that they are somehow poisonous, the Semang take really poisonous plants and turn them into good food. Surrounded as they are by plants that are in fact deadly, they have not added to the difficulties of life by inventing make-believe dangers. They seem to have no food taboos at all.

Each poisonous root requires a different treatment. One type of poisonous wild yam, for instance, is first rasped against a prickly stick in the same way that you might grate a nutmeg or a piece of cheese. Then the grating must be mixed with a little slaked lime, which chemically neutralizes the poison though it leaves the yam still inedible. Then the pulp is kneaded by hand into a sort of dough, a loaf of which is then wrapped up in a strip of fresh banana leaf, slipped into a cleft stick, and slowly roasted over the fire. Other roots have to be suspended in a basket for days in the running water of a river until the con-centrated poison is dissolved and diluted. Then the Semang squeeze both water and poison out of the roots by pulling and stretching the flexible woven basket, and finally dry them over a fire. Still other roots have to be buried back in the earth, where the natural fermentation destroys the poison. If it had ever been in the destiny of the Semang to develop their own higher civiliza-tion, it would surely have been particularly brilliant in the chemi-cal sciences.

The high points of the year for the Semang are the months in which the fruits of certain trees ripen and are ready for harvest. Then each small band, wherever it may have been wandering, comes back to its own home grounds. For though a Semang may shoot an animal or net a fish or dig up a root wherever he finds it, he will never think of picking the fruit of the mangosteen or the durian from any other trees than those that belong to his family. Even within the kinship band, to pick a durian or to collect ipoh poison from any other tree than one's own would be to invite violence.

The mangosteen is a fruit that looks very much like an orange, with a very thick rind and juicy flesh and a flavor somewhere between that of a peach and a pineapple. It does not, however, compare for popularity, among man, beast, or bird, with the durian, the favorite fruit of the millions of people in this part of the world. The durian is a very large globular fruit covered with a hard, very prickly green rind and sometimes weighing a couple of pounds. Its soft, cream-colored, cream-textured pulp is said to have the most delicious flavor, but, though it has been praised so much, there are not many white men who have finally brought themselves to taste it. For to European nostrils the durian has a most unpleasant pungent odor, so offensive even when fresh that European writers have said it is all but impossible to go into the crew's quarters of a Malay junk when the men have laid in a stock of the fruit. The seeds of the durian also may be roasted and eaten like chestnuts.

Harvesting the durian is a fairly simple matter. When the fruit is ripe it falls to the ground; then the Semang pick it up. They prefer on the whole not to climb trees, no doubt because of the unpleasant adventures one is likely to have up in the very populous second story of the jungle, with its thorns and poisons, snakes and cats, and stinging insects. The Semang are nonetheless expert tree climbers, running up the towering trunks like monkeys, using their feet and not their knees, with their arms out at full length. When tree trunks are too thick for this method, they use noosed ropes up which they clamber hand over hand.

The durian harvests are the time of the great feasts of the Semang. For once they will have more than just a few days' supply of food, and they are all in a happy, contented, generous mood. Though each man is jealously possessive about his own trees, actually the fruit is freely shared among the group. This sharing applies to all kinds of food once it is harvested, prepared, and cooked. If on one day a household happens to be well supplied, while the rest of the band is not, it will usually give so generously as to leave little for itself.

In this the Semang resemble most other primitive peoples who live in small groups. The common principle seems to be that the *catch* is the private property of the successful hunter, but the *food* is expected to be shared among those who have less than himself. The reason is, of course, everywhere the same: No man is always fortunate, and he who lets his neighbor starve while he has plenty will have no one to help him survive in future times of need. But the generosity of the Semang does not come from a cool calculation of this principle. He shares as naturally and spontaneously among his kinsmen as do the members of our own smaller families among themselves.

4. FAMILY LIFE

The naked little Semang child, named after the tree, flower, stream, or mountain near which he was born, lives a carefree, happy life. His extremely devoted parents may scold or correct but would never beat him. He is forever being fondled and kissed by all his relatives, which means of course the whole band. A mother will always see that her children have ornaments before she decorates herself. If a stranger appears in camp, all the mothers will immediately vanish into the forest with their children lest the young ones be enticed away.

Boys and girls are not real members of the community until they have married and established families of their own. Since everyone in the same band is too closely related for marriage, a young man will have to seek out his bride from some neighboring group. Throughout the world, among quite unrelated primitive peoples, certain courtship and marriage customs crop up again and again. Marriage is evidently regarded in some tribes as the capture of a bride by force, and in others as the purchase of a bride under contract; in still others (including some civilized nations of Europe) the husband must be paid a dowry to take the bride off her father's hands. In most cases, the capture or purchase or bribe may by now be only make-believe, a mere ceremony, but the ceremony at any rate is usually taken quite seriously. Among the Semang, the underlying idea is bride-purchase.

When the young man has come to some understanding with the girl of his choice, he will give his intended father-in-law some presents—a few bush knives perhaps, or a handsome decorated bamboo tinderbox. He will present the bride with a fine girdle. If she later leaves her husband, her father will have to return the bride gifts, but if the husband leaves his wife he will forfeit all the presents he has given. On the day on which the young man solicits the girl's hand, her mother becomes his mother-in-law, a person whom he must always avoid and never speak to on pain of committing a grave sin. She remains someone to avoid from then on, even if the marriage does not take place. After the marriage the bride must also avoid her father-in-law. This strange taboo, avoidance of one's in-laws, must be extremely ancient, for it is to be found in all parts of the world and among tribes who could never possibly have had any contact with one another.

It is customary for the Semang bridegroom to live in his father-in-law's encampment, helping him with his work, for a year or two after his marriage. Thus he acquires a little education abroad and escapes for a short while the exclusive influence of his own family, though the life he leads is no different from that at home.

Then he returns with his wife to his own people, never to leave them again except for an occasional visit to his father-in-law when the latter needs some extra help with his work.

The Semang home is among the simplest in the world. Since it is to be stayed in only a few days at the most, it would be foolish to build anything that could not be put up in the shortest possible time. Other nomadic tribes, under similar circumstances, have invented tents, but they usually also have horses or dogs to carry such equipment, the kind of country where such transport can be used, and the hope of staying a fairly long time at each camp. The Semang must carry everything themselves. On their choked jungle trails they must travel as light as possible. They have no time for frequent packing and unpacking of gear. So they build each shelter anew from the materials growing naturally around the spot selected for a camp site.

Camp is usually made in some small natural clearing in the forest or beneath an overhanging ledge of rock that will serve as a natural roof. On this camp site the six to a dozen household shelters will be arranged in a circle, each shelter being made by the mother for her own husband and children. She drives a line of three or four strong poles into the ground, at an angle so that they slope toward the central clearing of the camp, and props them against collapse with smaller forked sticks or with fiber strings pegged in the ground. She then weaves a thatch of big palm or rattan leaves over these sloping stakes, folding each leaf along its central stem to give double thickness. If there is a great hurry, one very big leaf will do.

This simple one-wall shed is all the shelter the Semang has from the frequent tropical storms. The angle of the roof or wall, for it is really both, can be adjusted up or down to suit the weather by moving the forked supports forward or back along the sloping poles. For extra protection against rain, more foliage can be piled on top and be held down with branches. Stuck up among the slats and thatch of the roof-wall are the few possessions of the owners, as well as a few yams or other surplus food.

The furniture of this crude dwelling may be listed in two words —bed and hearth. To keep the occupants off the damp earth the Semang make a couch of split bamboo raised from the ground by logs or forked sticks. On this all the members of the household sleep huddled together, with their heads to the back of the leaning wall, the whole front and sides of the little house being nothing but open window.

For added warmth and dryness a fire is built on one or both sides of the couch. The hearth consists of a few short logs laid directly on the cleared ground. Fire is made by rubbing together two blocks of wood or strips of dried cane or by holding down a branch of rattan with one's foot while a strip of cane is sawed back and forth under it with both hands until the wood dust catches fire.

This would be a very slow method of making fire even under the best circumstances, but in this moist climate it is even more tedious. So if possible the fire is not allowed to go out, and is carried by the Semang on their travels in the form of bamboo torches or of smoldering resin wrapped in palm leaves. For tinder the Semang often use the same downy palm fluff that serves for wadding in their blowpipes. Those of the men who have acquired flint and iron from the Malays greatly treasure these and keep them in special bamboo boxes carved with beautiful patterns.

On the hearth each woman cooks for her husband and children, serving the men before she herself eats. Game is lightly roasted over the fire in cleft sticks. The fruits and vegetables that are not eaten raw are usually baked in the fire wrapped in banana leaves or boiled in tubes of bamboo green enough to withstand the flames until the food is cooked. Banana leaves serve as plates and napkins, coconut shells as cups and bowls,

fingers as forks and spoons. There are no metal or clay pots to carry on the trail, and there is no kitchen- or tableware that cannot be replenished on the spot.

The only really permanent household equipment consists of the beautifully woven baskets of split rattan or bamboo, the making of which is the women's most admired and most important work. These are always artistically designed and skillfully executed, and they are of many kinds and purposes. There are back-baskets, like knapsacks, in which the women carry roots and fruit home from the field. For hanging cassavas and squeezing out their poisons, there are the baskets that work like children's "finger traps," pressure being exerted on the contents by pulling both ends of the basket. There are fishing scoops and basketry traps for birds and squirrels.

One task that the Semang woman is not overly burdened with is either the making or the carrying of the family's clothing. In this environment, obviously, the less clothing worn, the better. Even for keeping out the damp at night no clothes can compare with a warm fire, and indeed the Semang word for fire actually means "clothing."

The chief article of Semang clothing is the girdle or loincloth worn by both men and women. The older type of girdle, which is still most likely to be worn in celebrations and dances, is made from the long, shiny, black, leathery-looking strands of a native fungus. These strands, about as thin as shoelaces, are plaited together into strips of cloth several yards long, which are then wound about the body, with their unplaited ends hanging loose like fringed tassels.

From the Savage Malays, however, the Semang have learned to make cloth out of the inner bark of the poisonous upas tree; and this type of bark cloth, which is common throughout the South Seas, is replacing the old fungus girdle. Two circular cuts are made around the bark of a three-inch upas sapling, one very close to the ground, and the other a few feet above it. A vertical cut connects the two circles. Then the bark is pounded on the tree with a wooden mallet or cudgel until it is loose enough to be carefully peeled off in one piece. The inner bark is then separated from the outer, thoroughly washed to remove all the poison sap, dried, and hammered out with coarsely grooved wooden bats until it forms a strip of soft material about a yard long.

The rest of the Semang's wardrobe is purely ornamental, serving no more as protection against the weather than does his tattooing. The tattooing, or rather scarring, is made by scratching the skin with the sharp edge of the sugar-cane leaf and rubbing charcoal into the slight wounds. All over the world, including Europe and America, this painful form of decoration is very popular among human beings. It will usually be found that races with light-colored skins tattoo with colors, while darker races, such as the Semang, whose skins would not show rubbed-in colors, raise thin scars or welts.

For other ornaments and charms there are the necklaces, bracelets, and knee-bands, worn by both men and women, made of the shining black fungus strands, or of fibers from jungle creepers, on which have been strung small animal teeth, fruit seeds, and small wild roots.

The most striking articles of clothing are the tall Spanish-looking bamboo combs worn by the women. These have beautiful designs cut into them, each pattern being a magical protection against a particular disease. Although the Semang women never actually comb their short hair, they probably wear more combs than the women of any other race. A woman may own as many as twenty or thirty combs, and she will often appear wearing eight of them at once, and sometimes as many as sixteen, stuck in a double row one behind the other. She thus gets immunity from as many diseases as she thinks are going about at the time. She need not, however, always be wearing all her combs at once.

A whole group of women together, no matter how large, will be protected from any illness if only one of them is wearing the right kind of comb. The larger the group, the less combs each woman will have to wear. The women frequently lend them to one another or exchange them to meet special emergencies.

The men, whose hair is even shorter than the women's, do not wear combs, but they have the same magical designs incised on their bamboo arrow quivers and blowpipe-dart quivers, to protect themselves, and any women or children in their company, from the same diseases and accidents. The men also carry special charm holders—bamboo boxes containing magical sticks for the same purpose.

5 . THE INVISIBLE WORLD

The diseases against which the women are protected by their combs and the men by their quiver patterns are sent on the wind by Karei, god of thunder. Besides illness, what the Semang fears most in this land of tropical storms are thunder, flood, and wind. The great storms can tear his flimsy shelter to bits, turn his digging and hunting grounds into swamps, uproot the great trees on which he depends for food, often killing men under them.

When he is angry at a sinner, Karei takes up a flower and shakes it over him. This causes lightning, while the striking together of the bell-like flower cups makes thunder. When the thunder peals, every Semang who knows he has sinned pierces his leg near the shinbone with a sharp sliver of bamboo. He draws off a little blood, hastily mixes it with some water in a bamboo cup, and throws it up at the angry skies, crying, "Karei, it is enough!"

These are some of the things that the Semang consider sins: a father-in-law's approaching too near to his daughter-in-law, or a son-in-law's coming too near his mother-in-law (if they actually speak, they commit a very grievous sin); throwing a spear before noon; drawing water in a pot that has been blackened by fire. To mock captured animals is a sin, for, the Semang say, the captive beast cannot revenge itself; but it is not a sin to laugh at a human being, for he is free to reply in kind.

The Semang believe that their chief god Karei, who is of supernatural size and has a fiery breath but is invisible, created all things except the earth and mankind. He had his son Ple complete this part of the work; and so Ple made the Semang but Karei breathed life into them. Ple and his sister Simei lived among the Semang for many years, and Simei gave light to the fireflies so that they might accompany her by night when she visited sick Semang women. Since Ple and Simei have gone, the fireflies keep seeking for them among the bushes, and that is why no Semang will ever harm a firefly.

Karei used to punish sinners by sending the wind to give them diseases. Ple pitied the people, so he went to the land of the Chenoi. These are bright elf-like creatures who live in flowers on the other side of the world and who make flower ornaments that are magical charms against various diseases. Ple collected these flower charms and with the help of Simei planted them on the mountains to help the people. It is from these flowers that the patterns on the women's combs and the men's quivers are copied. When the wind spirit catches up with a sinner, he drops the disease on the sinner's forehead, but when he sees a quiver or comb that carries the charm against his particular disease, he must fall down and let the owner of the charm pass unharmed.

Though the Semang have no very clear-cut ideas or feelings about life after death, they say there are three parts to the afterworld. The highest heaven, where Karei, Ple, and Simei dwell, is, as one would expect, filled with durian and mangosteen trees always bearing ripe fruit. The second or central heaven is a sort of purgatory. It also contains wild fruit trees, but these are guarded by a gigantic baboon, who pelts would-be thieves with the hard, prickly, inedible fruit of the tree called "false durian." The third or nethermost region contains nothing but low and brooding clouds, which bring sickness to mankind.

Like their government, like most of their ways of working and living, the religion of the Semang is very simple, even for so primitive a culture. As we have seen, the Semang have practically no restrictions on what they may eat, no "food sins" or taboos, such as make up much of the religious practices of other primitive peoples. Aside from their small blood sacrifices during thunderstorms, Karei makes no painful demands on men and women. Even this bit of blood, the Semang believe, is gathered up by Ple and put to good use in fertilizing their fruit trees.

The Semang have no fear of ghosts and, unlike the Malays, do not believe in demons. To them the little Chenoi are friendly fairies. There is not much ritual or ceremony to the Semang religion, which seems to consist mostly of myths and legends. There are medicine men, or priests, called *halas,* who help the people to approach Karei, but the functions of these priests are rather vague. They enjoy no greater authority than the old men, and there does not even seem to be any regular ceremonial worship of Karei.

All this is a little surprising. One would surely expect to find a religion of terror in the depths of the gloomy jungle, where the restless search for food must go on unceasingly every day and the tools for finding and using it are so ill developed, where the sun is rare but the tiger and the python are not. Nor does it follow that primitive life always makes for a simple religion. In other parts of the world, among tribes equally primitive in their mode of life, there have been developed the most complicated beliefs about ghosts and spirits—religions crammed with countless terrifying taboos and full of elaborate rituals for appeasing the spirit world.

Among the Semang, however, there seems to be an almost

careless serenity about the other world. The dead are simply buried with their belongings but with no great ceremony and certainly without fear. Knowing of the terror of demons among the more civilized Malays, the Semang are even sophisticated enough to play upon these fears by pretending to act the demon parts expected of them.

The Semang in their legends seem to be quite as capable of laughing at themselves as at the Malays. They explain their own physical appearance thus: In the beginning all men were Malays. Then a rajah coconut monkey came into the land and kindled a great brand that he had stolen from Karei. He started a fire that raged in the savannah grass, and the people fled in panic. Some of them ran to the river, boarded rafts, and went downstream. These escaped people became the Coast Malays of today. The others were more lackadaisical, and the fire caught up with them, burning their skins and singeing their hair before they could escape into the forest. These were our forefathers, say the Semang, and this is why we now live in the forest and have darker skins and curly hair.

In spite of all the reasons against it, they remain a cheery little people. If their possessions are few, so are their worries. Each man knows that if he has bad luck his kinsmen will come to his rescue. And there are times of contentment and fun. After an abundant harvest of durians the little band may settle down on one of their better camp sites for a while longer than usual. There is a natural forest clearing here, and the sun shines down, bright and hot. The edge of a clearing is always the gayest part of the jungle, with brilliantly colored flowers growing from ground, vines, and trees and making a tapestry all around. Vying with the orchids in brilliance are the bright-plumaged birds that flash across this circle of sunshine.

Perhaps some young man has come from a neighboring band to marry the daughter of one of the group. In any case it is a time of festive feeling, and there will be a dance. The men and women have adorned themselves with bunches and tassels of fragrant leaves and flowers inserted under their bracelets, knee-bands, and girdles. Around their heads the young girls have wound fillets, into which they have stuck flowers and leaves to make natural crowns. Even into the holes of their pierced ear-lobes they insert small rolls of leaf, and across their bosoms are bandoliers of more flowers. The young men and women are dressed for the dance.

Men and women do not dance together in couples as we do, nor does the whole band dance together as do other tribes. The Semang give performances of two or three men or two or three women, and they make very graceful performers. The music is very simple. Some men chant the words of a song. Others beat time by striking two sticks of bamboo together. Another plays upon a long bamboo nose-flute, into which the wind is blown through the nostrils rather than through the mouth. Sometimes there is also a mouth flute, with only three stops, or a bamboo Jew's harp.

The music and the songs are gay, expressing not only the mood of the occasion but also the whole spirit of these people, their ready capacity to be lighthearted and happy. You can sense this in the words of the Kra Song, that is, the Monkey Song:

> He runs through the branches, Kra!
> Carrying off fruit with him, Kra!
> He runs to and fro, Kra!
> Over the seraya tree, Kra!
> Over the rambutan trees, Kra!
> Over the live bamboos, Kra!
> Over the dead bamboos, Kra!
> He runs along the branches, Kra!
> Peering forward, Kra!
> And dangling downward, Kra!
> He runs along the branches and hoots, Kra!

Peering forward, Kra!
Among the young fruit trees, Kra!
And showing his grinning teeth, Kra!
From every sapling, Kra!
Peering forward, Kra!
He is dressed for the dance, Kra!
With the porcupine's quill through his nose, Kra!

ESKIMO

"We fear those things that are about us and
about which we have no sure knowledge, as the
dead, and the malevolent ghosts, and the secret
misdoings of the heedless ones among ourselves."

II. POLAR ESKIMOS:
People of the Icecap

*Three-quarters of the way from the equator to the North Pole,
another imaginary line rings the earth. It marks the limit to
which daylight can reach in midwinter, when the earth's axis
is tilted away from the sun. Overhead, the Big Dipper or Great
Bear swings steadfastly round the Pole Star, the tip of its tail*

always directly over this line. Because the Greek word for bear is arktos, we call this the Arctic Circle, and all the land above it the Arctic zone.

This is the world's round skullcap of ice, with the North Pole like a button in its center. It is mostly frozen sea—the Arctic Ocean—but includes also the northernmost edges of North America, Europe, and Asia. Because the world is round, this is as far away as one can get from man's original home in the tropics. And since not only man but all living things originated in warmth and moisture, the farther life penetrates in this direction, the harder must it struggle to survive. Indeed, it was once thought that eventually one would reach a line of life, like the tree line on mountain peaks, above which reigned a frozen stillness, where nothing grew or moved but the wind.

We no longer underestimate life this way. We know that, given enough millions of years, nature can adapt her creatures to almost any earthly conditions, and it may be taken for granted that she has somehow also populated this arctic waste. Nor should we underestimate man. Let nature give him an inch, as the saying is, and he will take a mile. Let nature, in her infinitely patient and painstaking way, adapt just a few of her selected creatures to life under otherwise impossible conditions; let her open up another empty region to the most restricted animal colonization—and if those creatures are large or plentiful enough to be eaten, here comes Everyman, the uninvited guest, the eternal squatter, Johnny-come-lately, to settle down too and to take over besides.

Even in this far frozen north, there is no privacy for polar bear or walrus, no refuge from the unsolicited and painful attentions of men. What adds to the injury is that the men we are speaking of are no civilized explorers in electrically heated airships. They are primitive Stone Age food-gatherers, as little provided for by nature to live here as the Semang, and almost, but not quite, as lightly equipped by their culture.

They live on the northern rim of North America, from Alaska to Greenland. Their name for themselves is "Innuit," which means simply "the People." But it happens that we know them by a mocking name given them by the Indians—"Eskimo," that is, "eaters of raw flesh."

1. DISCOVERY OF THE NORTHERNMOST PEOPLE

The Eskimos had been known to Europeans ever since the Elizabethan navigator Martin Frobisher found them in the Hudson Straits and captured one to bring back alive to his queen. That was in 1577. Nevertheless, in 1818, the English explorer Captain John Ross, sailing through Smith Sound, off the northwestern coast of Greenland, in search of a northwest passage to the Pacific, was surprised to see a group of eight Eskimo hunters on the shore. He had not believed that human existence was possible so far above the Arctic Circle, less than a thousand miles from the Pole.

Even more surprised were the hunters. They had been in search of narwhal when they spied what they took to be some tremendous birds with vast white wings floating on the open water. Frightened but curious, they drove their sledges part way down the beach and then hurriedly drove back up again. It was not until the next day that they gathered enough courage to come closer on the sea ice. Then Ross's Eskimo guide came down the side of one of the huge winged beasts and paddled toward them in a small boat.

That this man looked and dressed and talked very much like themselves was not surprising to the hunters. Was he not a man? All the same, they regarded him with amazement, for they did

not know him. They had always thought their little tribe the
only human inhabitants of the universe. By turns they pleaded
with the strange Innuit and threatened him. "Don't kill us," some
begged, while one bolder one said, "I can kill you."

The stranger told them to have no fear. "I am a man like you,"
he said. "I am flesh and blood. I have a father and mother like
you." He told one of the natives to touch him. He pointed to
the south and said he came from a distant country in that direction.

"That cannot be," they said. "There is nothing there but snow
and ice." They pointed to the ships and asked, "What great
creatures are those? Do they come from the sun or the moon?
Do they give light by night or by day?"

Ross's Eskimo guide, Sacheuse, explained, "They are houses
made of wood." This, of course, the hunters knew to be a ridicu-
lous statement. There was not that much wood in all the world.

Besides, they said, "They are alive. We have seen them move their wings."

Sacheuse finally persuaded them to come into his boat and be taken to one of the floating wooden igloos. There they discovered men who were really strange, who dressed in curious garments not made of fur and spoke gibberish and had pale, ghostlike skins, pale eyes, and light-colored hair that also grew heavily on their faces. Politely and fearfully the hunters pulled their noses in greeting.

They were shown around the ship. At all the marvels they saw and touched, their mouths gaped wide in wonderment. What sort of ice, they wanted to know, were the mirrors and skylight and binnacle glass made of? The metals were equally strange. These things from another world—undoubtedly a spirit world—they did not try to understand. What impressed them most were the chairs and tables and chests—not as articles of furniture but as things which, as well as the ship itself, were made of wood. The only wood these people had ever seen was in small pieces cast up by the sea onto their shores. This rare sea fruit, as precious to them as amber or ambergris would have been to Captain Ross, was carefully hoarded to be combined with bone or ivory to make sledge runners. Their delight and amazement could have been matched only by the excitement of Ross's sailors if the Eskimos had appeared with sledge runners made of solid gold. Of only one thing could the hunters be contemptuous—of what possible use for drawing a sledge was the little terrier that was the ship's mascot?

Soon the aliens sailed off into the outer space from which they seemed to come. Aside from some trinkets and tools and little gifts of wood, they left behind no abiding influence. Perhaps now the shamans or medicine men were more easily believed and understood when they spoke of their own journeys to the spirit world and of their strange adventures there. Probably the vague traditions out of the misty past, as told by the old men, were now confirmed: the Polar Eskimos of Smith Sound were not the only people in the world.

2 . THE INNUIT

As a matter of fact, this little tribe of so-called Polar Eskimos were not even the only Innuit in the world. The Eskimo people are not numerous, as nations go. There are less than forty thousand of them altogether—the population of a small city—but they inhabit a truly vast domain. Scattered a third of the way round the top of the globe, they can claim as their home the millions of square miles from Alaska to Greenland, the whole upper edge of North America that lies within the Arctic zone. Until the coming of the white man in modern times, there was for perhaps two thousand years no one to dispute with them their sole possession of this inhospitable empire of extreme cold and barren, treeless ice. There was nothing to tempt any invader, not even the warlike Indians to the south. Nor was there anything to tempt the Eskimos from their own wintry world, to which they were so well adapted that in softer climes they would have felt lost, they would have had to stop being Eskimos.

Thinly dispersed as they are over this tremendous region, the Eskimos are very obviously one race. Physically they look quite different from the red men of America, being more "Mongolian" in appearance. They have the so-called "slanting" eyes, the sallow or yellow skin, the low-bridged nose and flat, broad, almost beardless faces, the coarse, black, straight hair, and the short stocky builds of the Chinese. Through the length and breadth of arctic America, along the thousands of miles of sea-coast, they speak more or less the same language. (That is why Sacheuse had no difficulty in making himself understood by the Polar Eskimos.) But what chiefly makes them one people is the remarkable sameness of their way of life. Almost everywhere are the same basic inventions, the same customs and religion, similar beliefs and attitudes and habits. Of course, where one small group has lost contact with others for a long time, as did the Polar Eskimos, there develop small variations in speech or tradition. Special local hunting problems give rise to special local hunting methods. By and large, however, the Eskimo way of living has held true because it has so successfully fitted the environment.

In this vast, drafty corner of the world the average temperature for the whole year is well below the freezing point. In winter it often falls in many places to seventy degrees below zero. There are other parts of the world where the winter cold is as intense, or even more so, but here what we call winter lasts nine months of the year. For three months of that winter, the sun never rises at all. Even during the three months of summer, when the sun, by shining twenty-four hours a day, finally brings the temperature above the freezing point, the melting snow and ice keep the air fairly cool. Winter is the time of constant howling winds and violent blizzards, with never a tree to break their force. If weather means everything to the civilized hunter or camper, it can be imagined what it must mean to a people whose whole life is one long hunting trip.

This climate has remorselessly driven out every animal not especially equipped by nature to cope with the cruel, enduring cold and the sparseness of food. It was only some thousands of years ago that the mighty mastodon was wiped out. There remain only the heavily furred polar bears, wolves, foxes, hares. Even the domesticated dogs wear thick pelts. The seals, walruses, and whales carry a thick layer of fat or blubber under their skins to keep their blood warm and muscles active in the icy waters, which are anyhow warmer than the air over the land. The birds are only summer visitors.

Yet the Eskimo has hung on. With skin and flesh no different

from any European's or African's, his fingers and toes are as
easily frozen off. He cannot by nature run any faster, swim any
longer, or do with less food or sleep than they. The natural equipment issued to him is the same, and yet it has sufficed, for it has
included the same priceless fingers and, to guide them, the same
resourceful brain. With these as his guarantees of survival he has
devised his own special arctic equipment. Long ago he invented
out of the most unpromising of materials some of the most elaborate and ingenious habitations, tools, and weapons known among
primitive people anywhere in the world.

In this heritage the long-forgotten tribe of Polar Eskimos
shared. Their ancestors had undoubtedly come here from Canada
over the ice of the narrower part of Smith Sound, bringing their
arts and skills with them. Some may have gone back; some may
have gradually drifted down to southern Greenland. Eventually
the connections and contacts on both sides were broken, and
their isolation lasted long enough for them to forget there were,
or ever had been, other Innuit. But that they were Innuit they
did not forget.

They were named the Polar Eskimos because they lived farther
north than any other people, and because they were directly on
the most convenient route for later dashes toward the North
Pole, such as Commodore Peary's. Actually they lived only halfway between the Arctic Circle and the Pole. When Ross discovered them, their world was a narrow strip of Greenland coast
a few hundred miles long, hemmed in at the back and ends by
Greenland's glacier-covered mountains. Beyond the glaciers, they
believed, was the end of the world, stopping at a great impassable
"ice wall," where nothing could live or move. This was a quite
reasonable belief, considering that the Eskimos lived on the edge
of Greenland's Icecap—the white, deathlike desert that covers
nine-tenths of that enormous island with a mantle of permanent

ice thousands of feet thick. On their narrow, high, rocky fringe of shore, between the Icecap and the ice-bound sea, lived two or three hundred Polar Eskimos in eight widely scattered little settlements. Each one of these consisted of a cluster of some half-dozen stone huts.

3. THE IGLOO

How, Captain Ross wondered, is it possible to carry on a human existence so deep in the Arctic? He did not, of course, mean merely staying alive on an exploring expedition, such as his own, or even on a hunting trip, such as that of the Eskimos he first encountered. He meant family living, with women and children and old people, in sickness as well as in health, in winter as in summer, in the performance of other work besides hunting, the kind of work that must be done in warmth and in leisure time. In short, he meant home life.

The Polar Eskimos could have answered that. For this climate and for their needs they had ideal homes. Their little villages were usually to be found on gently sloping beaches, close to stretches of protected water that would freeze into smooth ice in winter, instead of into storm-tossed hummocks and ridges. Thus the dog sledges would have no difficulty in hauling heavy seal and walrus carcasses across the sea ice up to the very huts.

There was no wood, and even in summer the earth, a few inches below the surface, was frozen too solid for easy digging. Nevertheless, there were building materials for permanent houses. On the beaches could be found slabs of sandstone or other rock. These, the best of insulating materials, were laid out in a rough oval to make the walls; the chinks between them were stuffed with turf. The ceiling consisted of two layers of skin with moss stuffed between, resting on rafters of long whalebone; it was topped with a roof of turf. Usually the back of the house was dug into a hill-side. The front, with its single entrance and lone window, faced the sea.

The low arched doorway in front of the single room had no door in it and did not lead directly outside. Instead, one stepped down into a covered passageway or tunnel and crawled on all fours down a gradual incline ten to thirty feet long. This made the simplest, yet most efficient, of heat locks. Since the entrance to the house was below its floor level, the warm air inside, al-ways rising, was trapped among the well-insulated walls. It could not escape with a rush into the frigid night outside, as it certainly would if entry were made by swinging doors or tent flaps.

The inhabitants in fact were in greater danger of suffocation than of freezing, so a well-regulated exhaust was provided in the roof at the back of the house. This was a small hole, not really a chimney, but more nearly what the Eskimos themselves called it, "the nose of the house," for breathing out the used-up warm air. It was ordinarily kept plugged with a bunch of moss. If any-one felt the need of fresher air, the plug was taken out for a while, the heated air escaped in a thin stream, and cold pure air siphoned in through the tunnel to take its place.

The house also had an eye, somewhat less efficient than its nose, in the single small window directly over the tunnel. This was simply a pane of dried seal gut sewed into a frame of seal-skin. It passed enough light to let those inside know whether the sun or moon was shining, without their having to put on clothes and crawl outdoors, and there might even be a pinhole in it to peep out through. Facing the sea, the window often had a more important use—the same one that Yankee captains of sailing ships may have had in mind when they built their houses with the biggest windows on the seaward side—to cheer and guide home the benighted traveler.

This, then, was the igloo, the winter home, of the Polar Eskimo.

Seen from above, the roughly oval shape and tunnel gave it the look of a long-necked turtle, its head stretching out to sea. Its basic principles of construction, never improved upon for arctic living on purely arctic resources, were the same throughout the length and breadth of Eskimoland, though elsewhere, where driftwood or whalebone was more abundant and the ground less difficult to handle, these other materials would be used instead of stone.

And of course all Eskimos knew how to use the most abundant housing material of all—snow and ice. When we think of igloos, it is usually these snow huts that come to mind, because our imaginations are captured by the sheer cleverness of fighting cold and snow with snow and ice. The Polar Eskimos could build these snow huts, which they called *iglooiaks*, but they did so only in an emergency, for temporary use on the trail for a few weeks at most. For their more permanent homes they had plenty of stone houses, built long ago by their more numerous ancestors on all the better wintering sites. Actually, when Ross found them, the Polar Eskimos were no longer stone-house builders, but, thanks to those pioneering ancestors, neither did they have a housing problem.

There were not only enough houses to go around among all the families; there were even houses to spare and to satisfy the Polar Eskimos' ingrained nomadic habits.

Every spring, when all the families moved out of their winter homes to set up housekeeping in skin tents, there was also a general exodus, a tribal moving day. Most of the families would have decided to spend their next winter in one of the other villages nearer to some special kind of game—bear or walrus. Some may have been running short of driftwood or soapstone for lamps and pots, and may have hoped to find these more abundantly on one of the other beaches. So off they would go, with all their household gear, to pitch their summer tents close by a stone house in another village—a house similarly abandoned by some other family also in search of a change. This was all it took to establish ownership for the next winter. And anyway, in case of miscalculation or need, there was always the possibility of building a snow house.

No hunter or family ever went on the trail in winter without snow knives. When time came to make camp, a site was selected

Snow knife

where the snow was of just the right kind for building. It must not be too grainy lest it crumble in handling, or too newly fallen lest it be too soft to hold its carved shape in carrying. With the bone or ivory snow knives, foot-thick blocks were cut out of the drifts and set up on edge around the builder in a circle from six to twelve feet in diameter, depending on the size of the party. The builder stayed inside the circle as he laid the blocks round and round himself in a continuous spiral that gradually sloped inward. It took a good eye to cut each succeeding block to just the right-fitting shape, for no two could be alike.

When the builder had completely walled himself in, and had built a dome overhead that might be nine feet high, and before the final block had been put in place, he could cut himself a low arch out of which to crawl. Meanwhile, others outside had been packing soft snow into all cracks and crevices, as a mortar to cement the blocks together. They had also been digging a tunnel through the drift up to this entrance, below the level of the igloo floor, so that one would have to step up into the room. A house for a family to live in for weeks could be built by experienced Eskimos in a few hours.

A hunter or wayfarer caught in a blizzard, even if he knew that his destination was somewhere only a short distance away, would

not ordinarily risk exhausting himself in aimless wandering
through the blinding storm. Quickly he would build himself a
one-man shelter of this kind, maybe six feet in diameter, and
wait out the storm, for days if need be, till the stars or prevailing
winds or known landmarks could show him his way.

The interior of the stone winter house showed the same efficient use of the country's limited resources as the exterior. A
visitor, having negotiated the tunnel on hands and knees, past
the growling dogs who lived in it all winter, would finally climb
up through the three-foot-high archway into the single room.
The room was lined with skins, the air space between them and
the walls acting as further insulation. From the entrance to the
back of the house ran a central aisle, where alone the visitor
could stand erect. Along the walls at his sides and across the
alcove in the back was a continuous series of broad low platforms,
made of flat stones supported by stone legs. These were all the
tables, chairs, couches, shelves, workbenches, and kitchen coun-
ters that the house could boast of. The spaces beneath them
served as closets, storerooms, pantries, and refrigerators.

The wide platform in the back alcove was the family bed—its
stone covered with a layer of dried moss or grass over which were
spread the soft skins of bear or seal. The stone tables at either
side could also be spread with skins to sit on, but mostly they
held the household equipment and kitchen gear, most important
of which were the lamps, one on each side of the house.

Of all his simple yet efficient devices for keeping warm, the
Eskimo's lamp perhaps looked the most primitive. Yet it too was
quite a remarkable invention. It was nothing but a big shallow
bowl or dish carved out of soft soapstone in the shape of a half-
moon and standing on three or four small stones for legs. Its
length could vary from one to over three feet. For fuel it burned
the oil crushed from the blubber of sea animals. This was stored
and carried in a waterproof bag made from a whole sealskin that

had been stripped off the seal with a minimum of cuts and slits. The lamp wick was dried moss which had been reduced to a powder by being rolled in the palms of the hands, then carefully laid, like a narrow trail of gunpowder, along the straight edge of the half-moon, in a ridge about a quarter of an inch high. As the wick sucked up the oil from the very shallow bowl, it burned in a long straight line of steady little flames, bright enough to give a soft yellow light to the room and warm enough to let the family take off their clothes in any weather.

If the wick was well made, and the oil kept replenished, it might last for an hour. Keeping the lamps burning uniformly and without smoke throughout the day and night was the housewife's major concern (aside, of course, from her duties as cook, seamstress, and general assistant to her hunter husband). For her family preferred to sleep warm and disliked sleeping in the dark. Besides, it was no easy matter to start a new fire in the dark by striking flint or operating the bow drill.

When the woman noticed that her lamps were guttering and burning with a darker flame, she knew that the air was becoming bad. She would pull the moss plug out of the "nose" in the roof and allow the fresh air to circulate from the tunnel through the house until the flames burned clear white again.

Besides being the source of all the light and warmth of the house, the lamps were its only cookstove and its only water tap. Practically the only method of cooking was by boiling in stone pots that were suspended over the lamp flames by thongs tied to a square framework of wood or bone. Fresh water was made by placing clumps of ice or blocks of packed snow on an inclined stone over the blubber lamp and letting the melting water drip into a sealskin cup. People on an exclusive meat diet need lots of drinking water, and this was a tedious process for getting it. Fortunately for the housewife, bathing was all but unknown among the Eskimos. (Indeed, some peoples might have regarded the Eskimos as a rather dirty, verminous folk, but it could not be said that they did not have a good excuse. Among the more dangerous things that could happen in this climate was getting wet, and the avoidance of unnecessary wetting could easily become as much second nature to a fur-clad man as it is first nature to a cat.)

The interior and furnishings of a snow house, if the family intended to stay in it any length of time, were on the same general plan as that of the stone igloo. The heavy stone lamp and pots, like all its household goods, always went with the family on its migrations by dog sledge. The sleeping and cooking platforms were, however, blocks of ice and snow instead of stone. The window could be a thin sheet of ice. The walls, like those of a stone house, were lined with a skin tent behind which there was left an air space for insulation, this time to keep the snow walls from being melted by the inside heat. A little melting that would soon freeze again to solid ice only made the house tighter and more snug. Whether the walls were made of stone or snow, as the winter advanced and the snow drifted over the house, stopping up every crack and crevice and making it more cozy, there was less and less by which to tell the two kinds of houses apart.

The interior might have seemed crowded, shut-in, and gloomy to an alien from warmer lands where the outdoors was not an enemy to be kept out at all costs. But for a primitive people depending on purely local resources, the igloo was a marvel of adaptation to the climate. For in this house, without an opening window or door and with nothing but the tiny flame of an oil lamp to heat it, the air remained delightfully warm, yet healthfully fresh, throughout the bitterest cold.

As the outside air seeped in through the tunnel, its temperature at the entranceway was still below freezing and could keep the blocks of snow standing there for drinking water, dry and unmelted. As the air pushed down the central aisle and under the platforms, it was still cold enough to keep the food stored under them refrigerated. But as the air was drawn upward by the open lamps, it was so warmed by them that it finally streamed over the bed platform almost at the temperature of a steam-heated apartment. As the cold air continued to roll in, displacing the rising warmer air, this set up a circulation that eventually heated the whole upper part of the room.

Most of their time indoors the Eskimos spent off the cold floor, lolling on the warm sleeping platform, without any clothes, as if they were in a Roman bath. Considering that the winter was so long, and that so much of it was spent indoors because of the blizzards and the darkness, the Eskimo could be said to pass a great part of his life in a temperate if not actually subtropical climate.

Only with the coming of the short summer, when the families abandoned their stone houses, to live outdoors and sleep in tents, did the primitive Polar Eskimos escape their purely man-made environment and surrender themselves to nature. Captain Ross need not have been so concerned about them.

4 . CLOTHES

As long ago as 1577, Frobisher's chronicler remarked of the Eskimos, "Those beasts, fishes, and fowls, which they kill, are their meat, drink, apparel, houses, bedding, hose, shoes, thread, and sails for their boats, with many other necessaries whereof they stand in need, and almost all their riches." And this was true, and remained true, until later white men brought the Eskimos wood and metal, cloth and cereals, tea and tobacco.

Stone and ice and snow can have their uses for human living, as we have seen, but such uses are after all rather limited. Yet the only other natural resource offered to primitive man by the Arctic was its thin population of elusive animal life. Aside from shelter, almost everything else that men needed to survive had somehow to be taken from these animals. Every mouthful of food, every calorie of fuel, every stitch of clothing must be chased or trapped or ambushed.

Take, for example, the clothing of the Polar Eskimos. This was not only entirely the product of the hunt; it was what made hunting in this climate possible at all. Hunting here meant leaving the igloo, no matter how snug and warm, to range far afield, often for days on end, in subzero temperatures, among the perils of blizzards and treacherously moving sea ice. Whether the hunter ever returned would depend in the first place on whether he was properly clothed to keep him warm and dry.

Among the more notable things that distinguished the Eskimos from most other primitive peoples was the extraordinarily high quality of their tailored clothing. This was the work of the women—indeed their chief task, occupying the greater part of their working time. The Eskimo woman was rated as a good wife on the expertness of her needlework. Every single article of apparel of her whole family was the product of her skill and labor. Trousers, coats, stockings, underwear, boots, hoods—all were of skin, fur, or feathers, and all custom-made to measure by the same deft hand of the woman of the house.

Even before she could begin her careful cutting and fine stitching, it was she who tanned and softened the raw skins, by the painfully slow method of chewing over every inch of them. An Eskimo girl would be set to chewing skins when she was only four or five years old, and all the rest of her life she would be at it frequently. By the time she was forty-five her teeth were usually worn down to the gums.

The woman's needles were made for her by her husband out of bone or walrus ivory. Her thread she made herself out of sinews of narwhal or caribou. This was the best possible thread for the purpose. When it became wet from melting snow or dashing spray, it only swelled up, filling the needle holes and making the well-sewed seams even more watertight.

Though the materials for clothes and clothes-making were thus copied and stolen from nature's better-clad children, the style was the Eskimos' own. It was so well fitted to human needs in the Arctic that later civilized explorers were glad to adopt it wholesale. As a matter of fact, it is possible that the Eskimos made and wore tailored clothing before most Europeans did.

First was the long, loose, frocklike sealskin coat, with long, wide, roomy sleeves, that was pulled on over the head like a sweater and worn fur side out. There were no buttons to come undone or be lost. The looseness captured and warmed a mass of insulating air. If an Eskimo felt a touch of frostbite on his hands or face, he could shuck his arms out of his wide sleeves, take his mittens off within the protection of his coat, warm his hands in his armpits, and bring them up through the neck-slit to press against the white frozen spot on the face until the circulation was restored. Around the neck-slit was sewn a pointed hood— the famous *parka*—with an edging of fur all around the face to keep the cold air from getting at the ears and the back of the neck. In warmer weather, the Eskimo would throw back the hood and go about bareheaded. When it was very cold, he would wear an outer coat of fox fur, or of the less perishable but stiffer caribou hide, with the skin of the reindeer's head, ears and all, left on for a hood.

The men's trousers were made of the glistening white fur of the polar bear. Hence, the word for polar bear, *nanook,* was also used for trousers. Bearskin wears like iron, and the oils in its hair shed water like rubber and prevent the fur from becoming matted. It is warm in winter, cool in summer, and easily washed in snow. Nanooks were knee breeches, held up by a drawstring very low on the hips. Despite the long skirt of his coat, an Eskimo bending down could expose the bare middle of his back to a temperature of ninety degrees below freezing.

Not even in the coldest weather did the men wear underpants, but they did wear undershirts of eider or other down. It might take hundreds of birds to make one of these luxuriously soft, warm shirts, which were also, unfortunately, a paradise for body lice. Stockings were made of the soft white skins of the arctic hare. These are rather fragile skins, and a man had to pull on his stockings with almost as much delicacy as that of a woman putting on nylon hose.

Over the stockings came the knee-high sealskin boots, perhaps the most important garment of all, calling for the seamstress's most conscientious care. The soles, of tough caribou skin, had to be resistant to the sharp-edged ice that can cut like knives. The sealskin uppers had to be warm and flexible, the seams absolutely waterproof. A frozen foot could mean the end of all hunting. A pad of dry moss between the boot sole and the stocking absorbed the penetrating damp of salt sea ice. Often, after a day's travel, this pad when taken out of the boot would be a solid cake of ice, while the fur stocking above it remained dry and flexible. The sealskin mittens, completing the men's costume, were also often provided with these protective pads of moss.

The women's dress was not very much different, except in materials and ornamentation. Women too wore trousers, but these were of blue and white foxskins that might have been worth a small fortune in the great cities of civilization. Also, unlike the men, women wore sealskin underpants, and their boots reached to their hips. These bulky, elephant-like hip-boots might not have seemed very feminine, but they were handy for carrying small valuables, such as a puppy new-born on the trail.

The children were dressed like their elders. Though they might be seen playing in the greasy snow around an igloo in dirty, torn clothes, they were sure to have at home a suit of clothing every bit as new and fine as those of their parents.

In the Arctic, dryness, not cleanliness, is next to godliness. The whole secret of keeping warm is keeping dry. The constant care of the Eskimo housewife was to keep the family's clothing and footgear mended, waterproof, soft, and flexible. Whenever an Eskimo came indoors he first of all beat the snow thoroughly out of his clothes with the household snowbeater—a flat piece of bone or driftwood kept hanging at the entrance. Then he gave his boots to the woman of the house to dry at the lamp. Otherwise the melting snow would soak into his clothes and freeze solid against his skin the moment he went outdoors again, sheathing him in ice. This was another reason for the Eskimo's custom of taking off all his clothes indoors. Even on the trail a snowbeater usually hung from the upright handles of the dog sledge, to be used whenever the traveler stopped to rest.

5. HUNTERS OF THE NORTH

Normally when we ask how some creature manages to live in a certain environment, we are thinking of its food—what it is and how it is gotten. It is only because of the extraordinary conditions of the Arctic that here our first thought was of dwellings and clothing, the problem of protection from the climate. We have seen how successfully the Polar Eskimo solved that problem, indoors and out. His family warmly sheltered behind stone and ice, himself warmly clad from head to toe in arctic furs, he was now ready to pursue his main business in life—the hunt.

It bears repeating that any people who chose to live on the resources of this land would have to hunt and fish, not only for its food but also for almost everything else that makes human life possible. There is no possibility of living by gathering plants, let alone by cultivating them. For all practical purposes, the only natural resource is the animal life. Hunting must supply not only the total diet, indoor fuel, and outdoor clothes, but also the means of hunting—the materials for the hunter's weapons.

Chief among the Eskimo's weapons was his harpoon, considered to be among the most remarkable of primitive inventions. It is illustrated and described on page 86. When you consider how this complex big-game weapon had to be assembled with almost machine-like precision—so that it would fly through the air as a single piece, true as a lance, and yet so that each part would do its separate job on contact—don't forget that it was invented by men of the Stone Age. The straightness and balance of the shaft had to be achieved by scraping with a sharp stone. The work of nails, screws, and hinges was done with lashings of skin string. The holes for the lashings were drilled through the hardest bone or ivory with still another clever Eskimo device, the bow drill, which is illustrated on page 87.

When Ross discovered the Polar Eskimos, their principal quarry was the seal. Its flesh was their staple diet, its blubber at once their bread and their lamp fuel, its skin their most important material for clothing, bedding, lines, and almost everything else for which other people use textiles and fibers.

And yet, in the long winter, no early white explorer would ever have guessed that this was seal country. For then the seals stayed hidden away in the warmer water under the thick ice. The Eskimos knew, however, that a seal must feed fairly close to shore and that, at least every quarter-hour, it has to come up for air. That does not make the seals any more visible, for they have their own inconspicuous way of doing this. In the short autumn, when the ice is still thin, each seal makes itself a series of breathing holes, which it keeps open all through the winter by returning to them very regularly for a draft of air. At each round of visits, it scratches and gnaws away the new ice that has meanwhile formed over its blow-holes. Then it pushes only

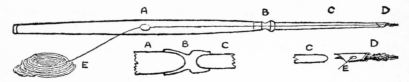

THE HARPOON

The Eskimo harpoon consisted of five separate parts:

(A) A heavy throwing shaft, preferably of driftwood, sometimes five feet long for the biggest game (walrus), with a knob halfway down the side for holding the line taut.

(B) A bone socket rammed firmly onto the long shaft, with drilled holes in its upper end, through which thongs were laced, holding in place

(C) a light shaft of bone or ivory, one to three feet long, onto the tip of which was stuck

(D) a detachable barbed harpoon head, held in place by

(E) a running thong line. One end was tied to the harpoon head through a drilled hole; it then passed tautly alongside the smaller shaft, was turned tightly around the knob on the heavy shaft, and ended in a coil at the hunter's feet.

The smaller shaft (C) was tied just tightly enough to the bone socket (B) to keep both shafts in a straight line while the harpoon was in flight. But there was enough play in the lashings so that, when the head struck the target, the impact made the connection give, the two shafts making an angle at the socket, like a bent elbow. This suddenly slackened the line (E), and the detachable head (D) was jerked from the light shaft. The barbed point turned in the flesh and held fast like a fishhook. As the wounded beast fled down into the water, the hunter paid out the coil until he could land his exhausted prey.

The Eskimo was very clever with string, for which he had a hundred uses. Taking a large section of uncured skin, he cut an edge of uniform width all around it, in a continuous spiral, the way one pares an apple, until the whole skin had been turned into a single length of line.

THE BOW DRILL

This ingenious substitute for a brace and bit looked like a toy bow and arrow. The bow had a slack string, the arrow a loosely fitted wooden block on its tail instead of feathers. The slack string of the bow was looped around the shaft of the arrow.

With one hand, the driller held the stone point of the shaft firmly over the spot where the hole was to be made. His teeth clenched in the wooden mouthpiece, he bore his weight down on the drill. With his other hand, he sawed the bow violently back and forth, thus rotating the drill.

The Eskimo also used his bow drill for making fire. He replaced the stone point by a wooden head and drilled it into a piece of driftwood, feeding the smoking sawdust with a tinder of dried moss until it burst into flame.

its nostrils up through the blanket of drifting snow that helps keep the ice from forming too thickly.

In doing this, however, as the Eskimos knew, the seal also leaves a scent for the hunter's dog. When a dog flushed such a blow-hole, the hunter carefully scraped away the covering snow, and could tell at once from the thinness of the ice whether the hole was in regular use. If it seemed promising, he would gently push the snow back over the hole and stick a bone pointer into it. The seal would have to move this when it thrust its muzzle through for air. Then the hunter might have to wait patiently for several hours for the seal's return visit to that hole. That is why this form of hunting was called *maupok*, meaning, "he waits."

It was in fact rather more like fishing than hunting. The hunter brought a little stool with him to sit on, or he might sit it out on a cake of ice, after building a snow wall as a windbreak for his back. He kept his harpoon ready to hand; he must be ready at the first tremor of the pointer to thrust the weapon through the snow and the small hole in the ice, directly into the muzzle of the invisible seal. As the seal plunged wildly into the sea, carrying

the detachable harpoon head with it, the Eskimo paid out his line and drew it in, exactly as one plays big fish, until he could pull the exhausted, air-starved animal back up to the breathing hole. Then he must chop in the ice—which was sometimes several feet thick—a hole big enough to bring in his catch. Obviously, under such conditions, the most high-powered rifle in the world would not have been a satisfactory substitute for the Eskimo's harpoon.

With the break-up of the ice in spring, the seals came out into the open, basking in the sun at the edge of the ice. Then the Eskimos could engage in a type of hunting that seems more familiar to us—*utok*, or "he stalks." The hunter crawled slowly and noiselessly forward, belly flat on the wet ice, hiding behind rocks and hummocks where he could, pretending to be a seal in all his gestures and movements when he could not hide, until he was close enough to launch his harpoon. Here too the harpoon was necessary not only to kill the seal but to hold it lest its body topple off the ice edge and be lost in the sea.

Since utok also took hours of patience and alertness, there was a special hazard from the glare on the ice reflecting the low rays of the spring sun. This could in a short time blind a man for days. Hence the hunter came equipped with still another special Eskimo invention—snow goggles. These were simply spectacles,

with "lenses" made of thin strips of bone, ivory, or wood, in which were cut slits just barely wide enough to see through yet narrow enough to shut out the glare. One naturally squints one's eyelids into narrow slits to cut down too dazzling a light and to protect the more sensitive parts of the retina of the eye, but this

action also makes for fuzzy vision and eyestrain. The Eskimo snow goggles were simply a device for permitting the hunter to keep his eyes wide open, without strain and without loss of clarity, while protecting his retinas.

Farther to the south, the Greenland Eskimos hunted even the whale with harpoons, but in Ross's time the Polar Eskimos were not seagoing (except on foot over the winter ice), and their biggest game was the walrus, the Scandinavians' "whale-horse." This tusked monster could supply almost a ton of meat, blubber, and bone, to say nothing of valuable ivory. But it took great daring and endurance to fight him, with harpoons and lances that could rarely kill him outright, out on the edge of the sea ice, which he could smash to smithereens in his struggles.

But the most exciting hunt of all—and one of the most important to the Polar Eskimos' way of life—was the hunt for the white polar bear. The Polar Eskimos looked upon Nanook as coming next to themselves in nature's ranks, and no boy was considered to have become a man or to have the right to take a wife until he had first killed a bear. Every hunter with a good,

strong team of dogs tried to go out after bear at least once a
year. This was usually during the first brilliant moonlight after
the forming of the winter ice or during the first bright sunlight
of early spring, for the bear's white coat is not easy to see at a distance amidst the snow, and he is very fast on the rough ice.

For this game the dogs were a necessity—to scent the bear,
chase him, attack and wear him down, and hold him at bay till
the slower hunter could come up and make the kill. The dogs
seemed to enjoy this sport as much as the men. Even when on
a journey for some different purpose, if they scented fresh bear
tracks, they could not be held back from setting off in pursuit.
The driver held onto the uprights of his sledge for dear life, for
no matter how fast they had to run, or how rough the ice, nothing
would stop the dogs until either they had brought the bear to
bay or it had escaped them into open water. If the driver was
shaken off the sledge, he would simply have to walk for miles,
maybe as many as twenty, after the dogs.

When he was actually out after bear, and the dogs gave chase,
the hunter would slip or cut the trace of one of his dogs so that
it might run ahead of the team as a pacemaker. He himself clung
fast to his sledge and cheered the dog on with cries of "Nanook!"
The dogs, if they finally caught up with this powerful, enduring,
swift ice-runner, would race around it in circles, baiting it,
nipping at its hindquarters. Often the great animal would catch
one of the dogs in its paws or jaws or throw it violently against
the ice. A bear hunt often cost the hunter dearly in valuable dogs
killed or hopelessly maimed.

For the hunter personally, too, the bear was his most dangerous
game. He must come close enough to strike it with a lance, sometimes even with a knife. Nearly every grown man bore the scars
of Nanook's claws on his body. Aside from the ferocity of the
bear, its long pursuit over the sea ice brought other hazards from
which the hunter might never return at all—being lost in a

sudden blizzard, or dying of cold and starvation. Many a Polar Eskimo had true tales to tell of heroic adventure and almost superhuman endurance suffered in the daily routine of making a living.

Of course, not all the hunting was dangerous, nor was it all done by the men. Among this race of hunters, all were hunters—men, women, and children. In winter the women made and tended the snares for arctic hares and foxes and such small game. The hares were caught in slip nooses hanging from lines stretched across their most frequented runways. The foxes were killed in stone deadfalls or captured in stone box traps.

In summer the women, as well as the children, the infirm, and the aged, spent most of their time catching birds with hand nets on long poles or with small spears. The whole village would pitch their skin tents near the cliffs where the northern birds congregated and nested in vast numbers—the dovekies, which were the most numerous; the flightless auks, which needed only to be knocked on the head to be taken; the black eider duck, from whose down the women made undershirts. All this small game, besides being valuable for furs and feathers, provided a welcome change from the monotonous winter diet of seal and walrus.

The surplus, even the eggs, could be cached away for some special feast, or for needier days, when the hunters would be storm-bound in the igloos. In winter, too, if the lucky hunter brought down more than the day's needs, or if it was more than he could carry and store at home, he would find some pit or build a stone cairn, safe from marauding foxes or bears, and stow the surplus in it. In this climate, these caches could well serve as a deep-freeze, and meat might often be preserved in them for a year or more. Even if a sudden thaw should unfreeze the meat for a while, the Eskimo would not consider that great harm had been done. He was not finicking about over-ripeness in meat.

Often the hunter would set up a whole string of caches on the trails he most regularly followed. In case of real need it was perfectly proper for any other hunter to help himself from any cache he might find.

Except when the game sought was too big for the resources and equipment of one man, the Eskimo was ordinarily a lone hunter. If you asked him about such things, he would tell you that he was alone responsible for the feeding of his family, and that what he caught was his own. Yet he did not mean by such ideas and words what they might mean to us. There is an old children's custom among us that is closer to the Eskimo way of thinking than our grown-up point of view is to either of them. If one of our boys finds a coin or other valuable treasure, he may say, "Finders keepers!" But if another boy happens to be along, he has the right to cry, "Halvies!" and to share in the finder's luck as a partner.

So, on a group hunting expedition there were strict rules and fixed customs for the division of all spoils. After an animal was killed, it was cut up into as many portions as there were heads of families in the party. The man who had actually made the kill or who had first harpooned it was entitled to choose his portion first. Second choice went to the man who first placed his hand on the game after the kill, the next choice to the second man who did so, and so on. But, in fact, almost anyone standing around when an animal was caught or brought home could expect a piece of it, especially if he helped to tow it onto the beach. Thus, calling the hunter's game "his" did not give him an absolute property right in it, to do with as he pleased, but seemed more a way of showing who were the good hunters, deserving the respect of the village. The honor was "his," not necessarily the meat.

Even after the hunter had brought his meat home, his lucky household was expected to share generously with the families of those that were not so lucky. It is undoubtedly this custom of sharing food that has kept the small race of Eskimos surviving for these thousands of years. If every hunter had to depend entirely on his own luck and skill, instead of sharing in and contributing to the luck and skill of the whole village, a hostile nature would very shortly have picked them off one by one, for in the Arctic no hunter's fortune can be consistently good for several years running. The Eskimo took the greatest pride in being a good hunter because his village gave its best hunters the greatest respect, and the village did this because the life and well-being of everyone depended on his efforts. To refuse to share with those in need would have undermined the hunter's very pride in his skill. He would at the very least have lost an appreciative audience for his favorite stories—his accounts of his own breathtaking exploits.

6. THE DOG SLEDGE

In this land where man's "bread" was scattered thinly over so wide an expanse and moved so swiftly on legs and flippers, his survival would have been unthinkable without the Eskimo dog team and sledge. Only because of these could he range as far and as fast as the game he chased. Because he had this means of transporting heavy loads, he could maintain a permanent base of operations for his family while he went great distances in pursuit of big animals. In winter he could hunt far out on the sea ice that bridged the many offshore islands and his narrow coastal homeland.

The sledge was a typically Eskimo piece of ingenuity in the way it turned difficulties into advantages. No wheeled vehicle could possibly have stood up to the terrain. Built low to the ground, the sledge was easy to keep from overturning even when it careened over the roughest ice. Light in weight, it could be carried over chasms that it could not jump. Intricately fitted together from many pieces of driftwood, bone, and ivory lashed together by thongs, it was as flexible as a snake, taking the contours of the land under it like the caterpillar treads of a tractor.

At the rear end were two upright guiding handles, often of caribou antlers, by which the driver steered the sledge and held it down to the ground right side up. Otherwise it was a simple narrow affair of two runners, five to fifteen feet long, held together by many crossbars lashed between them. The runners could be made of odds and ends of wood pieced out with bone, or even of frozen hide shod with ivory.

When the sledging was over soft or powdery snow, the runners would stick as if in sand or pick up uneven lumps of snow unless they were "iced" to make them glide more lightly. Since ice breaks off too easily from polished bone or wood, the driver would first cover his runners with a more cushiony layer of frozen mud, moss, or even seal's blood. Onto this, just before setting out on his journey, he would squirt mouthfuls of melted snow. Then, immediately, before this could turn back into ice, he must quickly smooth the already freezing water over the runners with mittens or bare hands. In a temperature of thirty to fifty degrees below zero, his hands had to move fast if they were not to freeze to the runners. Where the snow was level and soft, this layer of ice let the sledge skim over the ground like skates on a pond. But when the going was over sharp ridges of hard ice, the shoeing would of course break off and the whole process might have to be done all over again.

On a long trip the Eskimo would lay over the crossbars of the sledge big slabs of frozen blubber and meat a half-inch thick to serve as a kind of flooring. Over this he could, with pliant cords of walrus hide, strap a bearskin rug. Thus stowed away, the cargo of food would not spill if the sledge rolled over, and was

safe from the voracious dogs. When he stopped for a meal, all the traveler had to do was turn the light sledge upside down and cut himself a slice of blubber from between the crossbars. Often, too, he would use a slab of meat, frozen as hard as a plank, for his seat.

In the sledge the Eskimo again tackled and solved his problem in the typical Eskimo way. Just as with the snow house, difficulty was turned into opportunity, the enemy made into a useful ally. The very qualities that made snow and ice so very difficult for foot travel were what made them ideal for sledges. The efficiency of this invention *depended* on the extreme cold. Indeed, if there was one thing an Eskimo driver on the trail dreaded as much as an orchard grower dreads an unseasonable frost, it was an unseasonable thaw. Then, not only could he lose the icing off his runners, but also the skin lashings holding his sledge together would grow damp and begin to stretch, and his runners might

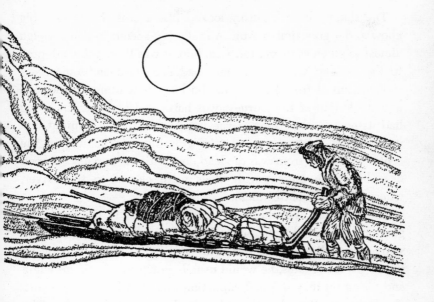

flatten out altogether, leaving him with an unwieldly raft in place of a trim, efficient, speedy craft.

The sledge could of course be dragged by men at their own plodding pace, but what made it the fast, wide-ranging vehicle of the hunter was the team of dogs. The dog is man's earliest domesticated animal, and has gone with man into every part of the world. But no primitive people has ever made better use of its companionship than the Eskimos. Frobisher's chronicler did not list the dog among the "riches" of the Eskimo, probably because Frobisher came in the summertime and could not see the huskies at work. Yet they were undoubtedly the Eskimo's most valuable possession, though the only one he did not acquire by trapping and killing. On the contrary, he had often to spend as much time hunting food for his dogs as for his family. Whenever possible, he fed the dogs as well as he fed himself, for on his dog sledge depended his having any food at all.

The shaggy Eskimo husky looked like a cross between a big chow and a gray timber wolf. A really big specimen could weigh almost as much as its master. Like him, it was thoroughly adapted to the subzero temperature and had enormous endurance.

The team of from five to nine huskies, depending on the load and the length of the journey, was harnessed fanwise. Each dog had its own leather trace of varying length so that it might find its own safe footing over the irregularities of the ice. In the center and out in front was the lead dog, with the females grouped near him. The more unruly dogs were closest to the driver, where he could control them.

The lead dog was the fiercest and strongest in the team. He got the choicest morsels of food and was expected to maintain some sort of discipline in the ranks. If a fight broke out between two of his teammates, he would usually pounce on both, growling and biting till they stopped. Sometimes he even had a lieutenant, also feared by the others but himself obedient to the leader. The best teams were usually made up out of puppies from the same litter, since the dogs were almost unmanageable if they did not know one another and acknowledge one of themselves as leader.

The team was guided mainly by means of a whiplash, often thirty feet long, with which the skillful driver could flick the ear or hindquarters of any dog not pulling its weight or straying from the course. The dog that had been hit would set up a howl, and the whole team would redouble its efforts. A good driver with a well-trained and harmonious team could also steer by cries of "right" and "left" while he held the sledge to the ground by the uprights. Braking his eager team to a halt might cost him more effort than driving it. For a short rest, the sledge would be turned over and each dog's trace looped around one of its paws.

These teams were capable of drawing a sledge ten to twelve hours a day for days on end, averaging four or five miles an hour over terrain that a man would be fortunate to cover at a mile an hour. Some dogs have been known to travel thirty-six hours at a stretch and to go three days without food. They seemed to have a special sense for ice danger, picking their way cautiously over uncertain ice and refusing to step on it at all when it was unsafe.

On the trail the dogs slept in the open, cuddled in a round ball, their noses and ears covered by their bushy tails—a trick that was copied by their driver, who often held a fox tail between his teeth while driving, in order to protect his nose from the wind. If the snow was drifting, the dogs would get up now and then to shake the snow out of their fur before it melted. For the dogs, as for the men, the secret of keeping alive and well in the winter was the same—eat plenty and keep your clothing dry. Nevertheless, at the end of a hard day of sledging, the dog's muzzle would be covered with a mush of ice formed on his fur by the freezing of his moist breath. Against this hazard the men at least could protect themselves by keeping clean-shaven, that is, by plucking out the hairs of their rather sparse beards.

When the going was over salt sea ice, which always remains somewhat damp by comparison with the more quickly hard-frozen ice of fresh water, the slush would pack in between the dogs' toes. Later this might refreeze, spread the toes apart, and split the skin, causing the dogs so much pain that they could not travel. Hence, on such terrain, the driver would stop the team now and then, to let the dogs bite out the slush. Sometimes the women even made little sealskin boots for the dogs.

In winter, between journeys, the dogs spent most of their time in the entrance tunnel of their master's igloo, protected from the bad weather, but only slightly from the cold, living on generous table scraps, and mostly sleeping. If visitors came to the village, the dogs would have to be tied up. Gentle and loyal to their master and his family, they were nonetheless dangerous animals, and all the dogs in a village would gang up, given the opportunity, for a savage attack on any strange dogs. In summer, when the sledges were put away, the Eskimos used often to put their dogs on small islands, where they could run at large but where food would be brought to them regularly.

There is one other Eskimo hunting vehicle as clever and as much imitated around the world as the dog sledge, namely, the kayak or one-man skin boat. If till now this boat had been mentioned only in passing, it is because, at the time of Captain Ross's discovery of the Polar Eskimos, they had no kayaks. To learn how this happened to be, and how the Polar Eskimos did acquire kayaks, we must know the story of how they were "discovered" a second time.

7 . THE ODYSSEY OF KRIDLARSSUARK

Hundreds of miles across the sea and due south from Smith Sound is a great island in northern Canada formerly called Baffin Land and now called Baffin Island, lying between Baffin and Hudson Bays. Now the coast of this island is a center of Eskimo culture, that is, it is one of the places where all the typical Eskimo arts, customs, and inventions may be found in their most highly developed state, and it is probably from here that many other Eskimo tribes originally spread out to the present fringes of the Eskimo world. Thus it bore the same relation to the Polar Eskimos of northern Greenland that Europe bore to the early white settlements of America.

Unlike the Eskimos of Smith Sound, those of Baffin Land were long accustomed to seeing white whalers and sailors on occasion. One day, about forty years after Ross's expedition, one of these whalers happened to mention to his Eskimo host that he had heard of an Eskimo tribe living far above the Arctic Circle in northern Greenland. The Baffinlander he told this to was Kridlarssuark, a mighty hunter among his people and a great magician.

When Kridlarssuark heard this tale, he was already a man past middle age. He was bald, and therefore already sufficiently striking to his fellow-tribesmen, for baldness is very rare among the Eskimos. In addition, he was an *angakok*, a shaman or medicine man; he could fall into trances and see visions and talk to the spirits, who forecast the weather for him, and told him where good hunting was to be found in times of famine, and revealed to him the names of those who had committed secret sins and thus brought disaster on the village from the offended spirits. He was held in great awe by his tribe as a powerful magician, a religious leader, and a good man. Men said that at night a white flame could be seen hovering over his bald head. They repeated marvelous stories of his hunting prowess—how many times he had saved the whole community from death by starvation because he was directed by the spirits to the one spot in the whole famine-stricken land where there was game to kill.

Once, they said, he was out hunting on the sea ice with a small orphan boy, and when they were far out from shore there rose a sudden gale that broke the ice around them into floating floes, and there was no way to get back. And then Kridlarssuark told the boy to lie down on the sledge and hold fast, and to keep his eyes tight shut no matter what happened until he was told to open them. And the boy did so, but he felt the sledge moving under him, and so he opened his eyes a crack and peeped. And he saw that the angakok had turned himself into a polar bear, who trotted ahead of the sledge, pursued by his own dogs, and that wherever the bear trod, the sea became ice, which bore up the dogs and the sledge. But as the boy looked, one of the sledge runners began to sink into the ice, and he could feel the sledge tipping him into the sea. So he quickly closed his eyes again and felt the sledge right itself and go on for a long, long while. And when the dogs stopped, he heard Kridlarssuark tell him to open his eyes and they were on the mainland. This story was known to be true because it had been told by the boy himself.

After Kridlarssuark heard the rumor of the little group of distant cousins living so far away beyond the Great Sea, where no one had imagined life could be possible, he could not sleep, and he could think of nothing else. It was as though a great sickness had come upon him, just the sort of arctic melancholy to which the Eskimos are prone and which he himself was accustomed to cure in others by finding some secret sin. He dreamed only of this faraway land and yearned to see these remote people. Columbus and many other great explorers would have understood his illness.

At last he told his wife and family that he had decided to go on a journey to find the strange Innuit to the north. He told others about his decision. "Do you know the desire for new countries?" he asked. "Do you know the desire for new peoples?" So persuasively did he tell of his dream that several others volunteered to go along. For so long a journey the men would naturally take their entire families, so among the party of thirty-eight bold adventurers who set out from Baffin Land in 1862 were many women and children.

The sledges were especially built for this expedition, each twenty feet long and four feet wide. They had to be so big because they were to carry the kayaks, the clothing, the tents, the hunting and fishing equipment, the lamps and cooking pots, the food for men and dogs, the children, and, when the going was good, the men and women themselves. Some of the sledges were drawn by as many as twenty dogs.

They set out toward the end of winter, when enough light had come to travel by but the sea was still frozen hard enough for sledging. Under Kridlarssuark's expert guidance they found plenty of meat along the way—seals, walruses, bears, and white whales. Sometimes they found long stretches of coast not covered with ice and so they had to make long detours out to sea or over huge glaciers. When summer came and the sea ice broke up, they made a permanent camp along the shore and hunted in their kayaks for supplies for the next winter's journeying. In autumn they built stone houses roofed with turf in which to spend the dark season. As soon as light came again they were once more on their way. Thus two years were passed traveling and camping.

Then one of the men, named Oqé, rose in protest and said he would go no farther. Oqé was homesick, not for his wife and family, for these were with him, but for whale meat. For they were long out of the country of the whales, on which the Baffin Land Eskimos depended mostly for their food and building materials. Naturally Oqé was ashamed to give this childish reason for his loss of heart and so he told the others that Kridlarssuark was deceiving them. There were no such people as the Polar Innuit and they were being led on a wild-goose chase. Oqé prevailed upon twenty-four people with five sledges to turn back with him. Five sledges and the faithful remainder continued on the journey, and among these was Oqé's own son.

We know what strength of character it took for Columbus to follow his dream across the unknown Atlantic for three months in spite of all ridicule and disbelief. What sort of man then was Kridlarssuark, who kept his little band going for *six years* across the unfamiliar icy wilderness of the Arctic, in quest of a promised land that had nothing behind it but a sailor's story? Often on the way, to give heart to his people, Kridlarssuark would go into a trance and send his spirit through the air to find the lost tribe. Finally, one day when they had made camp in a country full of caribou, they spied two tiny moving specks in the distance. "Sledges! Sledges!" broke the cry from the little band of explorers. Sure enough, on the two sledges that rapidly approached them were two Polar Eskimos.

They fell upon one another with eager questions, finding little difficulty in understanding one another's small variations in dialect. Here was no bewildering encounter between men of different races and speech, between "savage" natives and "civilized" men who came in hope of conquest or conversion. Kridlarssuark came not as a Cortez to rob and enslave and eventually to wipe out another people. He came in search of his lost brothers, and perhaps, underneath all that, out of the simple curiosity of the really great explorers—to see for himself and to settle a problem.

Nevertheless, the long isolation of the Polar Innuit from all other tribes did give rise to a few misunderstandings on both sides, the visitors being no better anthropologists or scientists of any kind than the natives. So when the Polar Eskimo who first came running to meet them turned out to have a leg made of driftwood—having lost his own in an accident—the Baffinlanders at first assumed they would all be like that, probably born with wooden legs. On the other hand, the tattooed faces of the Baffin Land women were equally startling to the Polar Innuit and gave them similar misconceptions.

The coming of Kridlarssuark was one of the two greatest turning points in the history of the Polar Eskimos, the other being not Captain Ross's visit but the events that had led up to their isolation from the rest of the Eskimo world. When Kridlarssuark and his companions had been royally welcomed by the hospitable northerners and had settled down among them and been adopted by the village, he discovered that these long-lost cousins did not have the bow and arrow, or had somehow lost the art of making them. How then, he asked, did they catch the caribou? Still more surprising was the answer that the Polar Innuit did not hunt the many reindeer that abounded in their country. They did not consider the meat fit for human consumption. If a Polar Eskimo did by chance kill a caribou or find a dead one, he would feed it to his dogs, and keep only the skin and antlers. Krid-

larssuark and his companions soon set about proving that the
flesh of the caribou was wholesome food, and that the eating of
this land animal need not offend the spirits of the sea animals if
proper precautions were taken to keep the two kinds of meat
apart. They taught the Polar Eskimos how to copy their own
bows—three pieces of antler lashed into a powerful springy
curve by wrappings of sinew—and their own small flint-tipped
arrows.

In time the Polar Eskimos revived the forgotten art of the
caribou hunt. Then, for two weeks in the early fall, when the birds
were leaving their cliff nests to fly south, and the sea ice had not
yet grown thick enough for maupok hunting of seals, and the
walruses and bears were still safe on their floating icebergs, all
the men and their dogs would go off together across the glacier
into what had once been to them no man's land. Here were the
last great grazing grounds of the big caribou herds, before the
flying snow covered the grassy plains. Soon the herds would
break up into little family groups, pawing through the snow
and ice for scant patches of frozen moss and drifting out of the
hunters' range. Now, too, at the end of summer, the meat of the
reindeer was at its fattest and juiciest, and their skins were most
thick and supple and had the shortest hair.

A whole herd could be stampeded and driven onto the new
thin ice in the wet bogs, where the hoofs of the caribou would
break through, slowing down their flight and making them easy
targets for arrows and dogs. Or the caribou could be driven
into narrow passes, the outlets of which had been blocked,
where many could be slaughtered at once. They could even be
driven to the edge of the cliff and made to jump to their deaths.

Then the men would sit down to a feast, gorging themselves
with fresh venison, seasoned with the half-digested vegetable
contents of the caribou stomachs—a rare and welcome addition
of greens to their almost exclusively meat diet—before returning

to the women with the great piles of meat, of tallow to burn and eat, of tasty marrow cracked from the bones, and of precious hides for tents and sleeping bags. And once home, of course, there would be another feast.

Kridlarssuark brought his adopted tribe many other arts and inventions that were so much more highly developed in his native Baffin Land. There was, for instance, the three-pronged fish spear for catching salmon in the streams. There was the trick

Fish spear

of building the tunnel into an igloo with a sharp angle at its mouth, the better to keep direct icy blasts out of the hut. But by far the greatest gifts he brought were the kayaks he had transported all the way from home.

To Kridlarssuark it was inconceivable that the Polar Innuit, living on the seashore, should not have the kayak. Without it, how did they hunt in the summertime, when all the winter's icy hunting grounds had turned to open sea and the seals and walruses were to be found only on distant isles or on icebergs? What sort of life was that for an Eskimo—depending on birds and their eggs that the women and children took from the cliffs?

The old men explained that the kayak had been known long, long ago to their ancestors, the same wise ancestors who had built their stone winter homes. But once upon a time a great plague had befallen their people, and the evil disease had taken off all their older men and best hunters. And so, when these men were buried, their kayaks were of course put in the graves with them along with all their other possessions. So it came about that no kayaks were left, and among the young people were none who knew the art of making them.

This the Baffinlanders understood; in their land, too, every dead man was buried with his prized possessions. In time, however, the Polar Eskimos learned again the forgotten art, and though they never acquired the skill of their teachers or made their kayaks as well as their models, they became once again sea-going hunters during the short summer season.

The kayak is a sealskin-covered one-man canoe. Its special virtue is that, like a ship, it is watertight on top as well as at its sides, and so can ride buoyantly through sea waves and spray without shipping water. There is only one small round opening in the top in which a man with a double paddle fits snugly. Around him on the narrow deck are loops of thong for holding his harpoons and spears and other hunting weapons. Behind him is fastened a hoop-shaped container for his coils of line.

On the water, the kayak and its paddler, both covered with sealskins, looked only like another small, floating, earth-stained cake of ice. The hunter would slowly drift as close to the game as possible before throwing his harpoon, and then back water with great speed if he saw that the game was anything as big and dangerous as a walrus. A wounded walrus was quite capable either of attacking or of plunging down beyond the length of line so suddenly as to drag the kayak under with it. Hence, there was usually attached to the line a big float, made of a whole sealskin —like the blubber-oil bag—sewed airtight and inflated with the hunter's breath. This hindered the diving of the wounded animal, showed the hunter where it was going, and kept its body from being lost when it died and sank. There were also drags, large square or round open-ended skin boxes, attached to the line so that the open end always faced the direction of flight, cutting down the animal's speed, submersibility, and endurance.

Many primitive peoples have myths about some god or supernatural hero who, in ages long gone by, came to them from "Outside" and taught them their most valuable arts and skills, enlightening their ignorance, saving them from extinction, and bringing them new foods or victory over their enemies or some new vision of life. These mythical beings are called by the anthropologists "culture heroes," for they are the people's way of explaining the mysterious gifts of their own culture. Hiawatha was such a being, and so was the White God for whom the Aztecs mistook Cortez. In Kridlarssuark the Polar Eskimos had a real, not imaginary, culture hero, one who came to them within our own historical times, so that later explorers could learn about him from many people who had actually known him. Yet in all things he followed the pattern set by his supernatural predecessors; he brought life-giving arts and skills, he did it for no other motive than love, and, still following the pattern, his mission accomplished, he set out for the other world from which he had come.

Kridlarssuark stayed with the Polar Eskimos for five years, and was an old man, with a fringe of white hair around his bald head, when once again he was seized with a great longing. It was a dozen years since he had left his homeland, and now he wanted to see it and his own people again before he died. So once more he set out, and all those who had come with him, even the men who had married among the Polar tribe, returned with him—all except his own son, who could not go because his child was sick. The son's place was taken by a native who must have become infected with Kridlarssuark's haunting song, "Do you know the desire for new countries? Do you know the desire for new peoples?" Indeed, the old magician must have also left a heritage of wanderlust with his adopted people, for many years later Commodore Peary was able to persuade a whole village of them to go with him as guides and helpers on the voyage that discovered the North Pole.

During the first wintering of the return journey old Kridlarssuark died. Now indeed his people knew what a great leader he had been, for from then on misfortune pursued the expedition. During the second wintering the food supplies gave out, and before the sun rose there was famine. They caught a few fish through the ice but not enough to keep some of them from dying of hunger. Then the hideous thing happened that was not new among the Eskimos, but of which they were always dreadfully ashamed. Those who survived ate the bodies of those who had died. Soon they might begin to kill one another for food. In the last extremities of starvation the Eskimos did resort to cannibalism but, unlike the cannibals of other lands, they practiced it with horror and loathing, and there was no greater insult than to accuse an Eskimo of having eaten human flesh.

Two of the men, brothers, decided to desert this ill-fated expedition and to escape back to Smith Sound with their wives and children. That first winter of their retreat they did not get very far. One of the women went astray on a glacier and was lost. The others built snow huts and managed to live out the darkness by eating their remaining dogs. When the sun came up again, they harnessed themselves to the sledges and trudged on. During the next wintering the other woman was also lost on a glacier and froze to death. It was five years after they had left the Polar Eskimo village that these men returned with their tale of horror. They never learned what happened to the rest of the expedition.

8. FEAR

It is sad to end the tale of Kridlarssuark on a note of disaster and suffering, but unfortunately such endings were the not uncommon lot of the men who dared the Arctic, whether as explorers or natives. There was no Eskimo family that had not suffered some tragedy—a father lost at sea, a mother frozen to death, a child starved, stricken by a mysterious disease, buried under an avalanche, engulfed by a glacier. Undeniably it was a life haunted by the twin fears of ever-threatening hunger and cold.

January and February were nearly always months of more or less severe privation. When the last morsel of food was gone from the igloos and caches, and the village hunters had again and again returned without meat from their perilous forays into the storm and dark—then the battle to stay alive until spring would become desperately grim. Little by little, the family's possessions and necessities would go into the cooking pot. Now it was indeed fortunate that nearly all its belongings were taken from the animals, for in need these could all be eaten. First to be boiled and eaten would be any spare sealskins the housewife had been saving for new clothes or much-needed mending, then trimmings from clothes already made, the sleeping rugs, the lashings of skin and sinew from tools. The man might have to give up the long whiplash of which he was so proud, and perhaps even the skin from his kayak.

Now when the hunter returned from fruitless sitting on the ice, waiting for the seal that had so strangely disappeared, there would be no welcoming gleam from the window of his igloo to guide him home, and no warmth when he got there. The lamp blubber would long ago have been eaten. Feeling the strength leaving his own body, looking at the pale thin woman who had been his round-cheeked wife, at his once plump greasy children now listless and without strength to play, the man would finally be faced by a truly desperate decision. Without his dogs, he would not be able to hunt, but the dogs were also starving and would soon be eating one another. So they would be killed and eaten, one by one, in the hope that some of them might be permitted to survive. Finally, as we have seen, even more terrible things might happen.

Though such terrors were by no means the usual experience,

they were always possible. It is no great wonder, therefore, that, when one Eskimo was asked what their religion was, what they believed in, he should answer, "We do not believe. We only fear. . . . We fear those things that are about us and about which we have no sure knowledge, as the dead, and the malevolent ghosts, and the secret misdoings of the heedless ones among ourselves."

Hunting is an activity full of unpredictable accidents, of pure luck, good and ill. Even the most reasonable of men, when he is hunting, becomes a little superstitious. Secretly he begins to believe that his success may depend on something he is wearing or on some words spoken by someone else or on the attitude toward him of the game—in short, something altogether irrelevant or impossible. Now consider a primitive hunter, whose very life depends on his success, and who has moreover been taught to believe that the animals he hunts are animated by wise spirits who know all there is to be known about him. Is it so strange that he should go about in deadly fear of saying or doing the wrong thing, even unknowingly? "Bad luck" is after all not an *explanation* of disaster. It *is* the disaster. And since a man, or a community, should rightly get what he or it deserves, it follows that for every piece of bad luck or hardship someone must be at fault. Someone, knowingly or unwittingly, must have offended the powers in charge of such things.

The Polar Eskimos had no form of what we would recognize as government, no chiefs or headmen whose commands must be obeyed, no council to lay down laws either for the tribe as a whole or for any village. For a people who were so clever at meeting the challenges of nature, they had done remarkably little to develop the machinery of living together in groups. Every family was free to come and go as it pleased, and the only restraints on a man seemed to be the good opinion of his neighbors and relatives. But if there were no outward forms of government, no judges or police, each man had implanted in him from early childhood an ever-watchful internal governor to tell him right from wrong and to make it extremely uncomfortable for him when he did wrong.

This was, of course, his belief in the world of spirits. True, these spirit powers, not being human, might have their own strange ideas of right and wrong. Being nevertheless Eskimo, their ideas usually revolved around food. A man might murder another and expect no worse punishment than being murdered in turn by his victim's relatives. But the sins that roused the spirits' wrath had mostly to do with food taboos. Every Eskimo tribe was forbidden to eat some particular animal or part of animal. In addition, there might be special taboos for women, unmarried women, married women, mothers, children, boys, girls, young men, old men, and even individuals. Food taboos, and harsh punishments for violating them, are as a matter of fact common among primitive peoples throughout the world.

The great female spirit Sedna lives at the bottom of the sea, and all the sea animals are her children, for the seals and walruses were created from her chopped-off fingers. Out of her kindness, she sends her children to be caught and killed by the Eskimos, so that human beings may have food. But let them beware of angering her by some thoughtless act she happens not to like. Let some wife in the village secretly commit the sin of working with caribou skin after her husband has brought home seal meat, and Sedna will wreak a terrible vengeance on all the village. She may withhold all her seals and walruses; she may whip up such a storm that there can be no hunting until the village has starved to death; she may smite the husband of the evildoer with a strange spirit-sickness.

Then the village would have to turn to the angakok, to find out what was wrong and who had sinned. The angakok, man or woman, was the one person with authority among these people without a government. This sorcerer was respected and feared because of his magic powers, which he had earned with great suffering and cruel privation. He had been initiated into his dread profession by another angakok, who had made him fast for weeks, alone, in a freezing little igloo until he had seen visions. Then the spirits had appeared and given him the power to travel to their country and to speak to them in their own language. They had taught him magic tricks to astound the other Eskimos.

Now all the village is gathered around the angakok in the yellow lamplight of the igloo. He begins by saying how poor are his powers, how foolish his tricks, all lies and humbug. Then he sings strange songs, accompanying himself on his little drum. He performs little tricks of magic. He jumps around and speaks in "spirit language." He grows more and more excited, his movements become more and more uncontrollable, until he falls down in a hysterical trance.

His soul leaves his body and journeys far into the spirit world. There powerful spirits, perhaps including Sedna herself, tell him who has committed a secret crime and what should be done about it. His soul comes back. He awakes, shaken and exhausted. He calls upon the wrongdoer to confess.

A woman whose husband has lain mysteriously ill for a long time steps forth and confesses what she knows can no longer be concealed. She has eaten liver, knowing it was forbidden her until she should have borne five children. She has already been punished, but this is as nothing to what she will suffer from the horror of her neighbors.

Eventually the wind shifts, the storms blows over, and the men go out and find seal again. The sick man recovers. All credit and honor to the angakok.

9 . THE BRIGHTER SIDE

In a life so hemmed in by real and imaginary terrors, one would naturally expect to find a people steeped in unrelieved gloom and misery. Yet nearly all explorers who have actually lived with the Eskimos agree that the truth is just the contrary. The hardships of their daily life seem to have called out in them the most admirable of human traits—not only ingenuity and industry, courage and endurance, but also generosity, kindliness, considerateness, cheerfulness, and good humor. Perhaps these latter qualities were just as important in combating the hunger, the dark, and the cold as were the former. Perhaps only a cheerful and optimistic people could have invented the igloo, the sledge, and the harpoon. At any rate, common as might be the experiences of starvation and tragedy, the Eskimo's mind did not dwell on them. The scene he lived for was one that was full of the joy of living—a warm igloo aglow in the lamplight, plenty of food, and friends and visitors to share it with.

The seasonal setting of this mellow picture was the darkest time of the year. When, toward the end of October, the sun finally set, not to rise again till the middle of February, this was the hunter's vacation time. This long-drawn-out Christmas he spent in visiting with friends, puttering about the house, and catching up on much-needed sleep. His mind was filled not with the gloomy picture of the unending dark outside but with the unchanging brightness of the never-extinguished lamps in all the homes of his friends a hundred miles up and down the coast. In the remotest of the settlements he had friends; knew almost every man, woman, and child by name; was eagerly interested in every birth, marriage, accident, and death. Indeed, in every village he had relatives, perhaps even a wife and children in two or more of them.

For ten or twelve days of each of the next three months there would be moonlight bright enough to travel by—if there were no storms—and the trip between villages need take no more than three or four days. Even the dogs seemed to know the way over the snow and to share the excitement of the visits. The drivers told the time from the circling of the brilliant northern stars, and every clump of ice or rock on the road had its name, known even to the youngest hunter. Expected or not, the travelers were sure of a warm welcome, and knew they would amply repay their host's hospitality with news of their own or other villages and with the chance they gave their host to have a party.

The woman of the house would rub the visitor's feet and dry his boots at the lamp before stuffing him with food. Because of the climate, the Eskimo was a very hearty eater. He compensated for the sameness of his exclusive meat diet, as well as for the simplicity of its preparation, by the sheer quantity of it that he enjoyed putting away. With an antler fork the hostess would fish a chunk of seal meat out of the boiling stone pot, cut off a favorite portion—say, the flipper joint—squeeze it dry between her fingers, and hand it to the honored guest. Then she would serve all the diners in turn, cut up the remaining meat, and lay the pieces on the edge of the cooking platform for second servings.

Instead of bread, there were pieces of fat, the blubber of sea animals, eaten boiled or raw, according to taste. This was also a favorite between-meals snack. A three-months-old baby would contentedly suck all day at a blubber nipple, and an older child would chew on a piece of raw bear gristle as if it were candy. Also considered a prize delicacy by the whole family were thin strips of fatty skin from the narwhal and the beluga, or white whale.

In the middle of the meal, a little girl would come in through the tunnel from a nearby igloo, bearing a freshly cooked seal flipper or other choice delicacy that her mother thought her neighbor's guest might enjoy. Then another little girl, from another family eager to share in feeding the guests, would bring something else. The hostess too would send her daughter with gifts of cooked meat to neighbors, particularly those who may have had poor luck in hunting. So the whole village participated in the feast and the entertainment of visitors.

The second main course of the dinner would be soup. When the hostess had fished all the meat out of the pot, she would pour seal blood into the boiling broth, stir it, remove the pot from the lamp, and throw in a handful of cooling snow from the snow block resting on the floor. Then she would pass around a bone or horn dipper so that the guests could help themselves, the host and hostess politely waiting for their turns last. The broth of boiled meat was the Eskimo's only beverage aside from water. He was very fond of it and always liked to take some along with him on the trail.

On this almost pure diet of meat, and with these extremely simple methods of preparing it—consisting mostly of boiling— as long as there was plenty of it, the men carried on their strenuous activities in subzero temperatures, and the children throve happily. There was of course some variety in the kinds of meat if not in the cooking. Seal, walrus, and bear were the staples, varied occasionally by narwhal, hare, and fox. In the summer there were birds and eggs, salmon, even a little scurvy grass or mountain sorrel to give taste to the soup. Then there were the meat, tallow, and marrow of the caribou killed in the late summer, though these could be eaten only in the summer tents and not in the winter igloos, where their contact with the flesh of sea animals might offend the spirits.

The absent vegetables and cereals, sugar and spices, even salt, were not missed. The reason that this diet of meat gave these hearty eaters all the food the human body needs for health was that they ate every part of the animal, much of it raw. Liver, brains, kidneys, entrails—vital organs especially rich in vitamins, especially if the vitamins are not cooked away—the Eskimos ate raw, either freshly killed or frozen.

Freezing is, after all, a kind of cooking, as can be seen from the tenderness of raw meat that has been frozen solid and then thawed. True, it adds nothing to the taste and might not be considered by more educated palates a satisfactory substitute for stewing, roasting, baking, broiling, or frying. The chief object of these delectable operations is to give taste and savor to food, but taste is only a matter of what one is used to. The Eskimo, for example, found nothing objectionable in the "high" odor of raw meat that had lain unrefrigerated for many days. He might even have found it most illogical on our part to turn away from its strong flavor in disgust when we had just finished pitying him for the blandness of his diet of boiled and raw flesh. In any case he would have no sympathy for wasting good food in any form.

When the guests had eaten all they could hold, the hostess might pass around bird skins for wiping greasy fingers. The bones would be thrown to the dogs in the passageway, and the pot might also be given them to lick clean. Then hosts and guests, their stomachs full, their bodies relaxed in grateful warmth, would settle back for an evening of fun, one of those jolly, noisy, talkative gatherings that formed the high point of Eskimo winter life. Then came the exciting exchange of news and views, gossip and history, the hunters recounting tall tales of their prowess, the old people retelling the ancient eerie tales of the spirits, all joining in the singing of old songs, dancing to drum music, playing games—all in all, a high old time that would be long treasured in the memory of all participants.

Ordinarily the most self-reliant of men, it was when the

Eskimo thus took his ease among friends, entertaining the traveler, or himself being entertained after a long journey, that he felt most expansive and sure that life was worth while.

10. THE FAMILY

During the longer part of the midwinter months, when there was no moon and the unbroken night outside was as likely as not to be filled with storm, hunting and visiting were both out of the question. Then the Eskimo family was igloo-bound and thrown entirely on its own resources. A great deal of this time was spent in sleeping, for, as the Eskimos said, "Adversity and storms are to be slept through." Sometimes the monotony might be broken by the chance visit of a hungry polar bear, and the whole village would turn out for the excitement of giving it chase by torchlight.

Mainly, however, this was the time for learning and practicing most intensively the household arts and the virtues of home life. The hunter made and repaired his weapons, tools, sledge, and kayak. His wife was busy at her endless tailoring and shoemaking. The children combined play with helping their parents. The dogs rested and built up their strength. Shut up in a single room for days on end, the family might have found life intolerable if it had not learned the importance of considerateness and helpfulness.

As an Eskimo household was unthinkable without a hunter to bring it meat, so it was inconceivable without a woman to clothe it and to care for it during the hunter's absence. Husband and wife made a single unit, not only for love and affection, but also for making a living, for survival.

Their marriage ceremony, like most of the ceremonies of the Eskimos, was very simple. At most, after the couple had agreed to marry, the man went through the pretense of capturing and

kidnaping her while she went through the pretense of protesting
lustily. The fact that the bridegroom might already have a wife
and home in some other village was no bar to the wedding. He
put his bride on a sledge and took her home along with the only
dowry he expected, a stone cooking pot and lamp and her nimble
tailor's fingers.

A greater fault in a wife even than being a lazy seamstress or a
careless lamp-tender was not having children. Barrenness was
always assumed to be the woman's fault, usually for breaking
some food taboo and thus offending the spirits who supplied the
souls for babies. She would then be taken before the angakok for
a spirit seance.

A newborn baby was carried by its mother next to her own
warm skin under her two fur coats. A little later the baby would
have an undershirt of its own of young blue foxskin. The mother
would sing it lullabies, called "petting songs," such as

> My own little newly hatched one,
> Nestle close to me on my back

or the latest spirit drum songs she had heard from the angakok.

The baby could never be left alone, lest a hungry dog make off
with it. On journeys it was carried either under the fur on its
mother's back or under a caribou skin on the sledge. When it
needed to be nursed, or to have its caribou diaper changed, the
mother would crouch down behind the sheltering sledge piled
high with household goods or meat, lean forward, and carefully
shake the baby out over one shoulder.

Since babies and very small children cannot get along on a
pure meat diet, their mothers continued to feed them at the
breast until they were about five years old. When the child was
two, however, the mother began to feed it a little meat that she
had first chewed herself until it was soft and very easy to digest.
A baby got no more bathing than its elders except that sometimes

the mother would lick its little face with her tongue and let its little sisters and brothers lick its hands.

Children were not merely loved, they were even respected as being under the special guardianship of the wise spirits of the ancestors. Their lives were carefree, one might even say spoiled. A child under seven or eight was never nagged for fear his ears would grow pointed like a dog's and he would grow up stupid. Besides, it would be disrespectful to the guardian spirits. Hence, too, parents seldom addressed their children by name but only as "my child" or "child," or even by the name of the guardian ancestor. Children on the other hand were not brought up to show special respect for their parents, addressing them as equals, and even using the disrespectful nicknames in common use in the village, as "Woman with the Wide Mouth." They would not hesitate to interrupt a conversation of their elders, or even to correct them.

No matter what the temperature, if there was no storm the children would be playing in the snow—coasting on sleds of ice, building igloos big enough to play in, carving snow bears and then "hunting" them with lance and knife, playing hide-and-seek among the ice hummocks, skipping rope with sinew cord, playing hockey with sticks of curved walrus rib and a ball of the seal's flipper joint, bowling a small hoop as we do, or throwing it up in the air and catching it on a stick.

Even the very young ones were wise in the ways of the frost. Suddenly one child might see a white spot on a playmate's face that the other had not yet felt. Frostbite! The first child would take its hand out of its mitten to place upon the spot until it became warm and red again. When the children got wet, they knew enough to run inside at once, put their clothes on the drying rack over the lamp, and slip into a fresh pair of boots. Usually they would also seize the occasion to take a snack, for the chil-

dren were not required to have regular meals but could eat
whenever they were hungry. A child of four would come in, take
in his hands a chunk of boiled meat weighing several pounds, put
one end in his mouth, and with a knife cut off a piece as close
to his mouth as was possible without slicing off his nose. This
very same child of four might still be nursing at his mother's
breast.

If a blizzard blew up, the children had of course to play in the
warm indoors, where, like everyone else, they took off all their
clothes. There they could play at seal-broth contests, the last
one to finish his cup being called the name of some old person
in the village. A favorite game was cat's cradles, at which the
Eskimos were very proficient, producing the most complicated
figures with their skin string.

The world over, much of children's games are imitations of the
serious work of their elders. Among primitive peoples these games
are at the same time their only education for their future life
work, for, unlike most civilized children, they know exactly what
they will be doing when they are grown up. An Eskimo boy
might be destined to be an angakok, but in any case he would be
a hunter, and the girl must grow up to keep house—to cook and
sew.

The baby's first playmate might be a puppy. As soon as the
child had learned to toddle, its father would have made him a
little harness and sealskin whip with which to drive the dog
around the igloo, dragging some small object as if it were a sledge.
The toys the father carved for his little boys were harpoons,
sledges, and maupok stools of bone and ivory. Very soon the boy
would learn to carve them for himself, beginning with dog-
harness rings and harpoon heads. At the same time he was learning to use them—to throw the harpoon and to hitch up a dog team.
Soon he would be making the whole harness and a whiplash

twelve or fifteen feet long, learning to snap it expertly over the dogs he was growing up with. He would also learn to make floats for kayak hunting.

At ten, a boy was considered big enough to trudge all day behind a sledge. He could shoot birds with a bow and arrow. Both boys and girls would be taught to stalk game by being taken on hunting trips. At twelve the boy would go along on his first walrus hunt. When he killed his first seal, his proud mother would make herself a pair of trousers from the skin and distribute the meat among the other families in the village. She would do the same with his first caribou. For the young hunter these were very special occasions, celebrated with a very special feast for him. For even these privileged children had their food taboos, and no boy could eat the entrails, heart, lung, or liver of any animal until he had himself killed one of that species, whether it was seal, hare, or bird.

For the girls, too, there was the same sort of gradual shading of children's games into grown-up activities. When the girls played house around the summer tent or on their mother's sleeping platform in the igloo, they burned real blubber in seashells or in miniature stone lamps, and cooked real meat. Their mother would teach them how to make dolls out of sealskin and how to cut patterns for their clothes. The little girl had very early learned to chew skins to soften them. By the age of ten she was already mending her own boots and clothes, and helping to make mittens and stockings for the household. She had been on hunting trips and snared small game and helped to build snow houses. At twelve she was almost ready to keep house on her own.

About this age, too, it was considered that the guardian ancestral spirits were ready to leave their young charges, having brought them through the helpless period of their lives. It was time for the child's parents to take full responsibility for its training and character. The new strict discipline from hitherto easy-going parents often came as a disagreeable shock, though the child had had warning from seeing the same sudden change happen to all its older playmates. What were games before now became work in earnest. But because this work had been learned as a game it would undoubtedly always be easy and pleasant to do.

11. THE YEAR'S CYCLE

Every year, in the middle of February, the heavens put on a dramatic little noontime ceremony for the Polar Innuit. The sun peeped over the southernmost horizon for the first time in three months, heralding the still far-off summer. It stayed only for a fleeting glimpse and sank down almost immediately. But each day thereafter it rose a little earlier and farther to the east, rode a little higher and longer, set a little farther to the west.

By the end of March the twenty-four hours were equally divided between night and day. It was still winter, however, and the sea ice was still firm. The hunters gathered at the mussel shoals for the big walrus hunt of the year. This was the last time for long visits between villages. Soon the sledges would be unusable.

The days continued to grow longer. By the middle of May sunset and sunrise were merging, and the sun was soon circling the horizon without sinking below it at all. At midnight it shone down from due north, from over the other side of the North Pole. Despite the continued coolness of the air, the direct rays of the never-setting sun were melting the snow off glaciers and hills, unlocking the frozen salmon streams, opening big leads and channels in the sea ice. The sledging season was closed, the kayak season opened.

Grasses, mosses, even flowers and the stunted shrubs of the Arctic began to give a touch of green to earth's sober winter dress of black and white. The birds arrived in clouds and laid their eggs, the seals and walruses had their young, and the Eskimos looked forward eagerly to foods they had almost forgotten the taste of. The children were as happy over the promised joys of summer as are children everywhere over knowing that school is soon to be out and the outdoor life about to begin. All was bustle and preparation at home, the men putting their kayaks and summer equipment in shape, the women preparing to move.

The move was a kind of spring cleaning, though of the simplest possible kind, the family removing itself rather than the accumulation of winter's dirt. Instead of airing the igloo, the family aired itself by moving off to an outdoor life in a skin tent. As the summer grew deeper and warmer, the family lived more and more outdoors, sometimes sleeping in the midday sun. The women carried on their housework outside the tent flaps. The naked babies crawled around on rugs in the sunshine until their skins were a warm brown. The children combined play and useful work by bringing in moss, hunting birds under the cliffs, and setting snares for small beasts.

But alas for the shortness of summer! About the middle of August, one day at midnight, the sun just barely dipped under the northernmost horizon. For the first time in three months it was absent from the sky, though only fleetingly. But from then on each night would be longer, each day shorter, as the sun rose and set farther south, and by September the day was again evenly divided between light and dark. It was already very cold. The more and more slanting rays of the southward-moving sun could no longer undo the freezing work of the frigid night.

More and more swiftly now the coast knit itself a thick skirt of ice that made the islands part of the mainland and turned the little beach settlements into inland villages. The birds began to leave. The winds grew stronger. There were snow flurries. The family cleaned out its chosen winter hut and laid on a new roof of turf before the turf should freeze too solid to dig. The women gathered final supplies of dry moss for bed platforms and lamp wicks. They busily sewed winter clothing. The men repaired harness and mended sledge runners.

Cold as it was, however, it was still the season of autumn and not yet of winter, and the family would not yet move from its skin *tupik*, until the men had had their big caribou hunt. Only when they came back from this round-up, loaded down with venison, skins, and antlers, would the village be ready to settle down to the idea of winter.

By the middle of November the Polar Eskimos were seeing the last of the sun for the next three months. The prospect of this long darkness did not strike them with terror. Even the children were maybe a little tired of the endless summer sun, and looked forward to the remembered fun and jollity of moonlight visits. The young men were hoping for their first bears.

It was around the winter that the Eskimos built their whole way of life. This was the "season of fast ice," for which they had fashioned their homes, their clothing, their sledges. Is it any wonder, then, that winter so dominated the imagination of the Eskimo that he reckoned his age not by years as we do, or by summers as do the Indians, but by winters?

MAORI

"Welcome to power [mana],
Welcome to sanctity [tapu],
Welcome to dread!"
        —Greeting to a chief

III. MAORIS:
People of the Pacific

The Pacific Ocean, some scientists say, was formed when a great piece of earth wrenched away to become the moon. If it were not for the great depth and size of the hole this left behind, the waters that now fill it would perhaps be spread over all the rest of the world, and we should at best all be Pacific islanders, living on the peaks of submerged mountains. Even as it is, there is more Pacific Ocean than there is land surface on all the six continents put together—*a vast emptiness stretching from the Arctic to the Antarctic and almost halfway round the world at the equator.*

The Pacific is not altogether empty of land, however, for it is speckled over with more islands than any other ocean. Indeed, its mid-ocean islands, islets, reefs, and atolls have never been counted. Some of these have been hurled up by violent submarine volcanoes; tens of thousands of others have grown by the patient building of millions of generations of coral polyps. Disregarding the groups of very large islands clustered at the southeast corner of Asia (the Philippines and Indonesia, for instance), which are considered to be part of that continent, the geographers have given to all the rest of the islands the name of Oceania.

This seventh "continent," which, like the human body, is composed almost entirely of water, is divided by geographers into three main groupings of islands, just as astronomers map the stars in the sky by constellations. Micronesia ("the tiny islands") extends in a broad band eastward from the Philippines for three thousand miles. Among these islands took place much of the sea fighting of the Second World War, and they have since been the proving grounds for atomic experiments. South of these and running parallel with them is another broad band of islands, starting with the big one of New Guinea (east of Indonesia and north of Australia) and ending with Fiji. These are called Melanesia, "the islands of the blacks," because they are inhabited mostly by a very dark primitive people with woolly hair. Finally, to the east of both these bands, extending deep into the Pacific, is the vast triangle known as Polynesia, "the many islands."

The northern apex of the Polynesian triangle is Hawaii, just under the Tropic of Cancer and two thousand miles from the North American coast. From here one side of the triangle runs some five thousand miles southeast, across the equator, to Easter Island, just south of the Tropic of Capricorn and two thousand

*miles off the coast of South America. The other leg of the triangle
goes an even greater distance southwest from Hawaii, skirting
Micronesia and Melanesia, into the South Temperate Zone, to
New Zealand, a thousand miles east of Australia. The base of the
triangle, joining New Zealand to Easter Island, is also some five
thousand miles long.*

*All this vast region, with its more than ten million square miles
of water, has for at least fifteen hundred years been the home of
a people whom we call the Polynesians. It is generally believed
that they originally came here from Indonesia and Asia, island-
skipping through Micronesia and possibly displacing earlier inhabitants on their route. They are a light-skinned people, with
straight or wavy brown-black hair, more European in general
facial and bodily appearance than any other large race of primitive folk.*

*Once they were the Vikings of the South Seas, the Argonauts
of the Pacific, a race of intrepid sailors and incomparable navigators. A thousand years ago they were already firmly established
in the heartland of their great triangle—in Tahiti, Samoa, and
the Marquesas. For them the sea had never been a barrier; it was
their broad high road, the natural bridge between the most distant lands. Then, five hundred years before the Europeans were
to do the same thing, they suddenly exploded outward. Their
Vasco da Gamas, Columbuses, and Magellans discovered and
colonized the three corners of their world—Hawaii, Easter Island,
and New Zealand. The next pages tell the story of how some Polynesians found New Zealand and made it their home.*

1. LONG WHITE CLOUD

A thousand years ago the Polynesians of Tahiti and Samoa were
already a great race of shipwrights and deep-sea sailors. Without

metals of any kind, they built boats capable of carrying a hundred persons, with their provisions and water, on voyages that were for weeks out of sight of land.

These were simply very long, slender, paddled canoes, the hulls made by painfully hollowing out tree trunks with stone adzes. The bigger ones, often a hundred feet long, were made by dovetailing two such trunks amidships, and their height was built up on the sides by long planks, also shaped with stone tools and lashed together with fiber ropes through stone-drilled holes. Waves from fore and aft were divided by very tall prows and sterns, also made of gracefully carved separate pieces.

For stability this slim craft often carried an outrigger, a long boom riding along one side and held to it with arched struts. Even better, two big canoes could be fastened together side by side, about four feet apart, by thwarts or crossbars. Over these crossbars was built a roofed deck, into which was stepped a mast forty feet tall. The triangular sail was of matting, for the Polynesians had no woven cloth, and it could not be furled but was swung around to catch the wind.

Fifty or more crewmen would swing their long, narrow paddles in perfect unison under the commands of the captain, who sat in the upraised stern, steering with a paddle eight feet long. They had neither compass nor astrolabe, neither charts nor written records of any kind, so their feats of navigation between the tiny island specks that were their homes were marvels of skill and daring. The crews always included star-reading experts who had memorized the times of the rising and setting of constellations and planets for every month of the year, and their navigators knew all about the prevailing winds and currents.

When Erik the Red, the Viking who would one day discover Greenland, was still a small child, a ferment of exploration and adventure seems to have taken hold of the Polynesian heartland. The same urge that had originally brought them to Tahiti and

Samoa and the Marquesas now set them once again to probing the watery immensity round about.

It probably began with the inevitable accidents to fishing and war parties—being blown out of course and caught in the inexorable drift of ocean currents. Many were thus lost, but a lucky few might make landfall on other islands. An even smaller number might manage to beat their way back home with marvelous sailors' yarns of distant lands inhabited by other Polynesian tribes, or of uninhabited island paradises.

These tales would be memorized and carefully preserved among the legends and history that were taught by word of mouth in the remarkable schools of the Polynesians. One day, maybe generations later, these chanted reports, remembered word for word, might inspire the outfitting of a new expedition to those unforgotten shores. It might be that there was famine or overpopulation at home, or that a quarrel had broken out among the sons of a dead chief and the loser was banished along with his family, or, most remarkable of all, there might be no other motive than the sheer love of adventure.

Thus there has been preserved down to our own days one account from those times of a voyage into antarctic waters, complete with strange encounters that were incomprehensible to the explorers from the tropics but that we can now recognize as having to do with icebergs and walruses. It was at this time too that Polynesian adventurers reached not only Easter Island, where they stayed, but probably also, two thousand miles beyond, to the shores of South America. There is no definite tradition of such a voyage, but, according to the botanists, it is only from that continent that the Polynesians could have acquired the sweet potato that was a staple of their diet. And about this time, we know with more certainty, Hawaii was found and colonized, and New Zealand was discovered.

Allowing for some embroidery by the priestly historians, the tradition of the finding of New Zealand is as clear, factual, and believable as the Greenland Vikings' accounts of their discovery of the American mainland. What gives it even more conviction is the fact that the tradition was the same in both New Zealand and Tahiti, which, when the white men connected the two, had had no contact with each other for hundreds of years.

This is the way the story went: Ten centuries ago, about the year 950, a Tahitian warrior named Kupe happened to be in Rarotonga, one of the Cook Islands some seven hundred miles southwest of his homeland, perhaps on some routine expedition. Here something aroused his curiosity about the possibility of undiscovered land still farther to the southwest. Perhaps he noticed the migratory birds that come from that direction. The legend has it simply that the god Io appeared to him in a dream, giving him orders and sailing directions. At any rate, he set out in two double canoes with his wife, family, and friends. After some weeks and two thousand miles, Kupe's wife saw on the horizon what looked like a long, low cloud bank. That is why, when they came to land on the northernmost cape of New Zealand, they named it Aotearoa, "Long White Cloud."

Kupe circumnavigated the two great islands that make up the thousand-mile length of New Zealand. Then he returned to Tahiti with marvelous tales of a land of high mist, a pleasant land un-inhabited by men or beasts except for a gigantic wingless bird twice as tall as a man. He brought back a great block of green-stone, a kind of jade much prized for making war clubs for chief-tains as well as necklaces for their wives. And he left two unfor-gotten memorials in the spoken tradition of Tahiti.

The first was a turn of speech, a part of the language. When many of his countrymen, excited by his tales, asked if he would not lead another expedition to White Cloud, the tired explorer merely answered, "*E hoki Kupe?*" meaning, "Will Kupe return?"

And this phrase became the traditional form for any polite refusal, thus keeping his name fresh in common speech.

His second contribution to oral history was the sailing directions he left for anyone who chose to follow his route: "From Rarotonga to White Cloud, let the course be to the right hand of the setting sun, moon, or Venus in February."

Two hundred years passed before anything was added to the priestly chants of the tale of Kupe. Then, they tell, one day in about the year 1150, a Tahitian elder named Toi was sitting on the shore of a lagoon with other old men, watching a canoe race among the youths. Unexpectedly a fog came down, a powerful wind arose, and the contestants made for shore. But though Toi waited anxiously, his grandson Whatonga and his crewmates were not among those who landed. Their canoe had somehow been swept out to sea.

Weeks passed and the boy did not return. It is typical that, for all his anxiety, Toi did not accept the possibility that his grandson might have gone down in the sea. It says something for the confidence of these South Sea islanders in their own seamanship that Toi merely assumed that Whatonga had been carried to some other island whence he could not return. Toi therefore decided to go look for him. He outfitted a seagoing expedition and scouted all the islands in the course the wind had taken. Thus he eventually came to Rarotonga.

Still no sign or word of Whatonga. But to be in Rarotonga, Kupe's jumping-off place, was to remember Kupe's directions for finding White Cloud. Could Whatonga have been swept on to Kupe's land? The persistent brave old man was determined to find out. He left word with the head chief of Rarotonga: "Tell whoever inquires after me that I go to seek my grandson in White Cloud, Kupe's land."

Naturally Toi's course was somewhat different from Kupe's,

and he landed first on the Chatham Islands, a little group about five hundred miles east of New Zealand and much to the south of Kupe's landfall. Nevertheless, Kupe's account must have been fairly detailed, for Toi knew he was not on White Cloud. So he ranged west and north until he finally came to where the city of Auckland now stands on New Zealand.

Here Toi found the country inhabited by people who may have arrived after Kupe's discovery. The legends say these people were not quite like the Tahitians. They were darker, taller, and more spare, with broader noses, and some had bushy hair like the Melanesians. But they spoke a language similar to Toi's, and they said their ancestors had been storm-driven here in three canoes from their home, a hot country in the west. They had no news of Whatonga. The old sailor was weary now of his many travels and disappointments. He could not face the long voyage back to Tahiti. He decided to stay.

Meanwhile, Whatonga, Toi's grandson, was very much alive, having drifted to an island not far from Tahiti, where he had been so well treated as an honored guest that he had lingered on. But at last he had grown homesick and, after awaiting favorable winds, had sailed for Tahiti, only to discover that his grandfather had gone in quest of him. Evidently as devoted a grandson as Toi was a grandfather, Whatonga immediately set afoot preparations for an expedition to find the old man.

Foreseeing a long search, he got a big seagoing canoe, renamed it the *Kurahaupo*, and gathered together a crew of sixty-six men— fifty-two paddlers, four ship's husbands, two anchor tenders, four sail tenders, two fire tenders, and two steersmen.

When the *Kurahaupo* finally reached Rarotonga, following Toi's track, and received Toi's last message, the undaunted crew at once set sail for White Cloud. This double quest had a happy ending, for Whatonga found his grandfather. Moreover, the whole ship's company decided to follow Toi's example and stay in New

Zealand. Some of them probably did get back to Tahiti with the story of these events, but in time all contact with the homeland broke off.

Gradually Toi's men intermarried with the *Moriori*, as the natives were called. The word may have meant simply "native," with just that touch of contempt that invaders always seem to use toward the original inhabitants of a country, especially if the invaders consider themselves somewhat more civilized. Eventually, however, the newcomers were to call themselves *Maori*, that is, "natives," with all the pride of old settlers.

Toi and his men founded a dynasty, or at least a group of tribes, which became dominant on New Zealand and even drove some of the earlier inhabitants off the land. Some of these went to the Chatham Islands and retained the name of Moriori. Meanwhile, the conquerors melted into the native population. They had not come as true colonizers, but only as explorers, and so had brought with them neither their families nor the seed plants, animals, or tools with which they could have simply transplanted their culture. The Moriori had not learned to cultivate plants but lived mostly by gathering food that grew wild. Toi has therefore gone down in Maori history as "Toi the Wood Eater," because he had to learn to eat the root of the fern tree, like the natives.

Meanwhile, back in the Polynesian heartland, the spirit of exploration seemed to subside or at least to be turned in other directions. For still another two hundred years the priestly chants had nothing to add to the odysseys of Kupe and Toi. Then, in the first half of the fourteenth century, a crisis seems to have hit the islands of central Polynesia. Perhaps the people had thrived too well, the population grown too rapidly for the resources of these small islands, and now there was not enough land or food to go around, so that there were endless wars and misery. In Tahiti a great emigration was organized, a fleet of five double canoes, besides three smaller enterprises of one canoe each, to find new land. This time all knew where they were going. They were deliberately setting out as colonists, following the track of Toi and Whatonga, to Kupe's land.

After six hundred years we still know the names of these canoes —of "the Fleet," composed of *Tainui, Te Arawa, Mata-atua, Kurahaupo,* and *Tokomaru,* and of the independent canoes *Aotea, Takitima,* and *Horouta.* For each of these eight *Mayflowers* (except one that was wrecked) landed on a different part of the coastline, where its crew established a new tribe or nation. Forever after, all honorable descent on New Zealand would have to be traced back to these pilgrims or be of no account. And these memorized family registers fit in so well with those remembered on Tahiti and Rarotonga that we know we are dealing with history and not mere legend in the stories of Kupe, Toi, and the Fleet.

Now the Polynesians had reached their southernmost "borders." And once more, as when they had come to Hawaii, five thousand miles to the north, the link to the homeland would soon be broken, and all contact with it cease, but it would never be forgotten. They would call themselves Maoris, but would always remember their Tahitian homeland, which in their traditional songs they called Hawaiki: "The seed of our coming is from Hawaiki, the seed of our nourishing, the seed of mankind."

Unlike Toi, the crews of the Fleet came determined to bring their way of life with them. They brought the taro and the sweet potato to plant, their skills as boatbuilders and sea rovers, their warlike customs and weapons, their dances and arts, their clothing, their architecture, their language, and their religion. Polynesians they would remain, even after they married among the mixed people who had preceded them, but in time they would stop being Tahitian immigrants and become Maori natives. For the more the things they brought with them depended on the physical world to make sense, the more they would have to be changed to suit the new environment.

It was a totally new environment in many ways. Most important, these immigrants from small islands had reached a land that was for them of almost continental dimensions. And since they had come here to escape their neighbors, not to seek new ones, all the energies of these pioneers would be absorbed for many generations in spreading over the uninhabited coasts, to say nothing of the mountainous interior. Expert boatbuilders they would remain, fine fishermen, sailors, and naval warriors, but they would no longer feel the need to explore the deep Pacific. Fighters they would remain—indeed, they would become even more warlike— but for the first time they would have to think primarily of land warfare, of attacks from the interior and of fortified defenses.

They had come to a climate that was harsher than that of their tropical homeland, with a different plant and animal life. They would have to become better builders of stronger houses, to forget their dependence on mulberry bark to clothe them and on breadfruit, bananas, and coconuts to feed them. Here their staple taros and yams would grow only in a few favored districts. Even growing their sweet potatoes would take more labor. They would have to learn to become "wood eaters" like Toi, and to weave their clothing out of wild flax.

Even their meat-eating habits would have to change, for these immigrants and their dogs, and a few stowaway rats, were the only mammals in New Zealand. On Tahiti there at least had been domesticated pigs. Here there were only birds, but of innumerable species, and some very strange. Because they had no enemies to fear on the ground, not even snakes, some of these birds, such as the kiwi and the moa, had lost the use of their wings. The ostrich-like moa was the fabulous giant bird that Kupe had reported. It did indeed reach a height of eight to twelve feet, but if it was not already extinct by the time the Fleet arrived, it was soon to be made so by men whom the hunger for meat quickly turned into expert bird-snarers.

Yet in all the basic customs and beliefs that did not depend directly on the outside world, the Maoris remained Polynesian, just as the much later white colonists would remain in all essential things Europeans. The language changed only enough to become another dialect of central Polynesian. Religion and myths retained the same fundamental point of view. The type of family and government was scarcely changed at all. In some matters—as in the love of warfare—the Maoris seemed even more Polynesian than their ancestors. This was especially true of Maori ideas of the nature of the world and of man's place in it.

2. MANA AND TAPU

In every society there are certain persons who receive more than the ordinary respect of their fellows. Those who enjoy this high regard are said to have "prestige." It may be given for entirely different reasons—in some cultures because of a man's birth, in others because of his achievements. Depending on the society, a man may become great by being a king or a president, a matador or a movie star, a saint or a millionaire.

Prestige is the result of concentrating and focusing upon a single living man the strong feelings that all the people who share his society have about the things considered to be most important in that society. No wonder, then, that the object of all this love and fear, admiration and envy, awe and reverence, seems often to reflect it all like a pinpoint of dazzling brilliance. People have often been sure that they could *feel* the royalty in a king, like some mysterious emanation. A sense of power more than ordinarily human seems to pour from his presence and crackle in the air. This does not seem such a fanciful idea after all when we consider that what we all really sense in the great ones is the awful power of our own society. What could be more natural among primitive people, therefore, than to identify this truly superhuman power with the supernatural? Royalty seems hedged about with divinity.

Prestige is something that is more sought after and thought about in one society than another, but no people in the world was ever more continuously concerned with questions of prestige than the Polynesians in general and the Maoris in particular. They not only combined the prestige of birth with the prestige of accomplishment; they also tied these up with what makes the world go round. They felt that all awe and wonder must be due to the same cause, whether aroused by a thunderbolt or by a man. They thought of this cause as a semi-physical kind of power or force, very like our own vague ideas about magnetism or electricity. They called it *mana*, and they considered the whole world to be more or less alive with its dread, invisible power. Like electricity, however, it had an affinity for certain things more than others—those things and persons that the Maoris considered most important. It could build up on these a charge of very high, dangerous potential that was quite capable of blasting ordinary people to death.

Gods were practically pure mana, for mana was what made them divine. All living things, including people, had some mana, for it was what gave them life. Chiefs were born with more of it than others, because that was the way it worked. In some respects it was like what we would call the soul, except that it was not personalized, being more a general kind of soul-stuff that could wax or wane in a man. Again like electricity, it could be passed on by physical contact between people or things.

It was this contagious quality that made life so dangerous for a Maori. He could really never know but that the most innocent-seeming thing he had to use—a tool or even his food—had somehow come into contact with a generator of powerful mana —for instance, the chief. If he used the tool, bad luck would come of it. If he ate the food, he would sicken, maybe die. Since he could not absorb so big a charge of invisible mana, these things that carried it were for him *tapu,* that is, "forbidden," "untouchable," "holy," "sanctified."

This word, under the form "taboo," has been adopted into English to mean anything that is forbidden, not by law but by custom. There is no earthly human tribe without its taboos. Many of them are strangely irrational from the point of view of all other tribes. On the other hand, there are some taboos, which seem no more rational, that are amazingly widespread over the world. Such is the taboo that forbade both American Indians of the Great Plains and the Negrito Semang of the Malayan jungle to speak to their mothers-in-law. Taboos that forbid the eating of certain kinds of food or of certain combinations of them or of certain foods on certain occasions are to be found everywhere from Greenland to Australia.

Among most peoples there are at least simple rules regarding food taboos that one can learn in childhood, but among the Maoris a tapu could be freely placed on anything at any time, and all one could learn was caution. It is all but impossible to understand the daily life of the Maoris without appreciating the part played in it by these ideas of mana and tapu. They were, for example, intertwined in all social relations, including government.

The Maoris lived in small villages consisting of several interrelated families. That is, every free person in the village claimed descent from the same grandparents or some slightly more remote ancestor. Hence, they were all uncles, aunts, or cousins of one another and felt this family relationship very keenly. But they were not all of equal rank; some were noble, most were commoners.

The nobles, or *rangatira*, were those most closely related to the chief or were themselves eligible to become chiefs. Chieftainship in this aristocratic society descended by very strict rules of primogeniture (the rule of the "first-born"), just as it did among the British nobility, from father to eldest son. If a first-born son died before his father, then the chief's second son would inherit the office, but on *his* death the chieftainship would go not to his own eldest son but to the eldest son of his older brother if the brother had left one. That is, the succession, whenever possible, must always go back to the eldest son of the eldest son.

The reason for this was that this was the way mana descended. All the children of a chief had some mana to start with, but the eldest son got most of it. And it was terribly important for a village that its chief should have the most mana possible. Peace and prosperity in the village and success in warfare depended on it. On the other hand, as a chief grew older and more experienced, as he chalked up each new victory in war, brought luck to the fishers or planters, gained in prestige by the size and number of his feasts, his mana grew, his spiritual power increased. Also, as we shall see, a chief could lose mana by defeat, bad luck, or humiliation, but never by exercising or spending it. Mana begets mana, as success breeds success.

If a village grew too big to support itself, or if a quarrel broke out as to the succession to the chieftainship, a younger son might lead his family and closest relatives out and start a new village. The leader would then be a chief in his own right, start a new noble line, and begin to collect mana to pass on to his eldest son. But among the chiefs of the new village and the old one there would always remain the relationship of younger and older brother. As long as they continued to recognize themselves as belonging to the same larger family, the older line would always have an edge on mana.

This process of the splitting up of villages would eventually create a large number of them covering a considerable area and all recognizing a common remote ancestor. They then constituted a tribe, all the village chieftains of which might recognize one among themselves as representing the oldest line of elder sons, and therefore as being the most potent, or tribal, chieftain. Most of the Maori tribes gave as their founding ancestor the leader of one of the canoes of the Fleet.

By the same process, of course, the commoners were created. A younger son of the younger son of a chief's younger son was already far removed from the possibility of chieftainship unless he went out and founded his own settlement. He had precious little mana to start with, and that little was easily lost by any untoward event. Nevertheless, the shading was pretty fine, and since all the villagers were related to the chief, most free Maoris would insist they were rangatira, or gentlemen. The only commoners who could not make such a pretense were the children of slaves, who made up the third class of Maori society.

Slaves were war captives and had no standing at all, regardless of their rank before capture. Being captured forever washed out of them all traces of mana, even if they had been powerful chiefs before. If they escaped from their captors, their own people would not have them or their bad luck back on any terms. Even if they fought on the side of their captors and performed valiant deeds of war, they could never recover their mana. If a woman slave was married to one of her captors, however, her children would not be slaves, but merely commoners. All the Maoris were born free.

A Maori chief was not a king in the European sense of the word. His "subjects" were after all only his cousins, and in any case his "reign" depended on his good behavior and the favor of the gods. He was not addressed by any epithets remotely resembling "Your Majesty." He was expected to be in the forefront of battle and an active leader in all peaceful pursuits. But

A Maori chief

in one respect he might well have been envied by most civilized monarchs, for he was believed very literally to have not merely the "divine right" of kings but the actual divine power. His mana, as long as he had it, meant that he could enforce his commands with supernatural police powers.

Did he want something left strictly alone? He needed only to touch it and declare it tapu. Then if he put up a proper sign understandable to all his people—a lock of his hair or a piece of flax—nothing on earth could induce them to come near it. His property was safe from thieves or vandals, because the punishment for violating tapu was sudden death or painful sickness. Even for minor offenses, the culprit's own hands might become tapu so that he could not feed himself but would have to be spoon-fed by his relatives like a baby. The beauty of this system for protecting the chief's property, or what he wanted to be considered his property, was that it did not depend on police or judges. The mere fact that there were no witnesses did not save the wrongdoer from automatic divine punishment, which was swift and certain, inescapable, not in the hereafter but immediately.

But, you might ask, even if the people believed in it, did the punishment really work? The answer, supported by many examples, seems to be that it did. Men did sicken and die when they discovered they had unwittingly eaten tapu food and when their friends turned from them in pity or in horror and loathing. For men's beliefs are made stronger when they are shared by others; and the stronger the beliefs, the more they affect the emotions; and the stronger the emotions, the more they affect the health as well as the actions of men.

So it is told that a famous and powerful chief was once on a war party in advance of his main forces. This is a time when the tapus surrounding a chief are more dangerous than ever. Naturally his food was carried separately in a special basket, for a chief's food is especially sacred, and naturally his ration of food was enough for three ordinary warriors. After stopping to eat, and in a hurry to be on the march again, he carelessly left the basket of half-eaten food beside the path instead of disposing of it as a thoughtful chief should. Soon afterward, the rear guard came up, and a hungry slave discovered the basket. Without stopping to ask questions, he gobbled down the unusually fine food. He had hardly finished when another slave, who had stayed behind from the chief's advance party, told him in horrified tones what he had done. At once, the greedy slave was seized with violent cramps, which did not cease until, at sundown, he was dead.

One episode like this was all that a Maori would need to confirm forever a belief which he and all the people he knew had held all their lives. It would outweigh a dozen other cases where no dire consequences had followed on the breach of a tapu, for these could all be explained away—as, for example, by the fact that the chief had somehow lost his mana. And, of course, where no one knew that a tapu had been violated, nothing was proved by the fact that nothing happened.

A really powerful chief could spread his mana fairly wide. There are cases of chiefs who, simply to show off their power, arbitrarily prevented all canoe travel on a river or all traffic through a particular forest by putting a tapu on them. Usually, however, the chief's motives for exercising his divine power in this way were more reasonable. He might, for instance, want to forbid the gathering of crops from certain fields in order to save up the food for a great feast he was giving that would bring prestige to the village. When Captain Cook made his voyage of rediscovery to New Zealand in the eighteenth century, one friendly chief protected the ship's gear and belongings from being pillaged simply by placing a tapu on the vessel. No Maori dared even set foot on it thereafter.

A chief's property was made sacred by contact with his sacred person. It was his body, and particularly his head, that was the seat of his mana, and other things became dangerous to touch to the extent that they could be considered a part of his person. Some chiefs were so mighty that, if their shadows happened to fall on huts or supplies of food, these would have to be destroyed. When a visiting chief made his rounds of a village, he had to be carefully directed where and how to go lest he inadvertently touch something valuable that could never afterward be used again.

The range of his capacity for harm depended of course on the amount and intensity of the individual chief's power, but his body itself was always fearsome. We have the account of one chief who went with others on a fishing trip. Evidently in this case this was all right, but on the return he had a nosebleed and the blood fell into the canoe. Not only the hard-won catch, but also the canoe, which had cost so many months of labor to make, had to be destroyed.

Being the repository for such sacredness could obviously be a burden even to the one so honored. It is always so when people are separated from one another by supernatural sanctions. Caste systems, such as that of old India, have prevented the most natural of human relations. Two hundred years ago, the Mikado of Japan could eat only out of the cheapest common clay dishes because they had to be broken after every meal for fear someone else might use them.

So it was for the Maori chief. His sacred head had often to be in a deplorably disheveled and dirty condition because no one but another chief would dare to put up his hair for him in the elaborate coiffure his dignity called for. The chief had always to eat out in the open air, regardless of weather or the state of his health, for fear of contaminating with his sanctity some object that others might use. He himself had to gather up the scraps from his table. If he asked for a drink, someone had to stand away from him pouring water from a calabash into the chief's cupped hands, which he held like a funnel before his mouth. In many ways it would have seemed to an outsider that a chief's people treated him not so much with reverence but rather as if he suffered from a loathsome and highly contagious disease.

Life, of course, must go on despite these self-imposed handicaps, and people anywhere, the more they are restricted by taboos, are the more ingenious in discovering remedies and evasions. The Maoris were too clever to be an exception. No matter how pious and careful a Maori might be, such was the snarl of tapu by which he was surrounded that he was bound to be enmeshed sooner or later. To make life endurable and to permit society to go on, there had to be a legal and reputable way out, at least for minor offenses.

In such cases the chief or priest could lift the harmful consequences of violating tapu. After the miscreant had submitted for a time to eating his food like a dog or a baby, without the use of his hands, the priest would light a sacred fire by rubbing sticks together and cook some fern root over it. The cooked root would be rubbed over the culprit's hand and then eaten by the leading woman in his family. The fern root thus picked up the charge of mana and the woman acted as a sort of lightning rod to ground it. A chief who had accidentally touched a valuable object could in some cases lift the tapu on it by touching it again, putting his fingers to his nose, and breathing back his mana.

An early New Zealand traveler tells a story of a less orthodox way of evading tapu, which is worth retelling because it illustrates both the kinds of problems the Maoris made for themselves and their flexibility in getting around them. Two canoes began a journey together, but one of them left somewhat earlier with all the women and slaves in the expedition. When the second canoe was about to embark, it was discovered that the provisions had not yet been loaded. It was also discovered that all the men in the second canoe were rangatira. Now, in any case, no self-respecting member of a chiefly family would lower himself by carrying a burden, but more important was the fact that a nobleman's back is almost as sacred as his head, and any food touching it would become inedible for anyone else in the expedition. In short, in this canoeful of strong young warriors there was not a single "back." Yet it was not possible to leave without the provisions.

The solution of this almost insoluble problem occurred to one of them who would undoubtedly have made a fine lawyer in some other civilization. In Maori there are at least two words meaning "to carry." *Pikau* means to carry a burden, and *hikau* means to hold or carry a baby. The suggestion was, not to *pikau* the food, but to *hikau* it. The man who had thought of this picked up a shark carcass, cradled it in his arms like a baby, and put it in the canoe. Amidst much laughter, the others followed suit. But these were only giddy young men with relatively little mana. No dignified older man would have got around his disability like this, and if he had, none of the younger men would have dared eat the food he carried.

There was one other peculiar Maori custom bound up with the ideas of mana and tapu, as well as with the Maori ideas of family, government, and justice. If a man killed his own slave, that was his own business. If he killed a man of another tribe, he had only to claim that it was in revenge for some recent or even traditional injury or insult, and his own tribe would rally round him to a man to defend him from punishment. But if he killed one of his own tribe or family, whether in anger or by purest accident, then all his property became forfeit to the first taker. As far as his possessions were concerned, he was an outlaw and was subject to raiding by all his kinsmen. This was *muru*.

Even if he lost a child of his own, through some accident, such as a fire for which he was not directly responsible, he was subject to muru. For had he not deprived the village and the tribe of a future warrior or the wife of a warrior? Indeed, the traditional occasions for muru were countless, for a man could injure his own tribe in countless ways, by malice, stupidity, or clumsiness. If he accidentally wounded himself, if he violated certain tapus, if he eloped with his bride instead of marrying her according to custom, obviously the man had lost his mana. He needed punishment (in addition to what the gods had already done to him) and he was fair game (being deserted by the gods). For certain kinds of bad luck there was no sympathy, only another excuse for tribal excitement.

The nobler the victim, the more he must be made to suffer, for the more he had injured his tribe. And indeed the pride of a rangatira would have been deeply wounded if the tribe had ignored his crime or misfortune or not treated it with all the attention his rank deserved.

The news spreads rapidly through the villages scattered over a tract a hundred miles square—"So-and-so has let his child be burned to death in a fire." Finally the news reaches the village of the child's mother. The people here have the first and greatest right to despoil the father. A marauding party is organized. The intended victim is told that a muru expedition is on the way. He asks anxiously if it is a large party and smiles happily if he is told it is. His importance is being recognized. He prepares a feast. He might as well, for when the muru is over, he will have nothing left anyway. When the party arrives, the dead child's father is challenged to a duel to the death by his brother-in-law. They fight with spears, but as soon as one is slightly wounded, they all sit down to the feast. After the feast the avengers systematically pillage the victim of all his wealth, his food, canoes, fishing nets, whatever they can lay hands on. Sometimes they burn the house to the ground and may even beat its owner with clubs.

Fortunately, such a stigma was not permanent. The offender might prove afterward that he had recovered his mana. In fact, he might soon recover some of his wealth by taking part in another muru against someone else. For the muru was not merely a sheriff's posse, a means whereby the tribal vigilantes punished crimes and mistakes. It was also a well recognized means for the exchange and circulation of property within the tribe—a sort of intramural substitute for war.

3. THE WARRIORS

The race from which the Maoris sprang—the Polynesians of the homeland Hawaiki—were far from being a peace-loving people. The history they so jealously remembered and taught their young was an endless account of war and warlike exploits, as is so much of our own early history and literature. The hero was the conqueror. The ideal was strength and skill in battle, love of battle, a sensitive code of honor, personal bravery, magnanimity in victory—in short, the ideal of chivalry. Moreover, the Maori nation was born of war, for when the Fleet came to New Zealand it was probably to escape extermination in the endless tribal conflicts of Tahiti.

But instead of finding peace in their new home, with its plenty of land for all and its harsher conditions for making a living, the pioneers went on to become the most warlike branch of all the Polynesian race. Their altered circumstances only gave them new occasions and pretexts for war, and new means and methods of warfare. Even after the descendants of the Fleet had overrun the country, absorbing or driving out or exterminating the earlier Moriori and the descendants of Toi, warfare became more than ever the preoccupation of the Maoris. It was in fact to become the chief business of their most important people, and the national sport of all.

The crew of each canoe of the Fleet had settled down on a different part of the coast, cleared it for planting, explored it for hunting, and forcibly dispossessed it of earlier inhabitants. Before the crew had grown into a tribe, it had probably lost all intimate contact with the descendants of other canoes. When this contact was finally restored, through the expansion of the tribes toward one another, it usually took the form of quarrels over boundaries.

By then the tribal land and shores were a sacred possession to be defended passionately with the lives of the tribe's warriors. Each tribe, on pain of being dispossessed by its neighbors, had to live in a constant state of military preparedness and to train its youth in battle-readiness. But with the warriors so keenly trained in the military virtues, and those same warriors the most important persons in the councils of the tribe, it was not to be expected that they would idly sit by waiting to repel an attack. Their history carefully retold every tribal defeat and victory, and there was always some ancient defeat to be avenged, or a victory to be made doubly sure of, before the enemy sought his own revenge. Then anything would serve as a pretext for war, and particularly some insult to the tribal honor.

A subchief weary of peace could practically at any time set off a tribal war by deliberately picking a quarrel with a neighboring tribesman, making some insulting reference to the outcome of a previous war, if necessary killing him. A subchief could thus start a war simply because he had some grudge against his own tribal chief, whose prestige he wanted to see reduced. This was known as "putting your own people in the wrong."

A mortal, and hence very effective insult was, "Your ancestors are still sticking to my teeth," meaning, "After our last war we feasted on your defeated dead." Any reference to someone else as food or even as a cooking utensil was a terrible curse or dire insult: "May your head be cooked!" or "Your skull is my cooking gourd!" Even a careless slip in etiquette could be construed under this touchy code of knightly honor as a justification for bloodshed.

One boy started a war because, happening to see an old man of another tribe planting in the hot sun, he thoughtlessly remarked that the sweat was steaming off the old man's head like the vapor from an oven. A chief more deliberately started a war by letting it be known that he had said that another chief's head (the most sacred part of his sacred person) should be beaten with a fern-root pounder! A disparaging remark about a chief (such as this insulting reference to a cooking utensil) was always an injury to his tribe, for he embodied its prestige. If a chief married a woman from another tribe, as frequently was done to cement political alliances between tribes, he could beat her with impunity, like any other wife, but woe to him if in his rage he insulted her family.

Back of all this were, of course, more solid reasons for fighting. Even the old Maori proverb ran, "By women and land are men lost." But by and large the men believed they fought simply because they had inherited from generation to generation a tribal feud or vendetta, or to improve their score in the king of sports. The warriors would have been no more grateful for a reign of universal peace than would King Arthur's knights have welcomed magistrates' courts to settle their disputes.

Whatever the cause or occasion for war, the chief could normally expect to get the support of all his blood relatives, that is to say, his village or tribe. It was not only the ties of kinship that obliged them to come to his aid, but also the need to protect the prestige of the tribal name. Nevertheless, the aid was purely voluntary and could be refused. The chief could only appeal to the sense of duty or to the love of glory of his kinsmen, perhaps also to their outraged sense of justice.

The chief would call the leading men and warriors into council and, brandishing his war club while he strode back and forth, harangue them on the wrongs the tribe had suffered from the enemy, its recent and most ancient grudges, the history of their previous wars, and the wisdom of immediate attack. It was not merely a matter of convincing his listeners by the reasonable force of his arguments. The men were also fine judges of pure oratory, an art as highly regarded among the Maoris as it was among the ancient Greeks. If the speaker was in top form in elocution, that was a good sign that the chief was filled with powerful mana and was the object of the gods' benevolence. It would be safe and proper to follow such a man where he led.

The war trumpet would be sounded and messengers sent to all the subchiefs to come to the aid of the tribe. From every village

the war parties would converge on the main tribal village. As they approached in battle array, they would be met as if they were the enemy. The home force, lined up as if for battle, would brandish its weapons and go into a war dance calculated to strike terror in the heart of a foe. Every muscle quivering, faces contorted, with bulging eyes and tongues sticking out, they would stamp, leap, and shout in absolute unison, like a highly trained ballet and chorus, until they sank to the ground in exhaustion. Then the visiting party would leap to its feet and execute an even more violent and ferocious dance.

Any break in the perfect rhythm of moving legs and shouting voices would be looked upon as a bad omen for the coming war, a reflection on their training as warriors and on the unity of their war spirit. That was, of course, what the dancing was for—not only to raise the pitch of enthusiasm of each individual fighter, but also to unify the common will to win, to make a perfectly functioning team out of them.

Finally, the army set out on the warpath. The warriors were now surrounded by the most potent tapus, the priests having blessed and baptized them and even had them touch and handle some of the most forbidden things. Women and slaves would go along to carry provisions or other burdens. If the party ran across a person—friend or foe, man, woman, or child—it would kill him outright. This, too, was a very good omen of success. If the victim was closely related to one of the warriors in the party, that warrior had the honor of slaying his own kinsman.

One of the many ways in which the Maori warriors resembled the knights of the Round Table was their preference for hand-to-hand combat. In their warfare they used no projectile weapons, no bows and arrows or slingshots, though these had existed in old Polynesia. Their chief weapons were the wooden spear and the short, heavy club of stone or bone called *mere*. The mere had a rather flat blade and a sharpened edge, and could be used for thrusting with the edge as well as clubbing with the flat. The handle end also had a sharp point that could be brought down like a blunt dagger. A thong through the handle was looped around the thumb. A warrior properly trained in this primitive-seeming weapon, thrusting, slicing, clubbing, stabbing, parrying, and feinting with both ends of it, face to face with his enemy, about whom he leaped and whirled in well-practiced footwork, must have looked like a dancing juggler, and was twice as dangerous as a white swordsman with saber or rapier.

The mere, preferably of the valuable greenstone or of whalebone, highly carved, was the chief's badge of office, which he carried about on all state occasions or whenever he addressed his own or other tribes as an orator. It usually had its own personal name, like Arthur's Excalibur, and its own mana, increased by the number and importance of the men it had killed. No cooked food must come near it, and during war the chief must eat with his left hand so as not to contaminate the hand that wielded the mere. Often inherited by the chief, his mere came to him with a history and personality well known to his own and other tribes. Chief Whegu, wounded and about to be slain on the battlefield, according to tradition, begged not to be killed by an inferior weapon and offered his own whalebone mere for the *coup de grâce*. His conqueror took the weapon and spared Whegu's life.

Even the four- to six-foot-long wooden spear was for close combat, man to man, as were of course the bone daggers the warriors carried in their belts. The rounded knob at the butt end of the spear was also used for striking, thrusting, and parrying, and the full use of this weapon included its employment as a quarterstaff. Here, too, intensive training in agility and special strokes began early in boyhood. Sometimes the fighter would wrap a cloak around his left arm to serve as a shield. Otherwise he fought almost naked except for his waist girdle, though a chief might wear his dogskin cape.

Again like the knights of old, the opposing armies would sometimes face each other across the battlefield, while a chosen champion from each side fought in single combat with spear or thrusting club for the honor of his tribe or to test the favor of the gods.

Nevertheless, battlefield tactics were also carefully studied, and many a chief was long remembered as a military genius. There were ambushes, feints, flanking movements, and all the rest. A favorite battle formation was the flying wedge, to crack up the other side's battle line, a Roman tactic also known to American football players. There would of course be much competition for the honor of being the single warrior at the apex of the wedge, or at least one of the two seconds immediately behind him. But once battle was joined, the fighting had to break up into individual combats, for there were no bowmen or slingers in the rear ranks, and every warrior needed elbow room for his art.

Special honor went to the warrior who made the first kill on the field. He would cry out, "I have the first fish!" Sometimes, then, the priest on the war party might cut open the corpse of this victim, pluck out the heart, and offer it to the gods. Meanwhile, the fighting would go on with redoubled fury now that blood had been shed. Eventually one side would be so far reduced that it would break and try to run, the other side in pursuit. At this point the victorious chief might decide that enough men had been killed to satisfy honor and he would lay his club in the path of his own men, or draw a line on the ground, and his warriors would stop the chase. Such chivalrous action was recognized as magnanimous on the part of the winning chief and could lead to peace and friendship between the victorious tribe and the defeated one.

This chivalry could not be expected, however, where there was a strong personal hatred between the chiefs. Then nothing would slake the war lust until one side had at least killed the chief of the other and eaten him—the supreme insult to him and all his descendants. Chief Ngatokorua was long remembered for the way he escaped this shameful fate. Wounded in battle and beset by many fighters, he managed to break off the point of a spear and hide it in his hand before being overpowered. His arms were bound behind him, and he was left lying on the field for later disposal. He succeeded in freeing his hands but kept them hidden behind him. After the fighting was over, he called for the chief of his conquerors; he wished to press noses with the conqueror in farewell before he was killed. As the victorious chief bent over the wounded warrior, Ngatokorua seized him by the hair, whipped out his spear point, and stabbed the chief in the neck. Ngatokorua's outraged captors killed him on the spot but not before the chief's blood had poured over him and rendered his body tapu. He died knowing they would never eat it.

An even worse fate for a chief than to be killed and eaten was to be captured and enslaved. After all, there was still some glory to being killed in battle, for battles were named and remembered after the chiefs and notable warriors who died in it. No matter how many others might lose their lives in it, a battle had no name and victory no fame if no chief was slain in it. Because of this the high chief Te Whakauruanga escaped slavery. After the battle the victorious enemy found him hiding in a thicket, wounded in both legs. He saw at once that, though they recognized him, they had no intention of taking his life. He asked for news of the

battle. Many had been slain, he learned, but none of his own brothers nor anyone else of great note. Raising his head with great dignity, he commanded his captors, "Kill me, so that your battle may have a name." Thus Te Whakauruanga won death instead of slavery and gave his name to a famous victory of his enemies.

If the Maoris often seemed to act like knights of the Round Table, it is because they fought under very similar conditions. In old New Zealand, before the coming of the white man, Maoris had only Maoris to fight with, men of the same blood and speech and culture. Though their battles could be bloody and the aftermaths exceedingly cruel and brutal from our point of view, all knew the rules of honorable combat and most fighters lived up to them. And if a great warrior went beyond what was expected of him, generously following the spirit rather than the mere letter of the rules, his nobility and magnanimity could immediately be recognized as such by both sides.

In one field of Polynesian warfare—that of defensive military strategy—the Maoris were innovators. In central Polynesia, a village was usually a rather loose scattering of houses, because each family head wished to build his house near his own grove of coconut or breadfruit trees. On these smaller islands, attacks could usually be expected from the sea, and the defenders could either go out in their own canoes to meet the raiders, fight them on the beaches, or simply flee to the uninhabited and relatively inaccessible interior.

The Fleet immigrants, however, were themselves invaders of a country already inhabited. It was natural for their pioneer villages to be more compactly laid out for protection. What they had to fear most were overland raids from the interior, which they had not yet explored. So they very early selected sites that were easily defended or from which they could have a distant view of approaching enemies—the top of a sea cliff or a dominating hill, an island in a lake or swamp, the bend in a river, or the tip of a cape. Then, as they themselves grew more warlike and the tribes spent more time and thought on raiding one another, the Maori village developed more and more into a fortified stronghold, called a *pa*. Every natural feature that could be used to render the pa more impregnable was worked into the defense plan. Some impressive feats of engineering and town planning resulted from this development.

Many villages were planted round with concentric circles of high stockades, with deep moats between them and watchtowers and fighting ramparts along their tops, and breastworks within, like any medieval castle. The outer ring of palisades might consist of huge tree trunks, many of them carved into the shapes of warriors with menacing heads, tongues sticking out in defiance. The main entrance was often a big, beautifully carved gateway, which was, however, barred in time of war, leaving only tiny, well-guarded exits. Slaves may have been sacrificed when the stockade was erected, and their bodies buried at the foot of the larger posts.

Some of these larger fortress villages were made to hold thousands of people during a siege. If such a large pa was built on a hillside, overlooking the fertile valley in which the tribe cultivated its sweet potatoes, the sloping land was often terraced to provide level ground for buildings, with the chief's home or the big meeting house on the highest level. Captain Cook, coming to New Zealand directly from Tahiti, was much struck by the sanitary arrangements of these pas, and found that they compared favorably not only with Polynesian settlements elsewhere but also with the European cities of that time. In some pas, every house had its own privy, and the garbage was collected and carefully disposed of in special dumps so that the village itself was kept clean and healthful.

At night the lookout towers on the stockades were manned by

Inside the pa

sentries who kept themselves awake and warned lurking enemies
of their vigilance by reciting out loud:

> O hither terrace, be on the alert!
> O yonder terrace, be on the alert!
> Lest ye be smothered in blood!

Or:

> This is the fort!
> Yes, this is the fort!
> This is the fort with high palisades
> Bound with the forest vines.
> And here within am I!

Usually, however, the news that war had been declared and that the pa was about to be attacked was brought in ample time by some neutral person or party. It was in line with the general sportsman's attitude toward warfare that fighting was usually engaged in only during certain seasons and after due warning. Only in the case of very bitter blood feuds were surprise attacks undertaken, or when the attacking force was definitely inferior in numbers.

When the imminent attack was made known, the war trumpets were sounded continuously and the war gongs beaten. Subtribes from outlying undefended villages came streaming in and took up assigned positions between the breastworks. All was noise, excitement, and furious activity as the stockades were mended with vines and ropes, moats deepened, houses in the way of the defenders knocked down, brushwood cleared away. Work would go on all day and all night by torchlight and the light of bonfires, to the doleful clamor of the trumpets and of the screaming women and crying children.

Meanwhile, the attacking force would have moved up and surrounded the pa. It might settle down for a long siege, building huts and a fortified camp, posting sentries, in the hope of starving the fort into submission. It might try tricks and maneuvers to lure the besieged warriors out into an ambush. It might try to storm the walls directly, braving the boulders thrown from the watchtowers and the weapons of the defenders. One of these was a special siege spear, over twelve feet long and often much longer, barbed with the terrible spines of the sting ray. Handled by two or more men, this huge spear would be thrust through a loophole in the stockade just when the attackers made a violent rush for the walls, and could sometimes transfix two or three of them at once.

The obligations of kinship, on which every military chief

depended for his fighting strength, could also sometimes be his weakness. It was, for instance, considered perfectly proper for the men in an attacking party, between battles, to pay friendly visits to their relatives in the besieged pa. Once, when a fortress was gradually being reduced to submission because the besiegers had cut off its water supply, it was able to keep on fighting because of such friendly visits. The dutiful relatives from the attacking force would simply soak themselves at the spring before dropping in for a chat, and their thirsty kinsmen would suck on their heavy flax garments while they exchanged news and gossip. The attacking chief, who could not stop the visits, finally broke the stalemate by placing guards around the spring and preventing his warriors from going bathing with their clothes on.

Another time, the chief Uerata had successfully stormed stockade after stockade and carried terrace after terrace of an enemy fort, when he paused to breathe his troops before the final assault on the last citadel. Then, faced by the annihilation of his people, the chief of the besieged garrison remembered that one of his remote ancestors had come from a leading family of Uerata's tribe. He went onto the topmost parapet of the last stockade and called down to the leader of the attacking host. "O Uerata!" he cried. "What token from the past have you for me?" Uerata immediately recognized this as a claim on his kinship. Raising his spear above his head in both hands, he brought it down across his knee, breaking it. Without a word he turned and walked down the hill, his warriors quietly following him. By this act of chivalry Uerata's already great mana and prestige were increased even more than they would have been by the total defeat of his enemy.

In other cases where the warring chiefs were kinsmen, an honorable peace was granted a besieged pa if the attacking chief called upon his foe to come forth as a cousin. Even if he was on the verge of being decisively defeated, the besieged chief could then go over to the other side with his garrison and be treated not as a conquered enemy but as an honored guest. It was thought no disgrace to accept such an invitation, and win both one's life and peace. The tribal histories also contain several instances of sieges lifted when the besieged chief gave his daughter in marriage to the besieging chief, lowering her down the battlements by a rope. The making and acceptance of such a gift were honorable chiefly gestures, for among the Maoris, as among European monarchs in former days, marriage was recognized as one of the principal ways of cementing peace.

But these chivalrous gestures, though proudly celebrated in history and song, were not the normal way in which wars ended. If honor and glory were one cause of the endless wars, the others were land, tribute, and plunder. To the victors belonged the spoils, and there was often much rivalry among them for the valuable loot. In this the chiefs naturally had a great advantage. If a warrior clapped his hand on a canoe and shouted, "This canoe is mine!" it was ordinarily recognized as an act of possession, but if a more powerful chief then came along and coveted the same canoe, he could render it tapu to anyone else by saying, "This canoe is my backbone!" or "That canoe, my skull shall be its bailer."

It was, however, in the treatment of the defeated people that we see the dark and savage side of the Maoris' knightly code. We have already mentioned the cannibalism. There are other primitive people who have been known to eat their fellow men out of sheer necessity; the Eskimos, as we have seen, were always deeply ashamed whenever they had done so. Yet, curiously enough, the Maoris, who seem to have developed the most exquisite modesty wherever the eating or preparation of food was concerned, who surrounded the subject of food with more taboos than almost any other people, would openly boast of the human flesh they had consumed. The only shame was connected not with eating others but with being eaten. Far from being taboo, as it was almost everywhere else in the world, the eating of a defeated enemy was a means of acquiring his mana.

Those war captives who were saved from the ovens—and they were, of course, the great majority—became slaves. Though the slaves did all the menial work as burden carriers and laborers on the land, they were not badly treated. There was no exhausting labor in mines or mills, and the work they did was not very different from that of the commoners and the women. Nevertheless, for Maoris of rank this was an even more shameful fate than being eaten, and slaves were, in fact, taunted as being "remnants of the feast," that is to say, mere table scraps not worth eating. For this reason, noble parents would sometimes slay their children to prevent their enslavement, and a wounded chief unable to fight or flee would often die on his own spear, like a Roman, rather than be captured. This was called "to die fighting like a shark."

Maori chronicles tell of battles after which the victors took as many as two thousand prisoners. Usually, however, if so many people were involved, the conquerors were satisfied merely to reduce the conquered tribe to vassalage after carrying off some of its women as hostages or slaves. This meant that, though the defeated people kept their land, they had to send tribute to the victorious chief. Such, however, were Maori notions of gifts that this usually obligated the conquerors to send back gifts in payment. Moreover, there was always the fear that the defeated tribe would husband its strength and someday seek revenge. This was one reason that the strongest and comeliest girls were regularly taken away by the ruling tribe—to prevent the raising up of warriors. When, however, the vassal tribe finally felt strong enough to challenge its rulers, it might bring its next tribute on the points of spears. Usually, when this happened, the conquerors took the hint and released their vassals of all further obligation to pay tribute.

4 . THE ARTISTS

Besides being born to the mana of a chief or becoming great in warfare, there were other roads to personal prestige and fame for the Maori. He could become a *tohunga,* that is, an expert or specialist in an honored craft, a skilled craftsman—in the widest sense of the term, an artist. For the Maoris were as artistic as they were warlike. They also saw the effects and workings of mana in the inspiration behind artistic creations, in the uncanny skill of the trained craftsman and the special knowledge of the learned man. They believed that such people were also in communion with the gods, and that their work was therefore tapu.

The priest or magician was a tohunga, and so was the architect, the canoe builder, the tattooer, the weapon maker, the orator, the poet or singer, and the teacher of music or dancing. The fame of many of these artists spread far beyond their own villages and tribes, and they were often invited, with lavish gifts, to perform their skills for distant chiefs. Sometimes they formed a special privileged class, for they alone could initiate new apprentices into the magic and mystery of their craft. In Samoa the house builders became a powerful guild or trade union that could challenge the power and prestige of the chiefs. Even in New Zealand the canoe builders and the tattooers represented a break in the otherwise all-dominating influence of family and kinship.

Such honors were gladly accorded the professional artists because most Maoris were themselves part-time artists in their own right. Every tool or implement of wood, bone, or stone made by the family itself was elaborately carved. The Maoris delighted in colors and designs on the mats and clothing woven by their women. They were an exceedingly musical and poetical race, and had, as we have seen, the highest regard for eloquence. A Maori orator would often, in the midst of a stirring retelling of tribal history or legend, break out into song. The people loved to chant in perfect unison to the music of trumpets, flutes, and drums. All the young women were trained in the graceful posture dances, in which the whole body danced and not only the feet, and the military exercises of the young men were as much perfectly drilled ballet performances as they were practice in the manual of arms.

Probably the oldest class of tohungas, or professionals, was, as it is among most primitive people, that of the priests and magicians. Indeed, though the word tohunga meant "expert," when used by itself it ordinarily meant priest. The priests were also the medicine men, or doctors, of the community and the historians and teachers of the highest learning.

These men were naturally also rangatira, members of the chiefly families, for not otherwise could they have learned what they were expected to know. First, they knew the names of all the gods, including those supreme deities who had created the world but no longer concerned themselves with the ordinary affairs of common men and were not even known to most of them. Of course they knew how to propitiate by proper ritual and prayer the actual working, or "departmental," gods—Tane of the forests, Tangaroa of the ocean, Tu of war, Rongo of agriculture. Finally, they could appeal to the lesser or ancestral spirits for small favors, and exorcise sickness and evil spirits from those who had broken tapu.

The priests were also the teachers of tradition and history. They were the living books who knew by heart the tremendously long pedigrees or genealogies of the chief families, and the marriages among them for many, many generations. It was they who kept recorded in their heads and taught the young all the crowded details of their tribe's military history. A young noble in whose presence someone should happen to make a slighting reference to an ancient defeat of his tribe was supposed to be ready immediately to mention a later victory that wiped out that defeat. This is perhaps one way of making the teaching of history by "dates" less dull than most people find it.

Any young man who hoped to become a leader of men had to be trained in oratory, a most important part of which was to have a well-stocked and ready supply of historical and literary references. He must know and play upon the relationships by blood and marriage among families, villages, and tribes, the treaties between tribes, and the history of the ownership of lands. He must use the proper figures of speech, the correct words of ancient heroes, the appropriate poetry and song to go with the occasion—whether he was making a welcoming speech to visitors from another tribe, or celebrating a birth or death or marriage, or making a political or warlike proposal in council. For whether he was facing his own tribe or another, he had a critical audience as quick to pick up a misquotation or a misstatement of history as to show its approval by joining him in the singing of a song. Because the teaching of history was in the hands of the priests, they played an important part in the political, as well as the religious, life of the people.

The striking artistic bent of the Maoris was best expressed in their carving, in the wood of their houses and canoes, in the bone and stone of their weapons and tools. Particularly in their treatment of wood, we can see the effect of a changed environment on the old Polynesian culture.

In boatbuilding, for instance, the Maoris were already master shipwrights before they came to New Zealand in their huge hollowed-out double canoes. The trees of Tahiti had not been big enough to give the length of hull needed, so each one had been made of two dugout logs butted end to end. The slimness of these hulls had also required that two canoes be fastened side by side, as described earlier, for stability under sail. Thus it had taken four trees to fashion the twin keels of each ship.

On New Zealand the immigrants found trees whose trunks, ten

feet in diameter, rose in straight shafts for a hundred feet and whose woods lent themselves to a great variety of carving techniques. The longest canoe could be made of a single log, with a beam wide enough for stability without the support of an outrigger. Besides, the Maoris no longer went on non-stop voyages of thousands of miles, and the extra width of double canoes only made them more difficult to maneuver up inland rivers and along complicated coastlines.

The result was a new Maori style of boatbuilding. It showed how flexibly the old Polynesian culture could adapt itself to a new geography and climate and new resources. But it also showed how an inherited culture can dictate the way in which new opportunities will be used. For the Maoris kept to the old ways of hollowing out their hulls instead of building boats of really different types, as, for example, out of planks, though they were quite handy at splitting logs.

The building of a war canoe capable of holding a hundred or more men could be undertaken only by the chief of a wealthy tribe or village, all the people of which would have to contribute labor or wealth to such a long-drawn-out enterprise. First, a suitable tree had to be selected, of the right size and shape, and growing not too far from the water's edge. Then the priest must, with the proper incantations, obtain the consent of Tane, god of the forest, and of all his attendant wood-elves, before one could think of chopping down one of his giant children. Otherwise, either the unlucky task would never be completed or the canoe would only bring disaster to the tribe—defeat in war or failure in fishing. For the building of a particularly sacred war canoe it might even be well to sacrifice a son of a chief and bury him at the foot of the tree to propitiate Tane.

A working space for the many men involved on the project must be cleared around the tree. If it was some distance from the village, the land near it was cleared and cultivated to grow extra food for the workers. When the priest had chosen an auspicious day, the chopping could begin. This was extremely slow work for men with stone adzes. They built small controlled fires around the trunk and then chipped away the charred parts. Days and weeks might go by before the breathless moment when the tree began to topple. If it split in its crash, then all the labor would have been in vain.

Meanwhile, the slaves and commoners had been busy building a skid road to the sea, clearing underbrush and laying down log rollers sometimes for miles. They would, of course, have nothing to do with such sacred work as the making of the canoe itself. That was only for the chiefs and the professional canoe builders, who may have been imported from outside the tribe and were repaid with many valuable gifts.

The trunk was roughly hollowed out with fire and adze where it lay, and then, somewhat more light and manageable, it was skidded down the rollers, which had of course also been blessed by the priests, to the accompaniment of sacred chants and special songs composed for the occasion. When the great hulk was safely on shore, the real work of hewing and shaping could begin. Only skilled and dedicated hands were allowed to do this work, and the chips were carefully burned in a sacred fire (like the fingernail parings or hair cuttings of people) to prevent their being used in black magic against the canoe.

The very best artists and craftsmen were engaged to carve out the separate tall bow and stern pieces and fit them to the hull, and to shape and curve the planking that built up the sides. To prevent the wood from cracking under the stone tools, the carving would be done in very small portions at a time, so that sometimes the canoe was years in the making. But, as with all true artists insistent on perfection, the Maori craftsmen were

patient. The double spirals carved on the bow over the figure of the hero-god Maui were considered just as important a part of the finished ship as the seaworthiness of its hull.

In the stern was a raised platform, the post of honor for the chief and the place of a tiny shrine to the sea god Tangaroa. On this sacred quarterdeck no food would ever be eaten. Indeed, in a war canoe it was absolutely tapu to carry any cooked food, and on long expeditions there would be separate canoes sent along as provision tenders.

Meanwhile, other workmen had been turning out the paddles, the bailers with carved handles, the big triangular sail made of matting, and a stone anchor with a hole in it through which ran the anchor cable of plaited flax. When the canoe was finally finished, calked, and painted, the thwarts and mast put in, and all the gear provided, it was ready for launching and baptism by the priest. He sprinkled water on it with a sacred shrub and recited a prayer for good fortune. The men took their places, sometimes five abreast—the three on the inside of each row as relief for the two outside paddlers—the chief in the stern, and the canoe was finally off on its maiden voyage at ten miles an hour.

In their housing the Maori woodworkers again successfully handled the challenge and opportunities of new-world conditions. In their tropical homeland their houses had been made of bamboo. Here there was no bamboo, and anyway walls made of it would have been much too well ventilated for the cold winters of New Zealand. On the other hand, the giant trees, with their great variety of hard and soft woods, lent themselves beautifully to solving the problem.

The Maoris gradually worked out a construction of solid planking split from the huge kauri pines. These they built into low substantial walls often over thirty feet long. They were half-buried in the earth that was banked against them and were covered with a heavily thatched peaked roof. The only openings were a single window and one low doorway, both giving out on a deep, roofed veranda in front.

There was practically no furniture of any sort in this long, single-roomed house. It was merely a dormitory or sleeping shed for several related families. In cold weather a small charcoal fire was kept burning on the floor, the smoke escaping where it could, for there was no chimney. The inner walls were lined with reeds or tree fern for warmth. Along the walls were laid logs to raise the sleeping places above the dirt floor; these were covered first with ferns, and then with mats. A string of flax might dangle from a rafter for hanging the garments of the sleepers. And that was all—no decorations, no furniture for family living, and certainly no facilities for eating or cooking.

Cooking, like all other family activities, was done outdoors or, in stormy weather, under special little cooking sheds, which were nothing more than roofed fireplaces or pit ovens open on all sides. Enough has been said already of the Maori attitude toward food to make it understandable that cooking and eating would never be allowed in a sleeping house. Some tribes were so sensitive about this that mothers would even go out into the middle of the night to nurse their babies. On the other hand, only a slave would be allowed to sleep under a cooking lean-to.

On these structures the Maori craftsmen did not expend a line of carving, though, curiously enough, on the little wooden storehouses for food, standing high on stilts in the middle of the village, there was often a great deal of elaborate carving and painting. But then, food was involved, so that not only animals and thieving men must be guarded against, but also all manner of magic and spirits.

It was, however, the village meeting house, its town hall, that was the glory of the builder's art. Maori meeting houses were the most beautiful and elaborate in the whole Polynesian world. As with the war canoe, it was the chief who was responsible for the building of the meeting house, and who gained the prestige and honor associated with it. But the whole village or tribe contributed to the labor and cost, and it belonged to all the people. A very large one might measure eighty-five feet in length, thirty in breadth, and twenty in height, and be capable of holding fifteen hundred people. One such building was called the "eight-year house" because it had taken that long to construct.

Once the decision to build was made, the village would begin to lay up stores of food and gifts for the workers and experts, planting for larger harvests, drying more fish, preserving more birds. Lumber, reeds, mats, paints, and other building materials would begin to be selected and collected. The proper woods for ridgepole, rafters, and side walls must be found in the forest, chopped down, and gathered for seasoning. A favorite wood for rafters was the "wet pukatea," so called because it took years to dry properly, and the favorite red paint was made from hematite, a mineral that it often took years to collect in sufficient quantities to decorate a really large house. Finally, the skilled craftsmen for dressing, thatching, reed work, paneling, painting, and carving had to be recruited, at home and abroad.

A famous master carver might be a very great man in his own tribe and, like any artist, inclined to be touchy and temperamental. He must be handled with great tact, and the gifts he received (payments for services among the Maoris were always "gifts") must be valuable and worthy of his dignity. They were even known to include the hand of the chief's daughter in marriage.

When the house was finished, every inch of visible wood, within and without, might be covered with carving or painting—the wall slabs, the pillars holding up the massive ridgepole, the frames of the single door and window. Inside, the rafters were painted with intricate scrollwork in red, white, and black. At the gable peak of the steeply slanting roof there was usually carved a great flat head. Around the wall slabs and at the base of the pillars the chief could point out to a visitor the carved portraits of his ancestors and the heroes of the tribe—all highly conventionalized, of course. Though the roof was thatched with rushes, and the floor was of beaten earth overlaid with plaited mats made by the women, the whole effect of the elaborate carving was of some enormous jewel box.

The meeting house did in fact contain something precious, for it was the fixed, visible symbol of the unity of the tribe. Here, or on the big open plaza, or *marae,* before it, were held all the meetings, councils, or celebrations of the tribe. Here the tribe met of an evening to sing and dance, to tell stories and recite history, to exchange news and gossip, for their own houses were only shelters to sleep in and not really homes as we understand them. The meeting house was the youth center of the village, where the young people gathered in the evening to play games and practice their posture dances, sometimes late into the night, without disturbing the older people asleep in their dormitories.

Finally, this was the village guest house, for the accommodation of visitors. Though no food could ever be brought into it, beds of fern and mats lined both sides, with a special bed reserved near the central pillar for high chiefs and very distinguished guests, which no person of lower rank would dare to touch. Etiquette required that the other visitors group themselves about this spot strictly according to their rank and prestige. It is no wonder, then, that the dedication of a meeting house should be attended by the most solemn ceremonies and the biggest feast and celebration the tribe could afford.

Carving was the great visual art of the Maoris; into it they poured much of their artistic energy. Pottery was non-existent. Textiles were not very highly developed, but when the Maoris had to learn to substitute the coarse fibers of the native wild flax for the inner bark of the Tahitian mulberry tree in making their dress cloth, this too involved a revolutionary change of techniques. From pounding out the papery wood in the manner of a plastic, they had to turn to working with threads, but somehow they stopped just short of true weaving with a loom. Instead, the fibers were plaited and tied after the manner of their basketwork and fishing nets. Eventually the women acquired great skill in this work and even cultivated the finer varieties of flax for the purpose.

The making of clothing is often an important outlet for the artistic impulses of a people, but the Maori wardrobe did not offer much opportunity for decorative display. Children went about naked until the age of ten. Men and women ordinarily dressed practically alike. Both wore a costume of only two garments: a knee-length fringed kilt held up by a belt and, when they were not working or fighting, a plaited mat or blanket draped over the shoulders to leave one arm free. Also, for the frequent rainy weather of this country, they might have a rain cape made of little overlapping tags or thatches that could turn water like a thatched roof, and for very cold weather a long cape of thick, rough matting. They wore no hats and usually went barefoot, though there was a sort of combined sandal and legging sometimes used in cold weather or for journeys over very rough ground.

In their basic wardrobe of kilt and blanket, even the chiefs were not very distinguishable from the other tribesmen, but their outer capes or robes often showed their rank, and in them the art of the seamstress could be seen to advantage. Many a chief married a woman simply because she was skilled in the making of fine capes. Sometimes measuring seven feet by ten, these ceremonial or dress capes often had beautiful borders of geometrical designs in black, red, and white. Only the chief could wear a cape of dogskin, and only women of high rank wore the showy capes made of the brightly colored feathers of birds—

pigeons, parrots, and kiwis—each feather individually tied by hand in what must have been most tedious work.

It was in the accessories of their costume that the Maoris expressed their love of adornment. Necklaces and earrings were worn by both men and women. Their ear lobes were pierced in infancy and the holes kept distended and sore for months so that they would later accommodate the large plugs of dried birdskins or dried sea horses that were especially popular. Necklaces would be made of the teeth of sharks, dogs, or even human beings. Chiefs and their wives might own necklaces and ear pendants of greenstone jade, priceless heirlooms that had been passed down for generations or were the loot of conquest. Women also wore tiny sachet bags of scented grass about their necks, and carried at their sides finely worked basketry pocketbooks slung from their shoulders.

The chief naturally permitted himself certain other small vanities to symbolize his rank. He alone wore in his hair the red and white tail feathers of the huia bird and carried the carved greenstone or whalebone club that was the badge of his office. Though he cut his hair short in war, in peace he wore it long and often done up in such an elaborate coiffure that he had to sleep on a wooden neck rest in order not to spoil it. In compensation, his sacred bed might be filled with scented grass and he could tapu a small pool so that he might use it for his private mirror.

But the chief personal adornment of the Maori was neither an article of clothing nor an accessory thereto. It was, in fact, as might be expected, a form of carving; it was tattooing. For this almost universally human practice, the English language has—as in the case of "taboo"—borrowed a Polynesian word, *tatu*. No Maori would consider himself a full-grown man, and certainly not a man of rank, unless his whole face—forehead, cheeks, nose, chin, and lips—was covered with spiral and geometrical designs. Many also had their thighs and buttocks similarly tattooed, as if

they were wearing patterned bathing trunks. The women tattooed their lips blue (red lips were not considered beautiful), with sometimes a design worked out on the chin. Ladies of rank also had designs picked out in the space between their eyes and on the backs of their legs, from heel to knee. The coloring used was the soot of certain resinous woods mixed with water or berry juices.

Tattooing, as practiced by the Maoris, was a most painful process, and could be done only a little at a time. A girl might not be able to eat with her painfully swollen lips for months, and might have to use the funnels especially invented for this purpose. A very young boy might have to be held down by a couple of his relatives, while the tattooer, with wooden hammer and bone chisel, tapped through his skin over a design previously drawn in charcoal. Whereas elsewhere in Polynesia the skin was merely punctured with sharp points, which were painful enough but left a fairly smooth skin, the Maori tattooer almost literally carved the skin deeply with a chisel that had a knifelike edge dipped in pigment. The skin between the fine, close-set colored lines was therefore raised in relief, like the wood on a canoe prow.

Though the result of covering the human face with cuts, punctures, and pigments was to make it look like a carved mask, the desired effect was far from being one of uniformity. Every chief's facial design was called his *moko,* a part of his individual personality like the natural arrangement of his features, or as a man's signature is considered to be among us. It was begun early in his boyhood and was continued for years until his face was covered, keeping pace with his growing experience and mana. One side of the face was done first, to establish the pattern. Sometimes a man, for one reason or another, might never get around to having the other side of his face finished, and would go about with the even more startling effect of a half-tattooed man.

It was, of course, a sacred work, for it involved the shedding of blood and hence much tapu. Besides, so permanent an addition to one's personality was not to be entrusted to amateurs. The tattooers were therefore among the most highly honored of the tohungas. The chiefly families sought out those most famous for the artistic excellence and magical power of their work, and loaded them down with gifts. After all, a botched canoe or house might, at worst, be got rid of, but what could one do with an unsuccessful moko? Hence it was not unknown for a slave to be sacrificed at the commencement of a tattooing, to propitiate the powers that dispensed mana.

5. MAKING A LIVING

It is never altogether true to say of any people, "They are warriors," or, "They are artists." Very few persons in any primitive society can give their full time, or even the major part of it, to such activities as war, art, or religion. Those who do are after all, as the Maoris say, specialists, experts, tohungas. Much as these men may be honored or be given power and influence, it is still true that the majority of their fellow tribesmen must spend most of their time simply in making a living—growing or hunting the means to feed and clothe not only themselves, but also their leaders and specialists.

The Maoris were at a transitional level of culture, where men have learned to cultivate crops as a main source of their food supply but have not yet given up the gathering of wild plants and the hunting of animals as equally important. Thus their two chief vegetable foods were the cultivated sweet potato, which they called the food of peace, and the wild-growing fern root, which they called the food of war. These made up the starchy basis of their diet, for they had not learned to grow the cereal grasses on which most agricultural peoples depend.

The fields, or plantations, for growing sweet potatoes were owned communally by the village, and at the proper seasons the whole village turned out together to clear the ground, dig up the soil, plant, and harvest. But each family was assigned its own individual plot in the common land and owned the produce of it. Everyone worked at the clearing and digging—men, women, and children, slaves, commoners, and even chiefs. With their love of group activities performed in unison, whether in paddling a canoe or executing a war dance, they would organize themselves in lines, chopping and chanting as one, like a well-drilled orchestra. Their tools were simple—stone adzes for clearing the ground of trees and brush, and, for hoeing, long wooden sticks with a footrest for applying the digger's weight to the hardened point. Until the white men brought steel axes and iron hoes, the Maoris knew nothing of the use of metal.

"Short fingernails," said the Maori proverb, "show the man of power." The chief did not, like kings elsewhere, live on the tribute exacted from his own people. He too had his allotment of land, and he was not above working. But he had, of course, a larger share of slaves than most and more wives than others. War and political marriages brought him land and slaves, and his wives, whom he might visit in turn, acted as overseers for his outlying plantations.

At harvest time, a tapu was put upon the harvested fields and even upon the village, and ropes were stretched across the pathways to warn outsiders of the danger. The ropes also discouraged snoopers from spreading rumors about the yield and thus perhaps arousing the warlike envy of villages with poorer crops. Even among themselves, the families of a single village were shy of advertising their harvest, and it was not considered good manners to pry. The sweet potatoes, after being dug up, were left heaped on the field, covered with leaves. At night the families would go out with baskets, bring the crop back, and fill their stilted storehouses before daylight. "Very poor crop," the ill-bred inquisitive person would be told. "Barely got back our own seed. We shall have to eat fern root this year."

The edible starchy roots of certain ferns growing wild on New Zealand could measure about three inches round and a foot long. They were usually dug up by the men, for this was heavy work. Then the women collected them and stacked them loosely in the shade to dry slowly in the wind. In about two weeks they were picked over and sorted and then stored away. If well dried, they could last for years, and hence could be taken along on war parties or long expeditions. To be made ready for eating, the roots were soaked and the black skin scraped off. Then they were roasted and pounded into a thick dough, and the long wiry fibers were drawn out. The result was a thick, mealy, rather tasteless dough, to which fish, flesh, or berry juices were usually added. Other wild plant foods were the tap root of the cabbage palm, the heart of the nikau palm, various berries, and—the most curious—the yellow pollen of the bulrush, which is supposed to taste like gingerbread. The only drink of the Maoris was water, sometimes sweetened with honey.

The tribes who settled and lived along the coast naturally

remained the expert fishermen their people had always been in the home islands of Hawaiki. In their canoes, they fished with hook and line, with hand nets, and with seines. The latter were often over a half-mile long, and their making, of the native flax, was of course a highly tapu undertaking of dedicated experts. The women gathered shellfish and did most of the preserving and drying of the men's catches. The coastal tribes exchanged their dried fish with the tribes of the interior for return gifts of preserved birds, usually at ceremonial feasts.

Birdcatching on a really large scale was something the Maoris learned and developed only after they had come to New Zealand. In this land, totally devoid of mammals, even of the primitive marsupials to be found in Australia, birds were the only large source of fresh meat. Fortunately, the country was very rich in bird life, both the migratory varieties and those that had permanently settled down—some, such as the kiwi, even to the point of giving up flight altogether. Of parrots especially there were many interesting varieties found nowhere else in the world —some that had given up the use of their wings and some that were as fierce and strong as eagles.

The hen-size, high-jumping, wingless kiwi, with its long, hair-like feathers, is perhaps the best known of New Zealand's birds. It was hunted with dogs or traps, like the forest rats that had come to this land as stowaways on the Fleet. The giant moa, which was so soon to become extinct, has already been mentioned. This heavy, ostrich-like bird, until its final disappearance, was hunted in bands whose technique was to knock its legs out from under it while it was poised to kick, and then to dispatch it with spears while it was on the ground.

The usual method of fowling for flying birds was by hand-operated snares. This called for no bravery on the part of the hunter but did require the utmost in agility and quickness of reaction, and was not a job for old men or untrained women. As the season came around when fat pigeons roosted in the trees, all was bustle and preparation in the village. Now snare cords were being rolled, plaited, and wound, new perches elaborately carved or old ones refurbished. The old men too feeble to climb trees took charge of this as well as of giving advice and instruction to the young fowlers. Women, children, and slaves collected firewood and stones for the ovens, and laid out the gourds for preserving the birds that were confidently expected.

Before leaving the village, each fowler stopped before a post that had been erected and painted red by the priest. He touched his snares with a switch which he then threw down before the post, saying, "Ill luck and indolent desire, be ye here heaped up. Cause me to acquire." This was to prevent the greedy thoughts of the lazy ones at home from winging their way into the forest and warning the birds of the coming of the fowlers. Such thoughts could not pass the magical post, and dropped before it. Naturally, also, the fowler carried only uncooked food with him, and he was careful not to let the feathers of captured birds fly about.

Each man went only to his own trees, whose forty or fifty feet he climbed by means of a shaky vine ladder. Up in the branches he fastened his bright snares, four to six alluring little perches for the birds to rest on as they pecked at the fruit, but each with a little noose for unwary feet. From each perch a trailing cord led to the branch where the fowler crouched, absolutely motionless, in ambush. With luck, a whole flock might settle in the tree, and, if he acted fast, he could pull all the nooses tight at once and capture four or more birds before they took flight. Holding his cords tight with hands, feet, and teeth, he released one bird at a time, killed it by wringing its neck, and dropped it to the ground. Then he reset his perches and waited for another flock. Primitive as this method may seem, a good fowler could bag several hundred birds a day during the season.

At the end of the first day, the fowlers gathered up their catch and returned to the village. There they were met by a silent crowd waving green branches at them, for they and their kill were tapu and must be purified. The priest made a new fire by rubbing sticks, mixed some of the feathers with fern root, roasted the mixture over the fire, and prayed that the birds would remain plentiful in the forest. The birds from which the feathers had been plucked were offered to the gods.

Meanwhile, three ovens had been prepared—one for the priests, one for the fowlers, and one for the rest of the people. The birds were cooked and the feast began. But if this was the first bag of a very young hunter, he would be content with a few bones and leavings, to show the gods that he was not thinking of his own stomach when he snared the birds, that he was not a glutton or— as the Maoris say, referring to the pest that destroys their sweet-potato vines—"a caterpillar always slowly eating." Among the coastal tribes, similar ceremonies and rituals were practiced after the first catch of the fishing season.

The fowlers were now free of the tapu, and the snaring season was officially open. Even women, to whom certain easy trees were assigned, might go out now to catch birds. At the end of each day's hunting, each family placed all the birds in its day's bag in a heap. Round and round the piles of birds strolled all the villagers, inspecting, commenting, criticizing, boasting. People with small heaps felt ashamed, those with large ones beamed. But this shame and pride were not over their *possessions* but over the fact that there was a village feast in the offing, and all were competing to make the largest contribution to it. It was fear of being thought stingy or lazy that explained their feelings.

For the feast, or for later use as gifts or delicacies, the birds were preserved. After the feathers and bones were removed, but not the lower beak, they were roasted, and sealed tight in decorative calabashes, with their own fat poured over them. These gourds, mounted on little carved wooden legs and wrapped round with a mat ornamented with feathers, made a dainty dish to set before important guests or to be given them to take home.

The highest peacetime virtue for the Maori was what we should call hospitality or generosity, except that it was often carried to such extremes and was of course mingled so much with Maori ideas of prestige that it might easily be called something else— the love of display, for instance, or the desire to impress others. Nevertheless, there is always something noble in the sheer fact of open-handedness, and it was at least one form of Maori rivalry that was not cruel or aggressive.

To be a great chief it was not enough merely to conquer in war; he had also to have a reputation for lavish hospitality, for making magnificent gifts, for expending large quantities of wealth with a casual air. This was indeed why the chief, whose standard of living was so little different from that of his people, so pressingly needed lands and wealth and sought them in war—not to keep, but to spend, to give away. His power was measured not so much by what he owned as by what passed through his hands.

This spirit was most satisfyingly expressed in the giving of feasts and the lavish entertainment of guests. If visitors were unexpected, no one asked them why they came. They would announce their purpose in their own good time, and meanwhile they were providing a welcome test of the chief's noted generosity. They would be stuffed with delicacies, showered with entertainment, and sent on their way loaded down with gifts.

There are many Maori stories to illustrate the chiefly obligation to keep open house. Chief Tutamure's brother-in-law, having heard the chief brag of his storehouses bursting with food, arrived with a large party of friends with the avowed intention of eating the boaster out of house and home. Never betraying the least anxiety or chilliness, Tutamure entertained the party, who stayed to the very limits that courtesy allowed, and he never let them know that they had achieved their purpose of impoverishing him. Then of course the brother-in-law was under an obligation to outdo Tutamure's hospitality.

On many similar occasions, a noble family cheerfully plied its unbidden guests with all the food that had been put aside for the winter. So inviolable was the code that one chief made his visitors stay on and enjoy his hospitality even after he had discovered that they were the murderers of his children.

Not to be able to behave in this chiefly fashion could be a cause of deep humiliation. There is a song still extant, composed by a great chief, which tells how the swamp hens and caterpillars had destroyed his village crops and how his chagrin at not being able to entertain visitors was driving him to hide away in one of his most remote settlements.

The idea of paying for services was foreign to the Maoris, and always took the form of returning a gift. Honor therefore demanded that the return should be more valuable than the original gift. Hence, the Maori never thought in terms of bargains; he insisted, so to speak, on overpaying for anything he received—a trait universally recognized as aristocratic. And not only the original giver, or the expert who had built the chief a canoe, must be recompensed; the chief's grateful generosity must be shared by the largest possible number of people. The best way to do this was to give a feast, at which the chief could show off at one and the same time his new victory or meeting house, or whatever the occasion might be, and the extent of his hospitality.

A great chief has been known to feast more than three thousand people at a time and in doing so to use up in a few days a year's work of planting and harvesting by his people. Nor did his people begrudge him the lavish display, for his increased prestige was theirs, as were the fun and excitement.

A dozen messengers would be sent to a neighboring tribe to invite them all to the feast. The invitation was extended in a formal chant and was accepted in an equally poetic form. Sometimes the invited chief would have to decline because he did not have suitably rich presents to bring his host. This was deemed a perfectly adequate reason, and no more would be said by the heralds. But no chief liked to put himself in such a humiliating position, and his people would go to great lengths to make themselves capable of accepting.

On the set day they would all start out for the party, sometimes leaving a whole pa deserted. Usually they tried to time their arrival early in the morning to allow for the proper welcoming ceremonies. If they reached the host village the evening before the feast, they would encamp in the outskirts. Food might then be sent them for an evening meal, but no formal meeting took place until the next morning.

The ceremonies of welcome had a great deal of magic connected with them, for the visitors must be fumigated of any evil spirits and black magic that they might have brought along even unwittingly. Fortunately, this ceremony was not as drastic as that of certain African tribes of the Congo, who throw pepper into the eyes of visitors to purge them of sinister powers. Among the Maoris, it was enough for the priests to perform certain rituals and incantations. After this, the visitors were at last welcomed by shouting and the waving of garments. Then came the formal speeches of the chiefs and leading orators. This could go on for hours.

Meanwhile, the host village had been in an orderly frenzy of bustling preparation. For days, extra firewood had been brought in and stacked high by the cooking sheds of each household. Bundles of green flax had been distributed among the women so that they could plait the circular dishes in which the cooked food would be served. Up to the last moment the men had gone out to catch the largest possible number of fish or birds, the women to collect shellfish or berries, and these had been distributed among the families. Each household had dipped into its own storehouse for sweet potatoes and preserved birds, and the women had been busy scraping the skins of great quantities of potatoes. With the Maori talent for organizing group activities, everyone was busy, yet there was no confusion and no one was in anyone else's way.

Sometimes, for the sheer love of display and out of pride in their labors, the village would erect a huge scaffolding, on which to show off all this food, like a gigantic restaurant window, that the visitors could see from afar as they approached. More usually the baskets of uncooked food were pyramided in appetizing arrangements around each cooking shed or fireplace pit, with the cooks grouped around them, waiting for the signal to begin. At the base of the pyramid were the baskets of sweet potatoes. Then came, in tier upon mouth-watering tier, the other vegetables, such as taro and fern root, or berries, all topped by the fish or preserved birds in calabashes. A preliminary tour of the village was made, calculated to put the guests into very good humor and appetite.

When all was ready to the satisfaction of the man serving as public announcer or master of culinary ceremonies, and when his turn around the village had alerted all the cooks, he stood up in the middle of the village and shouted, "Light up!" All together, the cooks applied the waiting fire to the wood already stacked in their fire pits. As the wood burned down, the oven stones that had been piled on top of it fell to the bed of live charcoals at the bottom of the shallow pit.

Then the public announcer shouted the signal, "Cook!" and all the cooks' assistants leveled out the heated stones with a rake, removing the unburnt wood, and sprinkled water over the stones. As the steam rose in clouds, flax bands were laid around the sides of the pit to keep out the earth, and the pit was filled with potatoes. On top of these was placed the fish or meat, and the mound of food was sprinkled with more water, covered with flax mats, and heaped over with earth to keep in the steam.

An hour later, when the master of ceremonies had been privately notified by the cooks that the food was ready, he announced, "Uncover!" The cooks' assistants scraped off the earth and carefully removed the mat covers. The flax dishes were heaped with potatoes from the pit, with fish or meat garnishing the top, and handed to the servers.

The girls of the village now lined up on either side of the plaza or marae, each carrying two of the flaxen dishes. The master of ceremonies signaled, "Carry!" and each line of girls slowly filed toward the little groups of guests on the plaza, singing in chorus special songs about the food, their bodies swaying in unison in a special posture dance. Thus were the guests both served and entertained on the first day of the feast. It can be seen that there was a military type of mind behind the organization of it, with every detail planned in advance as if in an army manual.

As to the food, all were treated equally, but if a visitor had relatives by marriage in the village, these could be expected to bring over some extra delicacy. The guests ate with their fingers, two or more sharing a basket, just as the Europeans of those days were accustomed to share a wooden trencher. There were no dishes to wash, the flaxen mats being thrown away after the meal, and the only pot a hole in the ground.

When food was plentiful, the Maoris ate twice a day, in the middle of the morning and the middle of the afternoon. So for the succeeding days of the feast, the uncooked food was usually distributed among the guests to prepare for themselves. Thereafter, the guests would separate into their family and tribal groups, at places assigned to them, to cook and eat their food. On their departure they would take home whatever they had left over, along with whatever other gifts their hosts might give them. Their heads would of course already be full of plans of how they would repay this hospitality.

By this means, for all their mutual enmity and traditional warfare, the Maoris managed to retain a sense of the unity of their nation. At these feasts they refreshed their knowledge of one another's historical claims, they made alliances, they arranged important intertribal marriages. The giving of feasts and the obligation to return them set up ever-widening ripples of contact, bringing together large groups of men, women, and children from distant areas. Most of all, it brought them together under conditions of friendliness and pleasure and without those feelings of caution and suspicion that are natural even to the peaceful contacts of trade.

6. MAKING A MAORI

A child is born of a Maori mother and a Maori father. Is this enough to make him a Maori? Yes, if we are thinking merely of the color of his skin and hair, the details of his facial features—in short, his biological make-up. But we have seen that a certain biological make-up is not enough even to make a properly human being, let alone a certain type of one known as a Maori. If by a Maori we also mean a man who speaks a certain language, has certain ideals of good conduct, believes in a certain theory of what makes the world go round, reacts in a certain predictable way to particular events or problems, has certain skills to cope with a certain kind of environment—then a Maori has to be made, not born. For then any normal human infant, no matter where he is born and regardless of his actual parents, can become a Maori. The process by which this is achieved is known generally as education.

All human societies, whether they know it or not, spend a great deal of time in educating their young, if only by letting them watch and imitate their elders and by correcting their mistakes. In this matter, however, the Maoris were rather unusual among primitive peoples. For their education was also deliberate and formal. Because they put so much stress on the prestige of the expert, they actually had schools for their young, where the process of education could be faster and more intense than it could be in the ordinary home.

Of course, every Maori without exception had to be able to do certain things for himself, even if he was not a specialist. This is made clear in a nursery rhyme that all children learned very early. For the boys it was:

> To bear the club, to carry the spear,
> To fight, to overcome;
> To storm the pa, to kill the first foe in the field;
> To climb the mountain, to ride the waves;
> To grow food for yourself;
> To build a canoe for yourself;
> To make a mat for yourself.

And for the girls:

> To grow food for yourself;
> To gather shellfish for yourself;
> To weave garments for yourself;
> To bear the burden for yourself.

The last thing one should do to a future proud, mana-filled warrior, the Maoris felt, was to break his spirit. Hence, a father would rarely, if ever, punish his child even if it were "an adze-breaking child," that is, a mischievous imp who ruined the family's most prized possession. Tried beyond endurance, the father might raise his hand in anger, but most likely he would lower it again in resignation. For it sometimes happened that a man's relatives, hearing that he had thrashed one of their future warriors, would come in a body to thrash him, the father. For them, the familiar maxim evidently read, "*Use* the rod and spoil the child." An adolescent who thought his parents were interfering unduly with his liberty would sometimes run away to the distant home of a relative, where he or she would be practically certain of a warm welcome and could stay for years. The Maoris were always ready to adopt children.

The care and first training of children was usually less in the charge of their busy parents than in that of their grandparents or other older relatives to whom were left the lighter tasks of the household. It was these older folk who had the time to sing them the old songs and tell them the old stories, just as it was they who led the village in community singing of an evening in the meeting house. It was they who would instill table manners in the children—not to stretch across the common dish to reach for a morsel, not to pass food behind a person's head, not to pick up a piece of fish or flesh before the potato, always to begin eating an eel or pigeon at its head, not to eat or spit before strangers, who might be sorcerers looking for a chance to practice black magic.

Since the public life of the community was carried on in the open—in the meeting house or the marae before it—even a small child, if he was at all bright, might soon begin to understand what it was all about. Fathers or grandfathers would often take their little boys with them to meetings and even on military expeditions. A chief's small son might interrupt an important debate to ask a question, and he would be given a serious answer. At public receptions and ceremonies, the children watched from the outskirts and learned what would be expected of them when they grew up. They mingled in the great feasts, and imitated them by inviting small guests to share food especially given them to encourage this spirit of hospitality. They learned the importance of oratory and so also of the tales and songs they heard from their grandparents.

As for the ordinary daily life of the community and family, the children, as soon as they were able, of course helped in gathering firewood and food, building, fishing, fowling, cultivating, basket making, and cooking. Here, too, under the guidance of parents or grandparents, they learned what adult life was all about.

These older teachers of the very young could permit themselves to correct and discipline their charges as the parents could not—as long as it was for sound reasons, such as training in alertness and agility. One grandfather woke up very early and left the house. When he returned, his grandson was still asleep, evidently not disturbed by the old man's going and coming. He bent down and slapped the boy awake. The next day the same thing happened, and the boy was again slapped awake. But the third day, when the grandfather returned, he found the boy watching him with open eyes. Good! The game went on for days, the grandfather getting up at different times to catch the boy napping, until he was satisfied that his grandson had learned the alertness expected of a fighting man, to be able to awaken at the slightest sound.

Another small Maori boy stumbled and fell and waited on the floor for his granduncle to pick him up and comfort him as usual. Instead his uncle came over and hit him with a stick. The surprised boy looked up to see his uncle raising the stick again, quickly rolled out of the way, and ran off. When this happened again, the boy knew it was a game. He began to trip deliberately near his uncle and to roll away, rise, and run before the man could bring down his stick. He got to be so quick at this that eventually he could fall right at his uncle's feet and escape. He had learned the agility that would be so useful on the battlefield.

The greatest emphasis was placed on physical training. Growing children were regularly massaged to make their muscles supple and their backs and legs straight. They learned to swim at an early age—a side stroke and an overhand—and to dive off trees, banks, and cliffs. A whole group would cross a river together, all breasting a long pole while they trod water. Wrestling was a favorite sport, even for girls. But for developing gracefulness in the girls and bodily control in the boys the chief means was the dance.

Even as very small children, the girls were already practicing the twirling of the *poi* ball and the graceful swaying motions of hips and arms; and the boys to stamp in unison, quivering their fingers, sticking out their tongues, and glaring with popping eyeballs. These were not yet the posture dances, only the gestures that went with them. But later, when the children were allowed to join the dances, they would easily fit these into the songs and rhythms, and learn the perfect timing of the perfectly drilled ballets.

The boys also began to train and drill in the use of weapons when they were still quite small, using harmless flax stalks or reeds under the tutelage of their grandfathers, and engaging in sham battles. Later in adolescence, they would practice with real clubs and spears and, if they showed enough talent for warlike games, would be sent to an expert teacher for a finishing course in thrusting and parrying. This, however, brings us to the subject of the schools.

To the Maoris, who so much admired and honored expertness in all the arts and crafts, and set such high standards for them, it was not enough that their children should merely pick up their knowledge and skills haphazardly and by mere example. Native talent was of course recognized as necessary for success in any field, but there must also be formal instruction by experts and, above all, initiation in the hidden mysteries at the hands of those to whom the gods had already shown favor. Thus there came to be schools in almost every line of endeavor—what we call vocational schools as well as the higher and more sacred schools of learning.

In the meeting houses during the winter the young people could attend courses in all the useful arts—cultivation, snaring, fishing, net making, weapon making, weaving, canoe and house building, navigation and astronomy. Even for such a common pursuit as the growing of crops, a boy could be apprenticed to an expert who would teach him the correct rituals for inducing the god Rongo to send plentiful harvests, as well as give him practical instruction in weather lore, the seasons, the soil, and methods of digging, planting, harvesting, and storing the different kinds of crops.

To be accepted as an apprentice by a real tohunga, however, such as a wood carver or tattooer, a boy would have to show signs of a genuine calling and pass a rigorous entrance examination. The master must, in a certain sense, accept his pupil as a son in order to bring him into the exclusive guild. The boy must show a capacity for acquiring mana. There would be ceremonies of purification, of overcoming tapu—baptism and magical incantations. Each traditional technique and design had its legend, usually of its origin in the supernatural, and these too the apprentice must take in along with the skill, and both must be fixed in him, so as never to be forgotten, by solemn ritual.

If a boy was to be dedicated to the war god Tu—and this was, of course, expected of the sons of the nobility—he would have received quite a lot of training in the use of weapons even before he was sent to school. He might in fact already have followed a war party and even killed his first enemy by the time he was fourteen. But the expert to whom he was sent had a special admission test—he had the right to give the boy one blow before accepting him. Master and candidate would spar a little with their weapons so that the latter could show his footwork, and then suddenly the master would aim his test blow. If the would-be student failed to parry it, he would not only be turned away as unqualified, he might also have to be carried home, severely wounded. If he passed, he must still await the final test of battle before he could be considered a full-fledged warrior.

Finally, there were the highest colleges of all, held in special houses of learning and reserved exclusively for the sons of chiefs and high priests. Here the entrance examination might consist of the priestly teacher's telling a Maori legend or two and then having the twelve-year-old candidate repeat them word for word. If the boy passed with a letter-perfect recitation, he could pursue his studies among what were called the three baskets of knowledge: first, tribal traditions, genealogies, and military history; second, sacred lore—the higher and more secret religious teachings and rituals; third, black magic. The school term was four to five months long, and the student attended courses for three to five years, depending on the number of baskets he chose to take. Many preferred not to take the third basket.

These were boarding schools, but the student arrived without any baggage whatsoever. Before entering he even had to take off all the clothing he had come in and put on a special school robe for wearing inside, for, as can be well imagined, both masters and scholars were under a very high state of tapu. Food was brought the boys daily by their mothers, who were, however, not allowed to speak to their sons. Nor, during the term, could the boys visit their families or come near any place where food was cooked.

Classes were held at night. There was no reading to make this a difficulty, and the darkness undoubtedly added solemnity and awe to the atmosphere in which the teachers sought to give their lectures. For some particularly sacred subjects the lectures could not be given indoors at all, and the boys were taken out into the forest or mountains. These were all means of giving the teachings such associations that the scholars would never forget them.

For the same reason the boys chewed on blades of grass as they listened; the knowledge they were hearing was supposed to go down into their stomachs too and to become a part of them. Or the boys held under their tongues small charmed stones, which they swallowed at a certain important point in the lecture, thus keeping the knowledge down for good. We, too, find that information absorbed in more than one way at the same time—as by reading and hearing—is often better remembered. Since the Maoris had no writing or reading, the idea of swallowing instruction while they heard it may not have been entirely useless, especially since so much of the learning was sheer memorizing.

The teachings of the priestly experts were so highly standardized that, if one tired in the middle of his lecture, his assistant could pick it up with the next word. Even the slightest change in the old teachings was strongly disapproved. Again, this is not surprising, considering the absence of a written literature. Where books have forever fixed the form of knowledge, and can always be referred to for correctness, a teacher has more leeway for his personal interpretations and methods. Where the teacher's own memory and spoken words are themselves the book, he cannot afford to depart a jot from what he himself was taught.

For the student who elected to go on to the third basket, there was a special series of examinations before "graduation." He was brought before a shrine, given a stone, and told to hit the altar with it. If the stone broke, he must repeat the term of instruction. If not, he must next show his power by making the stone shiver in his hand by reciting a prayer. If he succeeded in this, he must then kill a running dog or a flying bird with a spell. Now he was ready for the final and supreme test of his magic.

The candidate's hair was cut and he was led to another shrine.

Before it stood a man whom he must kill by uttering a powerful charm. Sometimes this was only a slave, but if the candidate was the son of a great chief, the victim selected for him could be one of his own close relatives. This final step in making a master of magic was meant to be an agonizing and shattering experience, one that would never be forgotten and that would forever remove him from the ranks of ordinary mortals. Since the priestly professor chose the victim, it is not surprising that the charm so often worked and the victim died—perhaps of poison? With the killing of a kinsman, the young neophyte was forever bound to the way of magic. Having paid such a terrible price, he would never henceforth question the reality of the dark powers he dealt in. And because he believed in them himself, so would all other men.

There was one other experience to be gone through before a boy could become a Maori. Birth was the first step, the long-drawn-out process of education was the heart of it, but the capstone was marriage. By taking a wife he took on all the obligations and responsibilities of a full member of his family and tribe. By having sons, he took his place in the genealogical history of his people.

For the children of chiefs, such an important step could not be left to chance. While he was still a young boy, the family council had carefully weighed the political advantages and disadvantages of certain alliances for the son of the chief. It had carefully gone into the lineage of certain suggested brides. Such a youngster would be betrothed and might even be already married before he had finished his education at the house of learning. His bride, if she was of a high chiefly family, would never have known the freedom of ordinary girls. She would have been constantly surrounded from childhood by attendants and relatives, to guard against her breaking any tapus.

There would be a feast at their betrothal, a great exchanging of gifts among the parents, and much ceremony and priestly ritual at the marriage. Later, when the groom had become a leader and warrior in his own right, he might take a second and a third wife, and these might be his first wife's sisters. They, by the way, had carefully stayed away from the marriage feast of their sister. This was, it was said, to avoid bad luck, such as never finding a husband or being barren if they did. But perhaps it was to avoid meeting their possible future husband under circumstances where he was marrying someone else.

Despite all this careful control over its higher nobility, there are Maori tales and legends, very like our own, that recognize the power of romantic love in upsetting the wordly arrangements of the elders. The high chief Papaku had a beautiful daughter with whom a certain brave young warrior of exalted birth fell hopelessly in love. He sent her many love messages, that is, knotted strings, her untying of which would signify that she returned his love. These messages fell into the hands of her horrified father.

The young man had, in his infatuation, forgotten that he was only a captive slave, whose high birth was totally without virtue! For some reason, Papaku did not have the presumptuous slave killed outright. Instead, he prepared a crushing reply. He sent back a little scaffolding, a miniature of the kind on which the food is displayed at the great feast. On this he placed little food baskets and on each basket lay one of the young man's love-knots. It meant, "Remnant of the feast, how do you dare address these to me?"

Even among the lesser rangatira, all the young man's relatives, down to his fifth cousins, felt they should be consulted about his choice of a bride. Often an impatient couple, to avoid the weary months of waiting while this went on, would elope. Either he would get up a mimic war party of his friends and abduct her, or they would simply run off together to some lonely spot in forest or mountain. This abnormal craving for privacy was severely frowned upon and considered a violation of tapu. The man's possessions could be subjected to muru—legal raiding by all his or her slighted relatives. But the couple would set up a little hut in their forest retreat, spend a happy honeymoon, and wait till they got word that their relatives were mollified and that their friends had arranged for their safe return.

The ordinary Maori boy and girl, however, enjoyed almost complete freedom in courtship and marriage. There were no bachelors or old maids among them, and the commoner rarely had more than one wife. Young men and women went about freely together. A girl might test her sweetheart's love and courage by running into tapu places—a priest's house, for instance, or the spot where the remnants of a chief's meals were buried— and expecting him to follow her. She would tease him to tell the secrets of the schools that he had taken a sacred oath never to reveal. Somehow even the Maoris excused young lovers for this.

In the evening the young people gathered in the meeting house, their youth center, to sing, dance, and play games. Once a year they had a public "proposal day." All the unmarried youths and maidens came to the meeting house clothed in their best—the men in their gayest cloaks, the girls with their faces painted red and blue. When they were all gathered, a priest would rise and say, in effect, "My children, this is a time for you, not your elders. Speak, children."

A young man might rise and say, "I shall have So-and-so." If the girl he named remained silent, this was her consent, which had most probably already been obtained in advance. But she could reject this public proposal, even with some scornful comment, and the young man would be ashamed but must take it in silence. "You have long fingernails," she might say, meaning that he was lazy.

Next a girl might get up and say, "I will have the son of So-

and-so," and the young man would consent by remaining silent. Or he could decline the honor politely. "I have no power," he would say. "My singing bird is So-and-so." This, of course, was also a public announcement of a forthcoming marriage.

For the ordinary Maori, it was all as simple as that, followed in a few days by an equally simple ceremony of marriage. The newlyweds would not even have to set up a new household. The young husband brought his bride to live with his family, to share its dormitory and its cooking house. Some day he might himself become the head of the family, or again, he might have to move out his growing brood and build another sleeping house. Usually, however, his life was set in its path. He was a Maori, and could look forward to being a father and a grandfather, a maker of Maoris.

7. THE REDISCOVERY OF LONG WHITE CLOUD

The descendants of the Fleet had Long White Cloud to themselves for more than three hundred years, during which only their traditions linked them to the world outside, before the arrival of the next visitors. These were, of course, the far-probing white men of Europe, now in the second century of *their* great era of exploration and discovery.

New Zealand was discovered in 1642 by the Dutch navigator Tasman during his voyage from Java, around the southern coast of Australia, in search of a great continent that was supposed to lie in the South Pacific between Asia and South America. Making very much the same kind of mistake as Columbus's, he thought New Zealand was the west coast of this continent. He had an unfortunate brush with the natives, during which he made the discovery that they were "murderers." He named the land New Zealand, satisfied himself that it offered no chance of profitable trade, and was glad to leave it in the condition he found it.

It was not until 1769, a century and a quarter later, that the great English explorer Captain Cook deliberately sought out New Zealand, sailing from Tahiti like the Polynesians before him, mapped its size and shape, and described the land and people. If Tasman was the white Kupe, Cook was the white Toi, except, of course, that he did not stay. English immigration, comparable to that of the Fleet, did not get under way until the nineteenth century, some five hundred years after the landing of the Fleet.

From then on, the history of the Maoris was in many ways similar to that of the Indians after the arrival of the white men in America. Here too it was not only the superior power and numbers of hostile invaders that would all but destroy the native culture. It was also the white man's gifts.

When Cook sent a ship's boat to shore to deal with the natives there, the Maoris first thought the approaching oarsmen must be evil spirits with eyes in the backs of their heads, for they were paddling backward! The natives gladly accepted the white men's gifts of Tahitian bark cloth and strange things to eat—sugar, which they took to be an edible pumice stone, and pork, which they assumed was human flesh. Tapa and pork had once been theirs, too, before that long-ago time when their ancestors had left Hawaiki.

The truly new things, Captain Cook noted with surprise—such as the iron nails he offered them—were at first received with indifference. The Maoris had no way of imagining the utility of these things as tools or their value as personal possessions. Since Maori culture had no words for such things, there was no way of grasping them mentally. Their novelty was invisible; iron nails were simply small splinters of some sort of stone.

The walking sticks that the white men pointed at distant birds, which then fell dead amidst a peal of thunder, could not be ignored in quite the same way. But then, Maori culture had a perfectly clear explanation for such a phenomenon. Cook's guns were doing no more and no differently than the magic devices of a Maori wizard, who could also kill at a distance. At first there would be no curiosity about the guns themselves, for obviously it was Cook's private magic that made them work, the guns being entirely incidental. But later, when it was seen that any white man could wield the magic instrument and get the same result, it could be thought of as a tool and become desirable.

Unfortunately for the warlike Maoris, this recognition came fairly soon. First, their threatening attitudes naturally resulted in a greater use of firearms by the whites. Then, inevitably, guns began to fall into the hands of the native warriors, by gift, trade, or capture, along with other of the white man's goods, such as strong drink. Firearms and firewater, in the hands of the Maoris, turned all their warlike aptitudes and virtues into a threat to their own existence.

With weapons of stone and bone, even their constant warfare had not been too lethal to themselves as a race. It had provided exercise in the manly arts and occasions for gaining prestige and mana. It had encouraged personal bravery and magnanimity and developed an aristocratic code of chivalry. War was merely a dangerous sport, dangerous to the warrior but not to the race. Actually it killed men at a rate that was scarcely higher than that of accidents or diseases. Firearms changed all that, and the result was slaughter.

In a few years, tribesmen armed with guns were able to settle, once for all, ancient feuds that had been going on for many generations, but it was done by wiping out whole tribes at once. Thus the warlike character of the Maoris, instead of enabling them to repel the encroachments of the irresistible white men, was turned against themselves.

At the same time, however, the Maoris were beginning to absorb the less immediately fatal gifts of white civilization. As soon as the uses of iron and steel had been thoroughly demonstrated, these too came into great demand. One member of an early landing party tells of crowds of Maoris following them about and begging for steel axes. One old chief offered his head in exchange for one—on credit, of course. The English officer would trust the Maori chief a little while, and collect his head when the old man died. So precious could steel tools be to a nation of wood carvers, of builders of great boats and houses, to say nothing of their usefulness in clearing land and cultivating the soil.

Finally, as in America, the white man was able to impose his peace on the native warring tribes and either to absorb their remnants into his civilization or to place them on protected reservations. Now the land is covered with white towns and cities that, like the rivers and mountains, often bear Maori names. New Zealand ships ply the world's oceans bearing names borrowed from the Fleet. Their cargoes of butter, wool, and meat are the product of animals that the ancient Maoris never knew existed and that nature herself had never got around to growing on New Zealand before the coming of the white man.

There is peace among the Maoris and no prestige to be gained in tribal warfare, but Maori culture is not quite dead. Even among those who have adopted most of the white man's ways, there still live on the Maori arts and skills—painting and carving, poetry and eloquence, canoemanship and knot weaving. The warrior is gone, but the tohunga will always have mana.

MAORI

HOPI

"*He is a good Hopi: he has a quiet heart and takes part in all the dances.*"

IV. HOPIS:
People of the Desert

The region where the four square states of Utah, Colorado, New Mexico, and Arizona meet is known as the Four Corners. It is part of the Colorado Plateau, a great desert tableland in the midst of the still greater desert known as the American Southwest. This mile-high arid plain is bracketed between two great river systems of the Southwest. On the east is the upper Rio Grande, where it flows south from Colorado through northern New Mexico. On the west is the Colorado River, coming down from Utah and then making a great western bend in Arizona as it winds deep down along the floor of the Grand Canyon. Between the two, but close to the Rio Grande, and parallel to it, runs the backbone of North America, the Continental Divide, which determines which drops of rainfall will find their way to the Atlantic Ocean and which to the Pacific.

Cutting eastward across the plateau in two converging arcs are two tributaries of the Colorado—the San Juan and the Little Colorado. The San Juan is like an "S" lying on its side and twisting in turn through all four states. It cuts directly through the Four Corners, on the point of which its double curve seems perfectly balanced, before it turns southwestward to join the Colorado. The Little Colorado, to the south, edges northwestward until it flows into the parent Colorado at the Grand Canyon. The rough circle defined by these four rivers contains some of nature's most awe-inspiring marvels.

It is rugged country but not mountainous in the grand way of the Rockies, of which it forms a western slope. The ruggedness of the Rockies comes from the building up of mountains. The plateau's ruggedness is due to digging down, to the erosion of wind and water. The surface is crisscrossed by deep gashes, or canyons, whose steep, naked sides have been carved by the fury of rivers now extinct and deepened by thousands of years of sandstorms and flash floods. Often one whole bank or canyon wall may have been ground up and washed away, leaving a long stretch of rolling hills of red and yellow sand—the Painted Desert. The other wall still stands, a tall straight-sided cliff, a flat table-topped mountain, or mesa (which is Spanish for "table"). There are some real built-up mountains, too, many of them extinct volcanoes of crumbling black lava.

It is a land of almost no rainfall. What little there is usually comes down in short, sudden, violent cloudbursts that work as much havoc on the soil as the drought and sandstorms. The rainwater roars down the canyons, the washes, and the arroyos, churning up their usually bone-dry beds, tearing at their banks, before it is soaked up and lost in the sandy ground. Only along the few *permanent rivers is there enough vegetation to hold back some of the water. Otherwise the land seems bare of any but the hardiest desert plants—leathery sagebrush, prickly cactus, and spiny yucca, the so-called Spanish bayonet. Large trees are to be found only on the sides of the higher snow-peaked mountains, or lying in stony fossil fragments on the sandy floor of the Petrified Forest. The lower slopes of the mountains, between the forest giants and the cactus, are covered with scrubby piñon and dusty juniper.*

By definition a desert is an uninhabitable region. This rock-strewn, gutted land of glaring heat and dry, sand-laden winds at once strikes the eye as most assuredly desert. So to the adventurous prospectors who are now scouring the land of the Four Corners in search of uranium it may come as a surprise that this was once the center of an Indian culture more advanced than any other that ever existed north of Mexico.

More surprising, it was a culture of farmers. Of all the Indians who lived in what is now the United States, these desert-dwellers alone grew all their food and built homes so permanent that they are still standing after a thousand years. They grew and built so well that, without enslaving one another, without even raising up an aristocracy, they found ample leisure for developing the peaceful arts and crafts and for leading the richest possible social and ceremonial life. Though they had neither writing nor metals, they had the nearest thing to what can be called civilization among the hundreds of tribes that shared the continent north of Mexico.

Most surprising of all, that culture has managed to persist down to the present time, against every challenge that nature and human history could devise. It has survived not only against the harshest of environments and the fiercest of human enemies, but also, so far, against the most subtle and persuasive challenge of all

—the influence of the all-conquering white man. "The Hopi way," as these survivors still call it after a thousand years, must offer something deeply satisfying to human beings.

1. A SHORT HISTORY
OF THE PUEBLO CULTURE

In 1540, the Viceroy of New Spain, the recently conquered Mexico, sent an expedition to the far north under the intrepid captain Francisco Vásquez de Coronado. He was to investigate some highly circumstantial reports that, a thousand miles from Mexico City, some three hundred miles above what is now El Paso on the Rio Grande, there were to be found seven Indian cities so rich that their houses and cooking utensils were made of gold. Coronado's mission was to find these Seven Cities of Cibola, annex them to the Spanish crown, and bring their inhabitants into the Christian fold. His party therefore included, besides a goodly company of soldiers, cavaliers, Indian guides, and some cattle to feed them and carry their provision, a few priests. After the loot of the Aztecs, nothing seemed less improbable than the accounts they had had of this new El Dorado, and no great voyage of discovery was ever set out upon with less scientific motives.

No wonder, then, that when Coronado, after untold hardships from desert thirst and hostile tribes, finally reached his destination, he had nothing to report but the bitterest disillusionment. What was it to him that he had found something altogether unique on the American continent and, indeed, in the whole world? He was used to marvels; he was looking for gold. He could find no gilded cities in Cibola, only some miserable villages (*pueblos*, in Spanish) whose square stone huts happened to be massed together and piled on top of one another like children's blocks.

Not for three hundred years would the white invaders themselves get around to building apartment houses like these, but to Coronado they were only primitive fortresses, from the walls of which misguided savages tried to drive him off with stone-tipped arrows and showers of rock. When the hungry Spaniards finally broke in, they found plenty of corn to loot but not an ounce of precious metal. Nor does it seem to have struck them as particularly remarkable that the desert in which they had suffered such thirst and hunger should yield up such ample stores of grain, vegetables, and cotton goods to a people who did not even know the use of metal.

About fifteen hundred years before Coronado's arrival—that is, about the time of the founding of the religion that Coronado brought with him to Cibola—some wandering tribes of seed-gatherers and rabbit hunters had somehow or other learned to cultivate corn along the river valleys of this desolate country. Probably the knowledge had come up from Mexico, where it was to lead to the building of the brilliantly rich cities of the Mayas, the Toltecs, and the Aztecs. Here in the desert, too, it meant that the nomads would settle down beside their fields, but only in villages of round wattled huts half sunk in the ground and roofed with brush and earth—the type of earth lodges that the Plains Indians were to continue to live in down to modern times.

These earliest corn-growers are now called the Basket Makers, partly because of the fine workmanship of the basketry that the archaeologists have dug up from the sites of their long-vanished villages and partly to indicate that they knew nothing of pottery. We also know from these diggings in ancient graves and trash heaps that their chief weapons were flat wooden clubs and long darts propelled by spear-throwers; that they plaited handsome sandals from yucca fiber and made robes from strips of rabbit fur or from the feathers of wild turkeys; that they stored their

grain in stone-slabbed shallow pits projecting above the surface of the ground; and that they buried their dead in a doubled-up sitting position, with their worldly wealth and ornaments beside them. All these objects, wherever they have been protected in caves, have been preserved by the marvelous dryness of this climate, where nothing ever rots or decays, just as the treasures and mummies of Egypt have been preserved in tombs.

The Basket Makers were the leading citizens of the Four Corners for at least five hundred years, a longer period than any European language has yet been spoken on this continent. They were not yet, strictly speaking, a Pueblo people. But Pueblo history must begin with them because it was they who proved that corn could be cultivated for a living in this arid land; indeed, that only by cultivating corn could a living be made here at all. We can only guess at how these Basket Makers thought and felt, but we know that in their long experience with what was always to remain the major activity of the peoples of this region—desert farming—they must have developed the same basic attitudes that have always gone with it here. Chief of these would be an emphasis on the Quaker virtues of industry, piety, and peace.

This is not always or necessarily the result of relying on agriculture. Corn also came to the tribes east of the Mississippi, possibly by a route different from Mexico, and also became a staple of their life. In those heavily forested regions, however, it was never the sole resource. It only supplemented the products of the chase. Its cultivation was therefore merely women's work. (Women were anyway the more peaceful half of the population.) The men were only made more free for the more dangerous and exciting work of hunting big game and, in their ample spare time, hunting scalps. Thus, corn brought no dampening of the normal Indian virtues—daring and ferocity in war, pride in heroic exploits, glorification of the leader, and hence a universal striving to be outstanding, every man touchy as to his personal honor, given to boasting and display, to suspicion of the outsider—in short, the warlike virtues of the noble red man that were in the end to destroy him.

Growing corn in the desert, on the other hand, was men's work. Planting, cultivating, weeding, and watering it; protecting it from sandstorms, drought, and flash floods, and from rabbits and prairie dogs; and, above all, praying over it—despite all the toil and heartbreak, this was a surer way of being fed than by hunting the scarce game and the almost equally scarce edible plants. But it would take all of a man's time, labor, and vigilance. It would take the wholehearted cooperation of his kinsmen and neighbors, and all the benevolence of nature and of the spirits who had influence with nature. It was definitely man's work, and possibly much too sacred to be entrusted to women.

For the six growing months of the year, the men would be too busy and anxious, hard at their common labors and prayers, to be thinking seriously of warlike exploits against their few neighbors, who, at the very best, had no better prize to offer than what was growing in their own fields. The type of man who would choose to go off on his own adventures for the pitifully small game or loot, to the neglect of the fields, would earn no credit as a mighty Nimrod. He would more likely be looked at askance as a lazy Rip Van Winkle. Even after the harvest had yielded enough to feed the village all winter in comparative leisure, why should the envious attention of hungry outsiders be attracted to the full granaries by beating the war drums? In fact, the archaeologists have been able to dig up very few signs of warfare in the history of the Basket Makers. Thus the serious, sober business of growing corn in the desert made for an attitude toward life that was altogether different from the warlike ones to be found in all the rest of the vast Indian land that was to become the United States. It would make these desert people seem curiously grown up in a world of small boys.

For half a thousand years or so the Basket Makers advanced along this path, when, rather suddenly from the archaeologist's long point of view, there began to appear a number of revolutionary changes. It is certain that these changes went hand in hand with the arrival of new tribes in the area. It is not so certain, however, which of the changes these immigrants brought with them—possibly from the direction of Mexico, where the great Toltec civilization was then getting started—and which ones they invented on the spot, by improving on the devices of the Basket Makers.

It is not even certain whether the immigrants themselves pushed out the Basket Makers, or whether they found them already dispersed by drought and their wattled villages already plundered and destroyed by wild tribesmen, or even whether the newcomers merely moved in among the Basket Makers, sharing the country as well as the new inventions with them. Most likely the immigrants did not come as a conquering wave, but rather seeped in, in small groups of different tribes and races. Some of them may have brought important new contributions to the culture, and some may have got their first taste of it by coming here and learning from the natives, then improving on it.

Chief among these new ideas and inventions were the bow and arrow, pottery, beans, better corn, the cotton plant and the weaving of cotton cloth, the domestication of the wild turkey, the practice of flattening the backs of the heads of infants by strapping them to cradleboards, and, most important of all, a new type of house building that was to give these people the name by which we know them—Pueblos. There were, of course, also new rites, customs, and myths, but it is only to the physical inventions that the archaeologists can put a definite date.

Whatever the changes were, and however they happened, there is no doubt that in the basic pattern of living there was no reversal of the old culture but only a quickening of development in the direction in which the Basket Makers were already aimed. Similarly the automobile, the airplane, and the radio have in a single lifetime changed the face of our own world without altering the basic ideas of our civilization. The changes they brought did not abolish the old culture but merely continued it at a higher level.

In the same way all the new inventions that suddenly flowered in the Southwest found a culture already prepared to appreciate and accept them. The new cultivated plants—the beans and cotton—could only bind the villages even more firmly to the agricultural life, since these plants required even more constant attention than the corn and squash already there. Moreover, the beans, by supplying the necessary proteins in the people's diet that were hitherto provided by occasional animal food, could only make hunting even less important than it had been, while the bow and arrow made it easier. (The turkeys, strangely enough, were raised not for food but for their feathers.) And the cotton weaving and the pottery could only add to the crafts and tasks that would occupy their already peacefully busy lives during the winter. In short, all these new improvements encouraged even further the sedentary habits of the desert people and their peculiar prejudices in favor of peace.

All this was perfectly expressed in the new architecture. The houses of the early Pueblo people were as permanent as they could be made, and they were as defensive as fortresses. The Basket Makers had lived in circular, rather flimsy, wattled pit dwellings, or earth lodges, but their granaries were mostly above ground and were more permanent structures of stone. The new houses could have been modeled on the latter, for they were entirely above ground and had walls made of solid masonry, courses of laid stone plastered with mud. The roofs were of beams cross-laid with a tight layer of smaller poles and twigs, and covered with packed earth.

Even the earliest of these buildings were already multiple dwellings, or apartment houses, with about a dozen square rooms, each housing a family. Sometimes the rooms were arranged in a single row, with no windows or doors, the only entrance being by ladders through holes in the roofs, from which attackers could be fought off. Sometimes they formed a circle, an oval, or a U-shape around a central patio. The outside would still be blank wall, but doors and window openings could give out on the inner patio. Except for the absence of doors and windows, these small groups of low continuous dwellings must have looked very like the motels now dotting the roads through the same countryside.

There was always one structure, however, that retained some of the character of the old pit dwellings. This was what might be called the chapel, though the term that is generally used for it is the Hopi word *kiva*. There is a world-wide tendency for religious objects to retain their oldest forms, so that, for instance, American churches are still built in the medieval style, and parts of the Old Testament are still read in Jewish synagogues from parchment scrolls. So here the kiva, though now built of stone, stayed underground, to be entered by ladders through the roof, and it was at first circular in shape. If the granaries of the Basket Makers served as the model for the Pueblo dwelling, their dwellings were the model for the Pueblo church.

The most interesting aspect of the new architecture, however, has not yet been mentioned. The houses described above showed an appreciation for the needs of defense against the Utes and other wild tribes that had harried the Basket Makers, but they were merely blockhouses set out in open country. Many of the new Pueblo people went further. They built their apartment houses high up on the mesas overlooking their fields on the valley floor below. Sometimes they were on the flat tops of the mesas, sometimes right in the middle of the sheer wall—in big natural caves that they enlarged, or under overhanging ledges wide enough to cover the whole village.

This meant that the villagers must climb up and down every day to tend their crops and to fetch their food, water, and fuel —a climb that had deliberately been made as difficult as possible to discourage attackers. It was a price they were willing to pay for safety. Secure in their inaccessible nests from surprise night raids, their sentries also had a clear view during the day of any distantly approaching marauders. The people at work below could, at the first signal of danger, hastily clamber the hundreds of feet of narrow rock-hewn trails, run up the notched-pole ladders, and draw these up after them. It is the frequency with which these castles were perched high in the air that has given the successors of the Basket Makers the popular name of Cliff Dwellers.

Gradually these small pueblos, whether on cliffs or on the

valley floors, came to dot the whole extent of the Colorado
Plateau, wherever there were rivers or springs to support them.
By the year 1000, when not even the Vikings had yet visited
America, the culture of the Cliff Dwellers and other Pueblo peoples extended as far south as the Gila River in southern Arizona
and halfway down the Rio Grande in New Mexico, and had pushed
north and west into Colorado, Utah, and Nevada.

Then came still another development. In the never-resting
search for peace and safety, the hundreds of little villages, each
the home of a clan or a related group of families, began to dis-

appear, to be replaced by fewer but larger concentrations of people into what might almost be called cities, made up of many clans or families. Perhaps the desert was growing drier, with fewer moist spots. Perhaps new waves of fierce nomads from the mountains and great plains made life too precarious for smaller groups. If so, they needed to combine their forces, physical and magical, to stand off their enemies and to bring more rain. Fortunately the high level to which they had brought their agriculture and other arts made it possible to support such large collections of people in a few choice spots. The boundaries of the Pueblo world contracted, still centering on the Four Corners.

This was the Golden Age of the Pueblo civilization, surpassing anything before seen north of Mexico. In the Chaco Canyon, in New Mexico, south of the San Juan River, there is a stretch of ten miles in which there are the ruins of thirty great pueblos from this period. They were D-shaped, with their straight backs against the cliffs, and rose four and five stories high, like terraced amphitheaters, around a central plaza containing a great underground ceremonial hall as well as many smaller kivas. The tall curved outer walls were blank and windowless. At least one of these pueblos had eight hundred rooms and thirty-two kivas. It housed more than a thousand persons, a family to each room or two. Because each floor was set back like steps in a stairway, every apartment had its own penthouse terrace, on the roof of the neighbors' room below, overlooking the great central patio. Such well-constructed apartment houses would not be equaled for size anywhere in the world until white Americans began to build similar habitations eight hundred years later.

The cliff dwellings of this period were necessarily smaller than the valley pueblos, being limited by the size of the caves or ledges on which they were built. But their bizarre positions in the rock walls make them even more impressive as ruins. Some of these, too—such as Mesa Verde on the San Juan River in south-west Colorado—were many-storied structures of more than two hundred rooms.

Here, between the years 1100 and 1300 there was the greatest flowering of all the Pueblo arts—in architecture, agriculture and irrigation, pottery, stone-tool making, basketry, jewelry, and no doubt also in ceremonial, as the great kivas would seem to indicate. Here, too, with their many families and clans crammed together, the Pueblo peoples received an intensive finishing course in getting along with one another at close quarters. This capacity for peaceful cooperation and for eliminating all harmful rivalries between close neighbors, without the help of rulers, police, or magistrates, is still as much a mark of these people as is their peacefulness and nonaggressive feeling toward outsiders.

Then, two hundred years before Columbus, the Golden Age collapsed. First, the great houses in the Chaco Canyon had to be abandoned because the extensive tree-cutting over hundreds of years had finally brought erosion and the silting up of streams and springs. Then in the year 1276 there came to the valley of the San Juan a drought that lasted twenty-three years! No people anywhere, no matter how civilized, not even these desert people, could stand up under almost a whole generation of thirst. Each year more people died or migrated in search of water—east to the Rio Grande, south to the Little Colorado or even farther, or to the Hopi and Zuñi country in between. The weakened remnants of the populations succumbed to the increasing attacks of savage tribes, no doubt themselves driven by thirst. Many of the emigrants looked on their going as merely temporary, for they carefully sealed their doors and windows with mortar against their return. But they never returned. For the drought hung on as long as the older refugees lived, and the younger ones, old or middle-aged when the crisis was over, must have lacked the energy to return or the memories to urge them back.

In search of water

In the next two hundred and fifty years, before its discovery by the white man, the Pueblo world became an ever-narrowing band, anchored on the upper Rio Grande in northern New Mexico and stretching halfway across northern Arizona. At first some even larger cities and cliff dwellings were built, though with none of the great kivas of the past. Then these too were abandoned, and by the time of Coronado's coming there were only about eighty pueblos in the whole region where there had been hundreds scattered over an area as big as France, and these were relatively modest in size and mostly concentrated on the Rio Grande. Today there are scarcely two and a half dozen villages left even of these, but the life that has never ceased to go on in them has remained essentially unchanged from that of the Golden Age—the peaceful cultivation of corn and of the civic virtues.

No doubt, in 1540, the Pueblo culture was in retreat from its high peak, but there were also signs of a renaissance. It is now no longer possible to know for sure whether Coronado merely broke into the final dying phase or whether he interrupted a new upswing such as the Pueblo peoples had experienced so many times in their fifteen hundred years of history. For this advanced and tenacious culture did not depend on any one race or nation to keep it going. It passed on by contagion, by attracting and infecting the uncivilized peoples and transforming them into its instruments.

To this day the surviving Pueblo peoples, for all the uniformity of their practices and beliefs, speak at least four distinct languages and belong to as many different stocks. In the Hopi traditions of the origins of their villages there is a basic pattern of welcoming newcomers who will agree to live in harmony and peace with their way of life. That must have been the chief way by which the Pueblo culture had always recruited its forces, and until the coming of the too-powerful and hence unconvertible white men, this might have happened again.

This is probably as good a place as any to answer a question that may seem already too long deferred: How do we know so much about the history of a people who left no written records and who vanished before they came under the observation of the white man? The answer is, in part, that they did leave records of a sort, and indeed in enormous quantities, though they never intended them as such. These are the physical things they made and left buried in the preserving dry desert soil—their buildings, pots and baskets, tools and weapons, clothing, and the pictures and decorations painted or carved or woven on them.

For many years archaeologists have been digging up these evidences, in scraps and fragments, out of graveyards (along with mummified bodies), long-buried town dumps, and silted-over mounds. They have been patiently arranging them in an order that makes a readable record of growth and decline. It was found, for instance, that styles and decorations of pottery differed distinctly between pueblos and between periods of history in the same pueblo. Thus the migrations of a single group could be followed from place to place. And if one pueblo was discovered to have been built on the ruins of another, it was obvious that the one underneath was the older. The archaeologists could even tell how much older, by comparing the tree rings in the house beams of the two pueblos—a method invented in this very region by Andrew Douglass, professor of astronomy at the University of Arizona.

Each year a tree grows another ring in its trunk that varies in thickness according to that year's drought or moisture. If there are enough rings, they make a recognizable pattern of thicks and thins that will be found in all the other trees growing in that neighborhood during the same years. For the Pueblo country this pattern has been worked out backward from the present time for almost two thousand years. Given a cross section of a house beam (or even of a charred log in a buried fireplace) and enough time to consult his tables for the area it came from, an archaeologist can tell in what year the tree died from which the log was cut. That is how we know so precisely that the great drought that ended the Golden Age in the San Juan Valley occurred in the years 1276 to 1299.

Thus, by telling us what these long-dead peoples made with their hands, and even in what order they invented these things, archaeology also tells us a great deal about how they lived, how they made and used these things, and why. Much of this would, of course, be pure guesswork, especially where it involved beliefs and attitudes, if it were not for the fact that the Pueblo culture is still living and apparently unchanged. Clever as the deductions and detective work of the archaeologists may be, they could never be proved if it were not that, as regards the Pueblo people, here one may "catch one's archaeology alive." When it is seen how closely the modern Pueblo people follow their ancient forebears in the things they make with their hands, it is only logical to assume that their religious and social ideas probably also follow the old pattern.

2. THE PEACEFUL PEOPLE

Today the Hopis live in nine villages that are strung along a stretch of less than twenty miles of the deeply scalloped southern rim of Black Mesa, in northeastern Arizona. This particularly forbidding region of the desert is almost in the center of the rough circle formed by the Colorado and its two tributaries, in ancient times the living heart of Puebloland. But even by Coronado's time the Hopis were already the isolated westernmost representatives of Pueblo culture. Because of that and the hundreds of discouraging desert miles between them and the Spanish settlement of Santa Fe, the Hopis would remain the least affected by the white man's disturbing influence. They would carry the old culture down to the present time in its purest form.

Archaeologists have traced the Hopis' history unbrokenly clear back to the age of the Basket Makers. One of their villages, Oraibi, has been continuously lived in, on exactly the same spot, for at least eight hundred years; it is the oldest still occupied community in the United States. Their ancestors may indeed have been among the original founders of the Pueblo culture. Yet the Hopis are a Shoshonean people, related to the nomadic Utes who have harassed them for centuries from the north and west, rather than to the other Pueblo tribes of today. They were, incidentally, also related to the warlike Aztecs, who originally came down from the north to conquer Mexico. But their own name for themselves, Hopituh, means "the Peaceful People."

Each Hopi village, perched high on an outjutting spur of the mesa and looking down on its fields in the valleys on either side, is a sovereign state. There has never been an all-tribal Hopi government, any more than there was a single government for the ancient city-states of Greece. Though all the pueblos follow the same unwritten rules of custom and have the same speech and culture, though their inhabitants freely intermingle and intermarry and acknowledge their common kinship, there is no national legislature or executive, no tribal supreme court. Each village runs its own affairs without interference from the others, without even the interference of war.

It may after all have been the Hopis who were unwittingly responsible for the legend of the Seven Cities of Cibola that brought the Spaniards in the first place, though most historians assume that this honor belongs to the villages of the Zuñi people in New Mexico. For the Hopis did, in fact, then live in seven villages of red and yellow sandstone, and they were famous among the other pueblos for a bright yellow pottery that may have been mistranslated into Spanish as "golden."

Coronado's men attacked one of those villages when the inhabitants tried to drive them away from its walls—very likely because a secret religious ceremony was under way. The hamlet immediately, and characteristically, made peace with the invaders —as soon as it was clear that this could be done at little cost. The white marauders seemed to be satisfied with only a little tribute in corn and textiles, easily spared, and wanted only to ask them searching questions about some yellow metal and about their spirit beliefs. The white men in polished stone clothing told them that the Hopis now owed allegiance to a great chief who lived on the other side of an enormous salt lake. (White men have ever since been known as the people from "the land of far water.") Other white men, in long black gowns, told them they must give their allegiance to a particular Great Spirit who lived in the sky. It must have taken all the Hopis' natural tact and gravity to deal with these astonishing creatures.

How the Hopis appeared to the Spaniards we do know, for the earliest explorers left records of their impressions. They found a tribe whose physical appearance and manner was quite easily distinguishable from those of the other Indians about them and even from those of the other Pueblo peoples on the Rio Grande. We can recognize the descriptions at once, for to this day the Hopis are one of the few surviving "full-blood" tribes, with very little intermixture of other types.

Their expression was grave and calm, their gestures slow and moderate, their voices unhurried and unexcited. The men were short, muscular, and stocky, averaging about five feet three or four inches in height, with short wide faces, slightly "slanting" eyes, and light brown skin. Their thick black hair was cut in short bangs straight down over the forehead but allowed to grow long on the nape of the neck, where it was gathered up in a heavy knot. Bound round the head was a fillet of rabbit skin or yucca fiber, which has since been replaced by a brightly colored band of cloth. The long hair of the women was either done up over the ears in the "butterfly whorls" of the unmarried girls or hung in the clublike double braids of the matrons.

The men wore short cotton kilts and woven yucca sandals, with mantles of cotton or deerskin to go over the shoulders in really cold weather. The women wore short black dresses made of a single square of cotton fastened over one shoulder, leaving the other bare, like a Roman toga, and gathered at the waist by a broad red embroidered cotton sash. Both sexes wore handsome necklaces, earrings, and bracelets, of shells, turquoise, seeds, and quillwork, much of the material in them obviously acquired in trade with distant tribes.

After their discovery, the Hopis were not seriously troubled

Hopi with throwing stick

by the Spaniards for the next ninety years. It was not until 1630 that the Franciscan friars established permanent missions in Tusayan, the Spanish name for Hopiland. By that time the Rio Grande pueblos were already groaning and muttering under the Spanish yoke. Soon enough, the Hopis also learned what it was like to slave under the commands of conquerors who forbade them the practice of their ancient religion and whose punishment for the disobedient was to cut off their hands and feet or to sell them into slavery away from the pueblo. So fifty years later, in 1680, the Hopis joined the Great Pueblo Rebellion, America's earliest war of independence, which swept the Spaniards out of New Mexico, killing the "long gowns" and destroying their mission churches. Never before or since in Pueblo history, so far as is known, have these independent city-states ever joined in such a common effort. The provocation must have been overwhelming.

A dozen years later the Spaniards returned from El Paso, where they had been driven (thereby coming to found that city), and quickly reconquered the pueblos of the Rio Grande. But not Tusayan, for the two hundred miles of waterless desert and hostile nomad tribes between Zuñi and Hopi country remained for them "the journey of death." Yet it was known that the Hopis were harboring numbers of recalcitrant and unreconstructed refugees from the Rio Grande, just as they had once sheltered the refugees from the Great Drought of the San Juan River.

Indeed, the Hopis had set up in business whole pueblos that had emigrated *en masse* rather than submit to the Spaniards, though these people from the Rio Grande were of a different race and language from their own. One of these has remained an independent pueblo to this day, and considers itself quite Hopi, in customs and thought, though these naturalized Hopis now speak two languages, having retained the old. The Hopis, welcoming them precisely because they were stubborn fighters, gave them a site on the easternmost mesa spur, the one most exposed to attack from Utes and Navahos as well as Spaniards. Meanwhile, also, those of the old Hopi villages that had been at the foot of the mesa, near the valley fields, moved up to its top.

It almost seemed, indeed, as if the Peaceful People would respond to their great crisis by changing their character entirely. When one of their villages, in 1700, succumbed to the blandishments of a new missionary and allowed him to baptize a number of them, the nearby pueblos attacked and destroyed it. This, too, was an event unique in Hopi history. They had as a matter of fact always rather welcomed new cults, as long as they could be added to the old ones. But the crime of the "long gowns" was to insist that their cult should be the only one, on pain of drastic punishment in this world and the next.

In general, however, it was by passive resistance that the Hopis carried out their now grim determination to remain Hopis. The mission churches were never rebuilt. Again and again the Hopis would receive the occasional visits of Spanish governors and Franciscan friars, politely, even cordially, and always promise to give serious consideration to adopting the Christian religion—and never do so. This Gandhi-like strategy went on for more than a hundred and twenty-five years until the Mexican Revolution of 1823 dispossessed the Spaniards altogether.

But while the Hopis were so successfully resisting the encroachments of an alien government and religion, the basis of their culture was actually undergoing a series of very profound changes at the hands of the white men. No matter how satisfied he was with his way of life, there was no reason for a Hopi to refuse to accept and use an iron hoe or steel ax in place of his wooden and stone tools. Such things could only make him a more successful farmer and hence a better Hopi. And there was no more reason for refusing to plant peach and apricot trees, once it was clear that they would grow here and bear the most delicious food, than it would have been for his Basket Maker forerunners to refuse to raise the alien bean. The same was true for melons, peas, and other garden vegetables, even for wheat, which might conceivably have been considered a rival of the sacred corn.

Even the Spaniards' domesticated animals gradually but surely made their way into Hopi life. The sheep, especially, which could forage in this desert, only reduced the need for hunting the occasional antelope, and the Pueblo people had always been ready to free themselves from the need for hunting their meat, while the sheep's wool readily lent itself to the Hopi techniques for weaving cotton. So, too, the little donkeys or burros of the Spaniards were most adaptable to the scanty herbage and the difficult trails, and the Hopis took to the burro as naturally as all the warlike Plains tribes took to the horse.

To balance these benefits, which might only have strengthened the Hopi way of life, the white men brought new dangers that even they did not intend. For along with their government and religion they brought new diseases. And along with the burro for the Hopi, they brought the horse to the wild Utes, Comanches, Navahos, and Apaches.

These age-old enemies of the Pueblos were thus not only enabled to become more effective raiders on the peaceful villages; they were also immunized against the Pueblo civilizing contagion. Whereas many of the predecessors of these wild hunters had undoubtedly themselves eventually fallen under the spell of the Pueblo civilization, for the now mounted marauders the Pueblo charm was gone. Not only were the Pueblos easier and even richer prey; they also had competition as an attraction. For the whites offered larger opportunities, not only for imitation, but also for pillage. On the face of it, the hard-working Hopi way could offer no prize as rich as what could be stolen from the white man with very little effort and much heart-warming excitement.

Hence, the civilizing role of the Pueblos was finished. There would be no more expansion of its way of life. The wonder is that it should survive at all, that the Hopis themselves should resist the temptation to give it up and join the general barbarization. That they did not join the rout—and hence saved their culture when the wild fling was over—is the reason that the four thousand people of the little Hopi nation are of such intense interest to anthropologists today.

"Know thyself" is one of those wise Greek maxims that we associate with high civilization and not with primitive folk. It is far from unusual that the Eskimos called themselves Innuit, that is, "the People." Many primitive tribes call themselves that, each in its own language. They are the Men; their way of life stems from that fact; there just is no other way for human beings to behave. The result is that, if they happen to be overrun by some more powerful people (like the white man), they are often morally shattered. To them it seems that the world has been delivered over to chaos and evil, and they are demoralized as we might be if the laws of gravity were suddenly to cease operating. They go to pieces, become ugly, become the "lazy, shiftless, thievish, childish, quarrelsome, untrustworthy, undisciplined lot" that the conquerors always seem to find the natives.

But the Hopis' name for themselves is "the Peaceful People," and there is something very sophisticated about that. It sounds deliberately chosen, no more an accident of language or geography than was the Quakers' calling themselves the Society of Friends. It recognizes that other ways of being human are possible. It means that their ideas of the proper life of man are based on comparisons. It means, in short, that the Hopis, without writing or books, have a genuine philosophy of life, that they have followed the Greek maxim.

The Hopi view of what is good and proper in men's dealings with one another and with the world in general may be summed up in the words "cooperation" and "responsibility." In the private dealings of the Hopis and in their conduct of village affairs, nothing is so frowned upon as agitation and heat—combativeness, self-assertion, envy, jealousy, quarrelsomeness, personal ambition, loud argument. The worst fault is to offend one's neighbor. All such traits and conduct are *ka-hopi*, that is, not Hopi, bad. The good Hopi is calm, self-possessed, and soft-spoken. He is modest but poised, law-abiding but strong. His highest ideal is again one that we associate with the Greek philosophers: moderation in all things.

The Hopi likes neither to give orders nor to take them and avoids both praise and blame. He has no difficulty in knowing his own duties and responsibilities, and in knowing and respecting those of others, for there is a right rule of behavior for every stage of life and for every situation in life. A good Hopi, in every undertaking, should be so intent on its proper outcome and upon his responsibility for bringing it about, that he has no time to think of personal prestige or benefits. He is expected to feel intensely about his goal but dispassionately about himself. Self-serving or self-admiring thoughts dissipate the mind's energy, and show up in whatever one does as imperfections in the result. This is irresponsibility; it is "two-heartedness," which is not merely ka-hopi, but also the Hopi definition of witchcraft. Pushing oneself forward in any common enterprise is especially "two-hearted."

Hence, a good Hopi cares nothing for personal prestige, is uncomfortable if personally praised for his achievements, and almost never seeks to be a leader. For him, the Maori chieftain with his thirst for mana would be nothing but a witch, and a man like Hitler a very evil witch indeed. Even nowadays, when a gang of Hopi workmen is hired for a job by a white man, it is extremely difficult to get one of them to serve as foreman, unless all are to be given a turn at it. The most skilled are content to receive the same wages as the inexperienced, preferring to avoid any invidious comparisons among themselves, though when dealt with as individuals they have the reputation of being quite keen traders.

All their lives they have worked quite well without any other supervisors or taskmasters than the village as a whole, and for no higher reward than the good of the village and the good opinion of their clansmen. Even their children, when they are sent to the schools run by whites, do their best work only when the teachers avoid introducing anything like competition in the classwork, and though they like team games, they usually manage not to keep score. They too know that praise and boasting arouse resentment and that all have the same duty to do their best.

On the other hand, the good Hopi will cheerfully carry out any extra responsibility placed on him by his clan, society, or village —even the responsibility of leadership. But the first requirement of a Hopi chief is self-effacement. He does not seek his position; it is usually thrust upon him by inheritance and age, by the consent and will of his clan or religious society, and by his own sense of responsibility. Concentrating on prayer for the welfare of all, he above all others must be without rancor or ambition, else the ritual for which he is responsible will be wasted if not harmful. He is neither a king nor a captain, but a priest. He has more responsibility than the others, not more power. He may guide but cannot command, for his following is purely voluntary. Indeed, most of the important work and ritual of the village is purely voluntary, performed neither from coercion nor ambition. It might almost be said that the Hopis are too democratic to have a government.

Of course, there actually is some compulsion to make a man do his duty, a moral compulsion that is nevertheless very strong. For nothing could make a man more miserable than to sense the gossip, or even the unspoken criticism, of his clan and neighbors that would result if he seemed to put his own advantage ahead of the common good. So, whenever he is at all free to do so, he gladly turns out to help on any new house raising or sheep shearing or crop gathering, which are all done by voluntary "work parties." He feels amply repaid by the fun of everyone's working together and by the feast that invariably follows. He tries to arrange his personal affairs so that he may take part in as many ceremonies and dances as possible, and is again repaid by the purifying feeling of having participated, along with all his people and all of nature, in a tremendously important spiritual experience.

All this is not to say that the Hopis are not human and that they have always lived without any bickering among themselves. Quiet-mannered and lacking in self-importance they might try to be, but timid or docile they are not. Besides, the purely democratic way in which they run their village affairs is bound to lead to some violent differences of opinion when group decisions have to be made, particularly where the problem is without precedents in their history.

We usually think of democracy as the rule of the majority and as a system of finding the majority by voting. Back of this idea is the assumption that all have agreed in advance to abide by the majority decision. There is no such assumption in the Hopi democracy. Here no one can be forced to do anything to which he does not freely consent, and if he does not agree with a majority decision, he has a perfect right to withhold his co-operation. To coerce him physically is unthinkable.

On the whole, it is remarkable how little internal conflict there has been under this system of government. It works so well probably only because in their small communities everyone is related to everyone else by clan ties or by certain religious ties (which are discussed later) and because the villagers are confident that their experienced leaders are not motivated by self-seeking ambitions. Therefore, in most cases, the careful, calm reasoning of the older priest-chiefs is enough to convince the village council, and the unanimity of the council is enough to persuade the people.

In larger communities, especially in the face of brand-new problems, opposing points of view have a better chance of picking up strength and leading to irreconcilable conflicts. When this happens, the Hopi system has no solution except to let the community split in two, each part going off to become an independent

village. As a matter of fact, many Hopi villages owe their origin
to just such a break-up.

One of the last such splits occurred as late as 1900, when the
United States government, pursuing a policy of "Americanizing"
the Indians and of doing away with their native culture, ordered
all the Hopis to send their children away to a government boarding school. In the eight-hundred-year-old village of Oraibi there
was unanimous disapproval of this harsh and high-handed measure, but two factions developed around the question of what to
do about it.

One side felt that this threat to the Hopi way of life must be
resisted by civil disobedience; this side came to be called the
faction of Conservatives or Hostiles. The other side—Progressives
or Friendlies—felt equally strongly that it was more correctly
Hopi to give in and not risk a violent clash with government
troops that were standing by to enforce the order. There was no
question of voting and letting the majority decide. It would not
have seemed sufficiently democratic to the villagers to let one
party impose its will on another, to let either the larger or more
numerous clans bully or dictate to the smaller.

So it was solemnly agreed, in the typically peaceable Hopi way,
that the two factions should hold a tug-of-war in the plaza, the
losing side to leave the village. The Hostiles lost, and they left to
found the new sovereign village of Hotevila not far away. In the
same way, according to tradition, old Oraibi itself had once been
founded as a dissident offshoot of the village of Shungopovi on
another mesa spur. At Hotevila they actually did refuse to give
up their children to the troops, and many went to prison for it.

In the end, the Hopis won the right to live their own lives. The
government, in the face of such determined passive opposition,
eventually changed its policies and established day schools at
the foot of each mesa spur. Since it is obvious that the government would not have been so conciliatory if it had been dealing

with an Apache tribe that was insisting on its ancient rights to raid and fight its neighbors, even this example of a breakdown in the Hopi way demonstrates its superior ability to survive.

3 · MOTHER CORN

If one fact is necessary to explain the character, religion, and culture of the Hopis, it is this: They are one and all farmers, growers of corn; for a thousand years their lives have depended on their growing corn in one of the world's greatest and driest of deserts.

To the naked eye, farming would seem to be the least likely way of earning a living in Tusayan. No large river flows here, as the San Juan once flowed past the pueblos of the Golden Age or as the Rio Grande still waters the land of the other modern Pueblo peoples. Besides, in these parts the only rainfall that amounts to anything comes in August, when the growing season is practically over.

Yet the Hopis, with no better tools than sharpened sticks, have always been among the most successful desert farmers the world has ever seen. All appearances to the contrary, there must be a steady supply of water.

Each Hopi village is perched on the sharp edge of one of three outjutting tongues of Black Mesa. Some hundreds of feet directly beneath their thresholds begins the sandy desert that stretches away into the southern distance. This is not for farming. Behind the villages the mesa inclines gradually upward until it becomes one with the snow-covered peaks far in the north. This dry, stony mesa is also not for farming. But in those faraway northern mountains there are frequent rainstorms and heavy snows that melt in the spring. It is from here that the Hopis get their water. It comes to them in two ways.

First, along the surface, after every mountain storm the water

comes rolling down the long incline of the mesa in violent
bursts. It races along the dried beds of arroyos and "washes"
carved out by previous storms, carrying fertile soil and rocks with
it, until it tumbles off the top of the mesa onto the desert floor
below. This violent action gouges great pieces off the southern
edge of the mesa, cutting deep wide clefts in its face, through
which the desert encroaches on the mesa, creating the long, sharp
spurs on which the villages stand. After every freshet these carved
ravines and valleys are covered with a layer of the more fertile
silt from above.

It is this somewhat moister soil that the Hopis farm. It is the
same sort of flood farming that has long been practiced in Egypt,
only infinitely more difficult and precarious. Here there is no
dependable Nile rising in some tropical rain forest and every
spring overflowing its well-defined banks as regularly as clock-
work. Here there is never any certainty when or where the waters
will come. A drought in the north may bring only a trickle of
surface water, with no flooding of the valleys at all. A series of
downpours in the mountains may send down such raging torrents
as to wash out the crops already planted, or the furious short-
lived streams may abandon the old channels and cut themselves
new ones.

Fortunately, the water from the north also comes by a second
route. The mesa is made up of a thick layer of porous sandstone
lying on top of a denser layer of shale, which, like the surface of
the mesa, tilts downward toward the south. Some of the mountain
rainfall percolates down through the sandstone and then seeps
very slowly southward between the two layers. It takes two years
for this water to reach the edge of the mesa, where it emerges
from the face of the cliff wall as springs. For the Hopi farmers,
the seeping water is like money in the bank. Even when Tusayan
itself is in the grip of a severe drought, these springs will flow
with life-giving water *if* there was no drought in the mountains

two years before. And if there was such a drought then, the chances are that there will not be one this year too, so that there will be surface water from the north, or local showers, to take the place of the springs.

Thus, the secret of the Hopis' survival is indeed an almost unfailing supply of water, the only such supply for a hundred miles around, though its source is neither in a permanently flowing river nor in local rainfall. It is never an overly generous supply, it is most thriftily doled out, but it is better guaranteed because it comes through diversified channels. This is in fact the principle of spreading out the luck on which all insurance companies operate; it also is the basis of the Hopi system of land ownership and land use. Nature and Hopi culture cooperate in a highly successful system of crop insurance.

Land here is useless without water, and though there is usually enough water to sustain the village as a whole, it is, as we have seen, too erratically distributed to maintain the fertility of any particular plot of ground. So the village cannot afford to let the land be owned by its individual villagers. To do so might mean that in any year half of the farmers would be idle for lack of tillable soil and might perish for lack of food. The next year the same thing might happen to the other half of the villagers. In so small a community it would not take long for the destruction of all of them.

So it is the village, and not the villagers, that owns the land. Each year the land is redistributed as needed among the families. Also each family is given the use of several plots, widely scattered, on both sides of the mesa, so that not all its eggs are in one basket. However unpredictable the course of the floods, however scattered the local rains and snowfall, all will share in each kind of fortune, and the village as a whole will survive. It should also go without saying that the village also owns the springs in its cliff wall, and that these springs are religious shrines.

In its unsuccessful attempt to "Americanize" the Hopis by force, one of the reforms the United States government had insisted on was that the land be permanently divided among individual landowners. This also was resisted by the Hostiles. After the government surveyor left the new village of Hotevila, they pulled up his stakes, ignored his boundary lines, and reallotted their land in the old way until the government gave in. Now, as for ages past, the Hopis practice their own system of crop and drought insurance, their eyes on the unpredictably moving waters and not shortsightedly on the fixed land.

Each February those fields are distributed that have had the benefit of winter snowfall or run-off mesa water or wind-drifted topsoil. The white man's burros and wagons, and the white man's peace, have made it possible to assign fields farther from home, and the men must often start out before dawn if they are to put in a full day's work. They weed their irregularly shaped one-acre fields of desert plants and put up low brushwood fences around them to keep out the drifting sand. In the middle of each plot is a stone slab set up on edge, with the clan (family) symbol on it, not so much a no-trespassing sign as a religious shrine. The soil is dug up with a dibble—a pointed wooden stick with a foot-rest for bearing down the digger's weight.

In April the first seed is planted. This is a most speculative crop, subject to late frosts, severe spring sandstorms, and lack of rain, which falls mostly, if at all, in late summer. But Hopi corn takes three to five months to ripen, a slow business for a staple on which the whole life of the tribe depends. Besides, the Hopis want green corn for the great Home Festival in July. Each week now a few more fields are planted until the summer solstice, near the end of June.

The Hopi farmer must plant his seeds at least a foot deep so that they can reach the subsurface moisture and root themselves strongly against the sand-blasting winds and violent cloudbursts.

He bores a hole with a sharpened wooden stick, loosens the soil at the bottom, and drops in as many as twenty seeds, in the hope that some will escape the gophers, mice, and worms. The rows of holes are several paces apart; there must not be too much competition for the underground moisture. This procedure is unlike not only the method used in the tall cornfields of Kansas, but also the usual Indian method of planting corn in hills fertilized by fishheads, as practiced in the well-watered soil of the East.

The Hopi result is a low bush of a dozen stalks, which are never thinned. Half the stalks are expected not to survive the leaf-tattering sandy winds but only to give shade and protection to those in the middle of the clump. After every flood, the farmer hurries down to his fields to scoop a low bank of soil around each clump to retain the water. All summer he is busy in the fields, trenching or leveling the ground to hold more water, or repairing the windbreaks, themselves shattered by the wind.

Between July and October the crops are harvested—if they have escaped destruction by frost or drought, sandstorms or flash floods, field mice or cutworms. Now in the early morning the farmer's wife and children join him in the clamber down the mesa trail. Sometimes the family puts up a temporary hut in the field so that it need not return to the village overnight and lose precious time.

The corn is husked in the fields, and some of it roasted and eaten on the spot. The stalks are left standing for next year's fertilizer. If this field is used again, the planting will be in the wide-spaced rows between last year's stalks. Carrying home the harvest, in back-loads and burro-loads, is a community affair. The day before, the village crier will have called a "work party," urging all who are free to go and help So-and-so. They will, of course, be repaid with a joyous feast.

The Hopi farmer knows his corn. Over the centuries he has bred this hardy desert variety out of what once was a grassy plant

with tiny nubbins of seeds. He has developed many different
strains and keeps the seed carefully separated. The range of
colors in his corn—white, red, blue, yellow, "black" (really
purple), and many-colored speckled varieties—is no accidental
mixture but the result of controlled breeding. Nor is the Hopi a
one-plant farmer. Corn is for him only the most important member of that great Indian trinity—corn, beans, squash—that have
always been grown together in America. And he has quickly
mastered the art of growing many of the white man's plants.

These less hardy fruits and vegetables he gardens nearer home,
around the springs. His people knew the techniques of irrigation
for these long before the white man came. The water from the

springs is stored in clay-bottomed reservoirs with stone retaining walls. Irrigation ditches run from these down a series of terraces, on which are plots of green vegetables and groves of peach and apricot. Here again the land is village common, but the trees—coming altogether new from the Spaniards, and hence falling outside traditional Hopi ideas of property—belong to the individual men.

So do the cattle and sheep, and for the same reason. The first sheep the Spaniards brought were slaughtered along with their missionaries, but in the end the Hopis gratefully accepted the former. Sheepherding is now important work for the Hopi farmer, but he allows it only the time he once devoted to hunting the scarce game—the small antelope, occasional deer, and rabbit. The business of herding and shearing the sheep, despite their being private property, has fallen into the usual cooperative pattern. The men combine their flocks so that they can take turns at being out on the range with them for two or three days at a time—and so be more free for tending their beloved corn. When the sheep are brought in for shearing toward the end of May, the village crier "cries a work party" for the next day. All the men join in the work while the women prepare huge quantities of food for the volunteer shearers.

The Hopis have never quite given up their love for the wild produce of the desert, on which they once lived entirely before the coming of Mother Corn. Their chief prize is still the sweet little nut of the piñon, though now they must go many miles north on the mesa, with burros, to find it. It is, however, mostly the women, helped by the children, who with knowing eyes hunt out, in this seeming desert desolation, the many kinds of berries and cactus fruit and edible grasses, seeds, and roots. Some wild plants must be sought for other purposes than food—wild tobacco for the religious ceremonies, yucca leaves for basketwork and yucca roots for soapsuds, rabbit grass for brooms and hairbrushes, certain berries for dyes, others for medicines.

The Hopis know their country well—the mesa behind them, the desert below—and all its resources for Hopi living, over great distances. Collecting firewood of juniper and piñon, which is men's work, requires journeys far into the northern mountains. Getting salt used to mean a twenty-day journey to the salt lakes in the West. Catching eagles for their ceremonial feathers still takes them far afield.

Skilled craftsmen, the Hopis have always been ready to engage in peaceful trade. Their men have carried their wares for barter not only to the other pueblos in Zuñi and on the Rio Grande, but also as far south as the land of the Papagos near the Mexican border and west to the friendly tribe of the Havasupai on the Colorado. All this travel and intercourse has, however, been only to bring back little extras, ornaments, and other things that do not seriously matter to the Hopi way of life. For, from the co-operation with nature that gives them corn, they have every-thing they really need. They are among the most self-sufficient people on earth. And that is the way they like it to be.

4 · CLAN MOTHERS AND PRIEST-CHIEFS

"Clan" is a Gaelic word, but it is used by anthropologists to in-dicate a type of family organization that is found among the most different kinds of peoples throughout the world. Clans reckon kinship only through one parent. In Scotland a clan in-cludes all those who claim descent, through their fathers and their fathers' fathers, from one common male ancestor. They therefore all bear a common surname—as, for instance, the MacGregors of the Clan MacGregor. Among the Hopis and many other peoples, the clan includes all those who claim descent, through their mothers and their mothers' mothers, from one common female ancestor. They bear the name of some species of animal or plant, or of some other class of natural or supernatural beings, to whom they consider themselves spiritually related.

There are about two dozen different clans among the Hopis, and most of them are represented in each pueblo. Each pueblo has its Snakes and Rabbits, its Corns and Tobaccos, its Clouds and Suns, its *Kachinas* (spirits), and so on.

The first law of the clan is that its members may not marry one another, being considered too closely related by virtue of their descent from the same original clan mother. It does not matter how remote is the actual family relationship as we would reckon it; all clan members of one's own generation are addressed as brother or sister, all older women as mother, all the older men as uncle. All the children of a marriage, boys and girls both, are born into their mother's clan, not their father's. Nevertheless, every Hopi considers himself also related to some extent to his father's clan, as well as to his mother's father's clan, and may not marry into these either.

The second great law of the clan is that the members must help one another. This proves only that they think of themselves precisely as we think of the members of our own smaller family of closest relatives. All the older women in the clan are indeed mothers to all its children, and all the younger people regard all their elders as parents. So as long as anyone in the clan has food, none may go hungry. The very old and the sick are taken care of as a matter of course, and it is practically impossible for a young person to become an orphan. On the other hand, everyone owes a duty to his clan not to become a burden upon it if he can help it and not to shame it by doing wrong. This wide family feeling makes for a generous hospitality. It also helps keep the individual person law-abiding perhaps even better than policemen and courts ever could.

Though the clan is an enlarged family, it is of course much too big to be accommodated under one roof but usually lives in a cluster of households or apartments forming a kind of ward in the village. Even the separate households of the clan we might consider unusually large for families. There may be, for instance, a grandmother and her husband, all their unmarried children plus all their married daughters and *their* husbands, all the children of these daughters except their married sons, and so on.

When such a household can simply contain no more additions of generations, even by building more rooms alongside or on the roof, then a branch will split off to start a new nucleus in another part of the village. But all these new households will continue to recognize the original grandmother as their family head. This is how the clans have grown and become dispersed among the various villages, and why, for each clan, there is always a recognized senior household whose head is the clan mother.

When a man marries, he leaves his mother's house and goes to live with his bride, that is, with *her* mother. This does not mean that he joins her clan or changes his name; he merely joins her household. Whenever his own clan requires certain duties of him, he returns to his mother's house to perform them. Such a duty might be disciplining his sister's children. These nieces and nephews, since they are of the same clan as himself, are felt in some ways to be more closely related to him than his own children, who belong to their mother's clan. He is responsible for his nephews' and nieces' growing up as credits to their clan, and therefore inclined to be a stern, strict uncle, unsparing in criticism and reprimand. But to his own children he can be merely an indulgent relative who happens to be sojourning in their mother's house.

"Their mother's house"—this must be taken literally. The Hopi women are the owners of whatever the clan possesses as a clan—the houses, the fields, the clan's religious objects. For the continued existence of the clan depends on the women. A clan without girl children would die out, no matter how many sons it had. So the birth of girls is welcomed, and the lands and houses pass to them from their mothers. The women will remain in those houses and on those lands, while the boys will go off to marry, to live with other clans, and to work for them. The men do all the work in the fields, using their own tools, but the harvest is their wives' as is the storeroom where it is kept. The men build the houses, but it is the women who own them and all the furniture in them. Only the cattle and sheep and the fruit trees introduced by the Spaniards have come to be treated as the personal private property of the men.

Because the house is the woman's, she can decide who is to live in it. Among the Hopis, therefore, it is the woman who divorces the man, simply by putting his personal belongings outside the doorway. When he returns from the fields, he understands the hint, picks up his goods, and goes home to Mother. When one of the clan's households diminishes in size while another increases, it is the clan mother who has the final say as to the redistribution of the clan's fields among them so that all may be busy and well fed and no land be idle for want of workers.

In short, in this society, women are bound to be treated with special respect and consideration, and motherhood brings special responsibilities and influence. This does not mean, however, that the women rule the community. Though being a father may not seem to give a man much importance, being a son definitely does. And being the eldest son of the clan mother, and hence eventually the eldest brother of the next clan mother, and thus the eldest uncle of his clan, makes him its priest and most respected member.

Family affairs revolve around the mothers, but religious affairs center in their brothers, and religion is the tie that holds all the different clans together. Religion is therefore the closest thing to a village government there is among the extremely democratic Hopis, who make no distinction between "priest" and "chief." The instruments, or organizations, through which this government is exercised are the men's secret religious societies, their ceremonial fraternities.

The Hopis' own traditions of how their pueblos came to be founded may not be historically accurate, but they do shed a clear light on the relationships between the clans, the men's societies, and the village, as the Hopis see them. This is how the legends go:

Long, long ago (or, as the Hopis say, "very, very when"), all mankind lived underground at the bottom of a seven-storied subterranean mountain. It was dark there, and wet, and the people had webbed hands and feet. Now the Spider Woman, the earth goddess who was also the wife of the Sun, pitied the people in their gloomy existence, and she sent her two young twin sons, the war gods, to bring them into the daylight. With their help, the clans of men finally emerged one by one through a hole in the earth. This hole was the *Sipapu*, the Place of Emergence, the navel of the world, under the San Francisco Mountains, whose peaks can be clearly seen a hundred miles away to the southwest from the top of Black Mesa. The people dried out in the sunshine, lost their webs, and each clan began to wander separately eastward toward the place of rising of "Father Sun." After many adventures with animals and spirits, which have given the clans their present names, they finally found their way together again at Tusayan. But many kinsmen had been left behind in the underworld.

The first to arrive at Black Mesa, and to settle down on one of its spurs, near a spring welling out from under the sandstone cap, would seem to have been the Bear Clan. Then, over the centuries, the other clans arrived, perhaps driven by drought or fleeing before the depredations of other nomad tribes. They asked

permission to join the pueblo and to have a share in the land
and water.

"Well," the Bears might say to the Snakes, "there is probably
enough land and water for all, and we could use some more defensive strength, and certainly we need more clans to marry into,
but will you be an asset to the community? Are you good Hopis,
or are you quarrelsome witches? How do you fit into the grand
plan of nature? What is your standing with the spirit world?
What can your clan *do*?"

"As to that," the Snake priest might answer, "through our elder
brothers the snakes and our sacred ritual, we can help bring the
August rains, and also we can cure snakebite." Other clans offered other ceremonies and rituals for bringing rain and for curing other diseases. The Cloud Clan passed the test for admission
to the village of Shungopovi by making a new spring gush out
of the rock. They did this by planting an olla or water jar as a
"seed."

The magical accomplishments of each clan come from its
possession of a certain sacred object obtained during its wander-
ings, along with the clan's name. The clan's *tiponi,* as the Hopis
call it, is very like the "medicine bundle" commonly found among
most other Indian tribes. (Such venerated charms are called
"fetishes" by the anthropologists.) But among the Hopis it belongs to the clan rather than to an individual. It usually consists
of a perfect ear of white corn wrapped up in cotton twine and
decorated with feathers.

The tiponi is the sacred emblem of the clan, the holy embodi-
ment of the clan's soul and history, and also the clan's means of
communication with its guardian spirits. The clan mother is its
custodian. It "lives" in her house, where she "feeds" it with offerings of corn meal. It never leaves her care except when its
priest, her brother, takes it to the kiva, the underground chapel

of his religious society, for the ritual that his clan promised the village as the price of its admission.

Now the priest of that ritual must obviously be a member of the clan that "owns" it. He is usually the clan mother's eldest brother, and the uncle of her children. Only he can conduct the ceremony through which the fetish exercises its power of bringing rain or curing disease, and then only if his own heart is pure and his devotion absolutely selfless. He has served a lifelong apprenticeship to this religious service, having been selected for it at an early age by his mother's brother. He has been carefully trained in all the complexities of the ceremony from childhood, and has tried all his life to remain a worthy instrument of the power in his hands. But that power must be exercised not merely for the clan's sake but for the good of all in the pueblo. All men are therefore free to help in it, regardless of their own clan membership. The greater the number of sincere prayers that are joined in a rite, the Hopis believe, the more certain and powerful its effect.

Hence, around each sacred ritual there has gradually been organized a brotherhood of like-minded, public-spirited men, a secret religious society, which any adult man may join if he is qualified and accepts its responsibilities. Sometimes a man joins out of gratitude, as when the Snake Society has cured him of snakebite. Some societies he may be obliged to join, willy-nilly, if he has "trespassed," that is, accidentally come into the kiva while the members were engaged in their secret ritual.

Thus there have come to be about a dozen such societies, including even three that are open to women. There are four societies to one of which every grown man must belong, regardless of his other affiliations. But he may join as many of the others as he has time or inclination for, or as his social conscience dictates. There are so many societies that their ceremonies have to be put on a strict schedule or calendar to fit into the year without overlapping, and even then some societies must hold their public rites only every other year. All the important societies have their own kivas, which the members treat as club rooms when ceremonies are not being held or rehearsed.

It is these men's fraternities that actually control the general affairs of the village, thus providing what government there is. Their kiva chiefs, who are also of course the priests of different clans, make up the "Chiefs' Talk," that is, the council of elders, who set the annual calendar of ceremonies and other village activities and who, if necessary, negotiate with outside groups such as the white man's government. Their presiding officer is the village chief, who is only the priest of the clan that founded the pueblo, and therefore usually of the Bear Clan.

There is no lack of "chiefs" among the Hopis, but the word indicates no power to command, only some priestly function. The town crier is also called the Crier Chief, and the Sun Watcher, who keeps account of the dates and seasons, is also a priest and hence a chief. There is even a War Chief in the town council, who does not have very much to do with war but who has some police functions when outsiders must be kept out of the village during certain ceremonies.

All in all, then, the Hopi way is not as much dominated by the women as would seem to follow from their leading role in clan affairs. Nor is the father likely to be intimidated by the fact that he is almost a stranger in his own household. There is a sort of balance and partnership between the sexes, each having its own sphere of influence and responsibility, the women in clan affairs, the men in village or inter-clan affairs. Yet there is no conflict between them, for, as we have seen, the religious society has grown naturally out of the clan. Together, the clans and societies provide the framework in which every Hopi lives out everything important in his life.

5· THE DANCERS OF TUSAYAN

To understand what their societies mean to the Hopis, we must first realize that responsibility, cooperation, and moderation are not only their ideal of good citizenship but also the basis of their religion, just as prestige and power were to be found at the base of Maori religion. For among primitive peoples, religion is rarely a neatly separated part of their lives, to be discovered by asking what church they attend. It is soaked clear through all their daily activities and attitudes.

To begin with, the Hopis see the whole world alive and full of purpose, like themselves. This is true not only of animals and plants, but also of sun and moon, wind and clouds, water and soil, and indeed everything that has any importance in their lives. A more or less vague feeling for the aliveness of all nature is very widespread among primitive peoples, but among the Hopis it is a very clearly defined belief. Even the world as a whole is in a sense an animate thing for them, since over it all, and all through it, broods the "Great Spirit," for which the Hopis have no other name.

Now, each of these living beings has its own duties and responsibilities toward all the others, just as the Hopis do in their pueblo, and it takes their mutual cooperation to keep the world going in its appointed way. And, of course, as long as each plays its proper part, it has the right to be what it is and to have that right respected. The universe is a democracy, a cooperative commonwealth.

So even the youngest children are taught never to waste or destroy any plant unnecessarily and to be protective of all life. If a Hopi must hunt the rabbit for food or the eagle for its ceremonial feathers, or cut down a tree for a roof beam, he will first speak to its spirit in silent prayer, explaining the necessity and rightness of what he is about to do. And the spirit of the victim, being also responsible and generous, will consent.

Since all things have life and understanding in *common*, men may *communicate* with them, that is, share their thoughts. The Hopis believe that a man makes himself part of whatever he thinks about, and so is able to influence it from the inside. That is why it is so very important to have good, quiet, reasonable thoughts that will spread calm throughout the world and not arouse the fear and enmity of nature. Unless a man approaches the things that matter with "quietness of heart," with "singleness of heart," leaving all his self-seeking desires outside, how can his mind enter into rain or sun, corn or snake, without making trouble? Unless he is an evil witch, he will not wish these things to be other than they are or to do what they ought not.

Prayer is simply the most intense form of communication. The Hopi word for praying means "desiring" or "willing," rather than "begging" or "pleading," but there is no sense of coercion in it. In prayer, the Hopi, by becoming part of nature's own will, wills nature to fulfill her own responsibilities. The power of prayer depends on its calmness, reasonableness, and "single-heartedness," and the power is multiplied by the number of those who willingly and unselfishly join in it.

In the whole cooperative commonwealth of nature, the heaviest responsibility of all rests on human beings, for they are its priests. Only men know the prayers and can perform the proper rituals that will keep the universe in its ordained path, balanced and healthy. But such an Atlas-like task cannot be left to a few consecrated priests, no matter how holy. All Hopis must share the burden, but they must do so willingly and in perfect harmony. And this is precisely the purpose of ritual and ceremony. They are prayer made visible for all to see. In their well-drilled words, gestures, and music and in their use of perfectly executed costumes and religious objects, all the participants can be sure that they are sharing exactly the same thought at exactly the same moment. Their individual prayers are fused into one mighty flood to drown out the discordant private thoughts of the selfish or heedless among them, the two-hearted witches. All their minds are pointed in a single direction, like an arrow made swift by the mighty bow of their combined wills.

Still another purpose of ritual is to give each man a part to play, so that he may forget himself and *become*, body and soul, what he is concentrating on—rain or sun, corn or kachina. This is why the Hopis believe that the most effective form of prayer is a drama, a dance. So also did King David believe when, dressed in priestly vestments, he "danced before the Lord with all his might." For the Hopis, "the dance of life" is more than a figure of speech. The procession of the seasons is a stately dance, repeated over and over again. That is why their own dances can make the spring return, bring the rain clouds in their due course, make sprout the corn and beans. The life of the Hopis depends on the corn, the corn on the rain, the rain on the dances of the Hopis. Nothing could be simpler, more circular, or fairer than that. Hence, a good Hopi is one who "has a quiet heart and takes part in all the dances."

According to their traditions, many of the clans earned their admission to the pueblo by bringing a rain-making or disease-curing ritual and letting all who wished share in it. The compact thus made is fulfilled and celebrated each year with a ceremonial dance sponsored by the religious society that was organized around that ritual. These ceremonies follow a fixed order, according to a calendar or schedule maintained by the village council. During each ceremony the village is turned over to the society involved, which becomes a sort of temporary government.

Scarcely a month passes without its big public dance cere-mony in the plaza, and there are enough dances to spread over a four-year cycle. Usually they take up the whole day, and the entire village is expected to attend as spectators and to assist with their prayers. For all their seriousness of purpose, these dances are no mere grim duties. Each ceremony in the plaza is a village holiday. It has been calculated that the Hopis, who have no Sundays, nevertheless manage to have more than two hundred holidays a year.

Probably no other primitive people in the world has ever spent so much of its time and energy in putting on and enjoying such a round of free public entertainments. Before each one, every housewife is busy for days making *piki* (the Hopi wafer-like cornbread) and other holiday food for guests whom she expects from other villages, as well as for the performers in the dance. Everyone shows up in the plaza and on the rooftops in his or her best finery and jewelry. The children run about in an ecstasy of excitement, for they are living in what is practically a circus.

Fortunate it is for the work that must be done in the fields that not every Hopi is expected to belong to every society. The men in any one family generally arrange it so that they join different fraternities and are not all occupied with religious duties at the same time. Each of the public dances, most of which even outsiders are cordially invited to attend, is only the climax, the grand finale, of a secret ceremony that has been going on in the underground kiva for days or weeks (four or eight or sixteen days, always multiples of the sacred number four). Here the society members have been practicing their secret rites every evening and sometimes all through the day, praying and purifying themselves and building an altar. They scarcely return home; their wives bring them food unless they are required to fast.

Since these religious ceremonies, both public and secret, are also the tribe's highest achievement in art, and the public ones are its most popular entertainment, the performers are as conscious of their artistic as of their religious responsibilities. These dances are no mere spontaneous outbursts of animal spirits. They are dramas as carefully prepared and conscientiously rehearsed as any theatrical shows on earth. For all that the Hopi way frowns upon any striving to become a "star," nothing less than perfection is expected of the chorus. Songs and music must be learned letter-perfect, an infinite number of steps and evolutions must be practiced, a vast variety of masks and costumes must be made, ingenious stage props have to be contrived. All are working under the pressure of deadlines to be met, for the dances are part of the calendar of the Hopis, telling them when to plant and when to reap. They are more important than an almanac, for they do not merely predict the weather, they make it.

The annual cycle begins with a ceremony that is felt to be so fundamental for the village—indeed, so far-reaching for the whole world—that it goes beyond the powers of any one clan or society to "own" or conduct it. This is the *Soyala,* for which the officiating priest is the village chief himself, that is, the priest of the clan that founded the village. It is celebrated in the fourth week of December, at the winter "solstice," when, in the Latin meaning of the word, "the sun stands still," having retreated to the lowest, southernmost point in its risings and settings, and seems to hesitate before turning back on its northward climb.

All northern peoples who know something of the cold of winter and its long dark nights have always felt this to be a critical moment for the world. What if, for once, the sun should continue to sink and disappear altogether under the horizon, never to return? For the Hopis it is a time when all men of good will must pool their spiritual power until it is as strong as the Sun himself and as sharp and swift as his rays, to turn him back and start the new year.

For many days the Sun Watcher priest has been carefully observing behind which cliff, notch, or other landmark on the horizon the sun has been rising each morning. When it reaches a certain position, he warns the village council that the solstice is only so many days off. The next dawn the crier chief chants the announcement from the highest housetop. Warning standards—black-painted sticks from which flutter the feathers of the red woodpecker—are posted over the kivas: the uninitiated must stay away; powerful magic is at work.

Down in his kiva, the village chief has already retired to fast and pray. He prays continuously, purging his mind of every selfish thought and every trace of ill will toward anybody or anything. He is becoming a center of calm and pure benevolence in the wintry violence of the world. He is becoming a human sipapu, an earth navel, opening up the way into the spirit world for others to follow. He tends the fire in the kiva, night and day, and will not emerge until the final day of the ceremony.

Now each grown man will spend the next four evenings in his own kiva, with the members of his own society. They will be inviting the gods, preparing an altar for them and costumes for themselves, and making prayer sticks and prayer feathers. These appear to be only variously painted wooden wands from which hang by bits of cotton twine the feathers of eagles, turkeys, or other birds. But the kind of bird, the kind of feather—whether from wing or breast or down undercoat—the way the feathers are tied to the stick, the symbolic colors the stick is painted, are all different for different purposes, rituals, or prayers.

They *are* prayers, made visible like writing, and, like the written prayers that Tibetan monks turn round on their prayer-wheels, these wind-fluttering offerings to the spirits carry specific, unmistakable messages. There is nothing mechanical about them, however, for they are worthless unless made with good will and unless the maker has breathed a sincere and worthy prayer into them.

Prayer and good will must go even into the capture of the birds that provide the feathers, for the birds must consent to be so

261261261

used. Every clan has its own mountain, often several days' journey away, where it alone may hunt for eagles. These are captured bare-handed, alive, usually as eaglets, in their all but inaccessible nests—a dangerous undertaking. They are carefully tended until their feathers must be plucked for the ceremony. Afterward their naked bodies are reverently buried in a special cemetery.

Prayer sticks are made for all their relatives and friends, for the dead, for the sun and moon, for their houses and fields, for their springs and their livestock, for everything in which the Hopis recognize life or an aid to life. During the whole Soyala ceremony no animal may be killed, no plant cut down; everything must be left as it was created; one may not even cut one's hair. The well-being of everything must be prayed for, nothing forgotten or left out of the universal blessing.

The altar set up in the kiva is an elaborate work of art. On the floor the men draw a sacred picture by strewing white and colored sands and powdered charcoal in striking traditional designs. On this sand painting they place a bowl of water and around it ears of corn—symbols of life because they are the means of life, the very things for which above all else the Hopis are praying.

Now the men sit around the altar, dressed only in loincloths, their hair unbound, sprinkling corn meal and water and blowing clouds of sacred tobacco smoke over the altar, in all six directions. They sing a song of corn and its growth for each direction—about yellow corn to the north, blue to the west, red to the south, white to the east, black for above, and sweet corn for below. A young man in an ancient cotton kilt races out to the springs and other shrines to invite the gods, kachinas, for whom all is ready.

During the next four days the rites are still continued in the kivas, but now they are in the hands of the gods, as represented by the men in their masks and costumes. In each kiva a different dance-drama is acted out about corn and rain and the good life.

The next evening, each group gives the same performance in another kiva, and again the next night in still another, until all the people have seen all the dances.

There must not be a hair's breadth of deviation from one performance to the next, or from one year to the next, for these dances are prayers for abundant crops, children, health and long life, and peaceful security for all. They are much too serious to permit of personal touches or individual prominence; the Sun himself is involved, the life of the heart of the world. Yet these extremely complex dances are not the work of professionals or even of a trained priesthood. All the men in the village participate fully, from the many months they have spent in making their own masks and costumes to the four nights of dancing.

Finally, before dawn of the morning of the solstice, the masked men emerge into the upper world at last. They exchange prayer sticks and distribute them to others, much as gifts are exchanged and bestowed at Christmas. There is an overwhelming sense of peace and good will among those who give and those who receive. The sticks are planted at the springs, before the little shrines in the fields and corrals, on the houses and in the storerooms among the seed grain.

From the shrine at the spring the chief sprinkles a line of corn meal to the east. Everyone deposits his offerings at the shrine and follows the road thus made toward the rising sun. The world is renewed, the sun will come back, a new year has begun. The men who have been the kachinas must now purge themselves, with water and corn meal, of every trace of the awful sacredness in which they have been steeped. They invite the gods to go home again, for it is not well for the two worlds to mingle intimately on an everyday basis.

The Soyala is the first, and perhaps the most solemn, of the year's fixed ceremonies, but from then on, not a month will pass without some similar splendid occasion in which the whole people will join as one to identify themselves with the life-giving forces of nature and thereby to keep those forces in their proper path.

The rites will be different, to suit the stage of cultivation of the corn that has to be helped. The dances, costumes, songs, and dramatic "plot" will change, as well as the priests and societies responsible for them. In some the spirit of the occasion will be more merry, even farcical, a purely holiday spirit appealing especially to the children; in others it will be more somber, even terrifying. But all will have their periods of secret preparations in the kivas, with their sand paintings and altars, their purifications and fasts and smoke-blowing. All will call for, and bring, rain when needed, the renewal of crops and herds and children, health and long life, and peace.

6. KACHINAS AND SNAKES

The next important ceremony is the Powamu, the ceremony of germination and early growth, which comes in February. The Powamu celebrates the return of the kachinas, the spirits of the rain clouds, from their winter home in the San Francisco Mountains, where they have spent the past six months.

In that underworld home, the seasons are topsy-turvy. When it is winter here, it is summer there, and they celebrate the Soyala at our summer solstice. It is as if the underworld were on the other side of the equator, in the southern hemisphere, though such geographical concepts are beyond the Hopis' knowledge. That is why the kachinas, who, like the Greek Persephone, come to herald the spring and to stay half a year, are able to bring with them, in the cold of February, fully sprouted beans.

Actually it is no secret, except to the uninitiated children, that the priest of the Kachina Society has forced the growth of these sprouts in the warmth of his kiva. This is of course done not merely to mystify the children; the success of next year's crops are distinctly felt to depend on the priest's success in growing his hothouse sprouts. He has spent practically all his time for two weeks tending the kiva fire and watering the seeds, all the while praying and avoiding salt and meat. He has distributed the sprouts to all the other kivas, where more were grown, and to the clan houses, so that they might be placed among the seed corn to give the latter magical encouragement to germinate when they are planted.

At the public Bean Dance, which climaxes this ceremony, the kachinas again distribute sprouts to the villagers, who this time bury them in the fields, with the same magical purpose of encouraging fertility. This sort of practice may seem pretty far removed from scientific agriculture, but it is general among all races of mankind, civilized as well as primitive, and is known as "sympathetic magic." It attempts to induce nature to do something by setting her an example, by exerting the power of suggestion, so that she will respond out of sheer sympathy with the idea. We know that the trick works on people, so why not on other living, animate things? So sailors whistle for a wind, and many farmers are convinced that planting should be done only at the beginning of a waxing moon.

For the same magical reason, the Powamu, because it is the ceremony of germination, introduces the foot-racing season. The whole village watches from the mesa top as the young men of the various kivas race one another among the fields in the valley below. Foot racing is practically the only really competitive sport among the Hopis, but the purpose at this time is not so much to encourage the young men's will to win over their competitors as to encourage the corn, exposed to such examples of speed, to a swifter growth. Probably if the Hopis had had stop watches, they would have had their young men race against time rather than against one another.

The kachinas open their season on earth by arriving in procession from the west and gradually filling the public plaza. There may be a hundred of them, each with its own well-known name, its own awesome or comic mask, headdress of spruce boughs or dyed skins or feathers, and body brightly painted in weird designs. They are loaded down with precious necklaces and bracelets (to which all their friends have contributed loans). Each has attached to his right knee a turtleshell rattle, which gives a stirring effect when they all stamp together in the dance, and each holds a gourd rattle in his right hand. The village shimmers with their color and resounds to their songs and music.

All day they dance, from sunrise to nearly sunset. After short breaks for food and rest, they roam about the village with kachina dolls (just like the "real" ones) for good little girls and bows and arrows for good little boys and baskets of pink piki and other delicacies for all. The kachinas are very human gods and sometimes insist on racing a small boy for his present. Sometimes they come knocking at the doors demanding that bad children be given to them to take away. (But the parents always beg the kachinas to give the child another chance and to accept some gift instead.) Nearly all the fairy tales have kachinas not only as their heroes but also as their foolish characters. The children naturally stand in awe of these strange beings, but not in terror, for most of the kachinas are so obviously kind, and it can be seen that the grown-ups, too, love them, for they bring the lovely rain. Since the kachinas are also the spirits of ancestors, or angels in a sense, children speculate on what kind of kachinas they will become when they finally return to the underworld. In short, for the Hopi child, the kachinas are a combination of Santa Claus, fairies, ogres, angels, ghosts, and Punch and Judy—and all in the flesh, actually there to be seen and touched and talked to.

The village is full of visitors, in their best bright finery, watching the show from the housetops, feasting with friends and relatives among the villagers, and sharing in the undisguised general sense of happiness. No one may quarrel during the kachina dance. Even silently harboring ill will, and thus endangering the good effects of the ceremony, would be a piece of inexcusable irresponsibility.

At last, the kachinas file out of the village, their life-giving work done. As they go they distribute consecrated ears of corn to the villagers, who will place them in their storerooms among the corn set aside for seed, to ensure their germination. When the dancers reach the spring shrine, they take off their masks, scrape a little paint from the left eye, plant prayer sticks, and strew a corn-meal road to the west so that the kachina spirits may leave them.

This time the kachinas do not go home to the San Francisco Mountains. They will stay at the spring or other shrines near the mesa for the next six months, ready to come back whenever they are summoned for another dance. Until the end of the corn-planting season in July the mesa practically belongs to the kachinas, who may be found dancing in one of the pueblos at any time, in an almost unbroken round of dance and song in the kivas at night and in the plazas by day.

There is no fixed calendar for these events, nor any fixed order for the many kinds of dances that they perform. At the end of the Soyala ceremony of the winter solstice, anyone may present a prayer stick to the Kachina Society chief and ask to be allowed to sponsor a particular kachina dance after the Powamu. The village council will then schedule it, to prevent overlapping ceremonies. When the date approaches, the village crier will announce the coming event, to give the kachinas time to prepare and the sponsor's womenfolk time to make ready the big feast. The sponsor's family must feed the kachinas and load them down with gifts and delicacies, not only for themselves but also for them to give the children. Also, friends and relatives will come flocking in from

other villages, expecting to be feasted in their turn as they have
feasted others. It is no wonder therefore that the kachinas are
associated from earliest infancy in the Hopis' minds with ideas
of hospitality, generosity, peace and good will, and, in general,
a good time.

Though the fundamental purpose of the kachinas is to bring
rain and health, and is therefore of the utmost seriousness, the
feeling of well-being they bring often spills over into sheer fun
and good humor. For comic relief, the stately dances of the
kachinas are often joined and burlesqued by a group of clowns,
who also sometimes appear in the intermissions. They come out in
comical masks, stumble in their dances, fall all over one another,
and even address silly, childish questions to the kachinas. The
kachinas pretend not to notice the clowns until the very end,
when they may whip them. These clown characters are not bound
by the traditional costumes, steps, and songs of the kachinas, and
are constantly being invented freshly for each occasion. Their
originality surprises the normally silent and respectful onlookers
into loud laughter, and visitors will note the more successful ones
and imitate them in their own dances.

In July comes the last of the kachina ceremonies, the Home
Dance, the farewell rites for these guardian spirits, who must now
return to their homes in the San Francisco Mountains to take care
of their own spring planting and ceremonies. Like the Powamu,
when the kachinas first came, this is again a village affair, a nine-
day ceremony more important than all the intervening summer
shows. Again the kachinas arrive at sunrise, escorted by the Kachina priest, to dance in the plaza all day, with scarcely a let-up,
after having stayed up all night in the kiva in song and prayer.
This time they distribute the first green corn already ripened
in the fields, and loads of melons for the children. That evening
they are blessed with tobacco smoke, corn meal, and water, and a

corn-meal path leading west is laid for them. They leave now, carrying to their cloud parents the fervent prayers of the Hopis for rain and good health.

What is for white people the eeriest and most spectacular of the Hopi ceremonies is held in August, to bring on the late summer rains, without which the last crop of corn would surely die. This is the Snake Dance, the mysteries of which have by now attracted the fascinated attention of visitors from all over the world. It is given every other year, alternately, on two of the mesas. The priest of the Snake Clan, who is therefore also the chief of the Snake Society, has been observing the weather signs carefully for some time when he finally informs the village council that "the snakes want to dance." The village crier then announces the beginning of the sixteen-day ceremony that commemorates the arrival of the Snake Clan on Black Mesa.

The people of this clan say that after the Great Dispersion following the emergence from the underworld, their families lived for a while in snakeskin bags hanging from the rainbow, from which they dropped down on Navaho Mountain. Since then the snakes have been their elder brothers, giving them power over the August rains and a secret medicine for curing snakebite.

For eight days the members of the Snake fraternity scour the country round about for snakes, first to the north, then to the east, and so around the compass. Anyone who "trespasses" upon them during the hunt must join it and the society. They gather all the snakes they can find, young and old, poisonous and harmless, and bring them down into the kiva to be prayed over and to have their heads ceremonially washed in preparation for the dance. In the kiva even the rattlers are handled with the utmost unconcern for danger by even very young boys, who pick them up fearlessly and keep them herded on the sacred sand painting. If the Hopis have an antidote for snake venom, as is quite likely, it is still a secret from the white man.

On the final day of the ceremony, that of the public dance, all the snakes are put into a little brushwood shelter in the plaza. Now while the men of the Antelope Society, who hold their ceremony jointly with the Snakes, sing a series of songs, one Snake dancer after another reaches unhesitatingly into the little brush hut, pulls out whatever snake comes to hand, holds it in his mouth, and "dances his elder brother" around the plaza. The men wear no masks, but their faces and bodies are painted, their kilts and moccasins are henna-colored, and they are heavily bedecked with turquoise jewelry. With each snake-carrier dances another, who keeps one hand upon the carrier's shoulder while with the other he brushes the snake's head with a feather, as if to keep it from striking.

Then all the "elder brothers" are dumped into a corn-meal circle in the middle of the plaza, a squirming, terrifying mass, from which they are gathered up in armfuls, blessed with corn meal, and carried down from the mesa to the four directions whence they came. The human dancers then take a strong emetic to make them vomit away the dangerous sacred power which they have been handling. Not the least impressive part of the ceremony for white onlookers is the fact that rain nearly always falls right afterward.

On the alternate years when there is no Snake Dance, it is the Flute Dance that is held in August. The contrast between these two dances can hardly have been greater, though the purpose of bringing rain is the same in both. This beautiful, sunny ceremony, too, celebrates the advent of a clan, the Rain Makers, and the organization of a society, the Flutes. Here the kiva rites are focused on the singing of songs to flute music, and the main performers at the public dance are the young children in the morning and the youths and maidens in the afternoon, while the older men sing for them and coach them. After the dance, all repair to a sacred spring, into the reservoir of which the priests dive, in order to plant prayer sticks on the bottom.

During and after the harvest, in September and October, there is a sort of women's interlude in the ceremonial year. It is as if the Hopis, so intent on keeping a fair balance between the sexes, had realized that the men's secret societies had perhaps gone a little too far in counterbalancing the women's clans and had themselves upset the balance. So there are these few women's secret societies, too, with ceremonies that celebrate women's work and thanksgiving for the women's harvest. They too have their eight-day kiva rites before the public dance, and they too acquire members by curing a disease or by "trespass."

In some villages the women's societies may even have their

own kivas; in others they borrow them for the occasion. But the women's costumes, their prayer sticks, their sand paintings and altars, must still be made for them by men—for in the Hopi division of labor it is the men who are the priests—just as the men must turn to the women for their sacred corn meal and for birth, marriage, and burial rites.

The ceremonial year closes in November as solemnly as it began. The *Wuwuchim,* or grown-man ceremony, like the Soyala or winter-solstice ceremony that opened the year, requires the participation of all, since it is conducted jointly by the four societies, to one of which every man must belong. The Wuwuchim is marked not only by the initiation of the young men into the full status of Hopi adulthood, but also by the lighting of the New Fire. When all the trails to the village have been closed off, and the women and children hidden in the houses, all fires in the kivas and homes are extinguished. Then the village chief kindles a flame by the ancient method of friction, and embers from it are distributed throughout the pueblo. It is a promise that the world will come out of the darkness of winter—a promise of the coming Soyala and the rekindling of the sun's flame.

Rich as the ceremonial life of the Hopis is, it does not exhaust their love and capacity for putting on public shows and dances. Since there is no major ceremonial dance in January, there is a purely social one called the Buffalo Dance. Similarly in summer there is the Butterfly Dance. In these, both young men and women, and even children, take part, dressed in gorgeous costumes and wearing towering wooden headdresses painted in vivid colors.

The Butterfly Dance is the traditional occasion during which a young girl is expected to announce the name of the young man she is going to marry. Even for these joyful occasions, the spirit of which is like that of our country dances, there have been

weeks of careful rehearsal, and there is the never-forgotten prayer for rain. In the Butterfly Dance, one of the songs, to the accompaniment of drums, goes as follows:

> Come here, Thunder, and look!
> Come here, Cold, and see it rain!
> Thunder strikes and makes it hot.
> All seeds grow when it is hot.
> Corn in blossom,
> Beans in blossom,
> Your face on garden looks.

Thus, whenever these people have something to say to the Great Spirit that concerns all of them, they dance, like David, "with all their might." They act out a drama, the highest of their arts, since it includes all their other arts—of story-telling, music, song, painting, and sculpture. They thus enter into the ever-recurring drama of nature, play their allotted role, and help bring it to a successful conclusion. They do not imitate nature;

they become part of it. They do not merely tell a story; they make it come true.

They *all* dance. Everyone is both an artist and a priest. Everyone has the opportunity to express both himself and the common desire, and everyone has the responsibility for helping to direct nature in the path it should take. Naturally every man feels *good* as a result of the dance. He has expressed his deepest feelings; he has played his part and done it for the public good. In doing so, he has forgotten every thought of petty jealousy and personal gain. Is it any wonder, then, that the primitive culture that can offer its people such an exciting and satisfying social life should win their firm allegiance despite all its daily hardships and despite all the attractiveness of the white man's way?

7. THE ROAD OF LIFE

The Hopis see every man's life as a journey on the same road. It is a well-mapped, clearly marked road running due east from the Place of Emergence to the rising sun. Birth is coming up out of the underworld. The soul then travels the road through the four well-defined stages of childhood, youth, adulthood, and old age. Then it turns westward, on what is now the road of death, back to the Sipapu, the navel of the earth, to rejoin its ancestors and the unborn souls in the underworld.

Four is a sacred number among nearly all Indians, perhaps because they recognize four cardinal directions in the world— north, east, south, and west. But just as the Hopis have added the directions of up and down in all their rituals, so to the four stages of life they have added those of before-birth and after-death.

Each stage of the road is thought of as a necessary, slow preparation for the next. But the actual passage from one to the other is always an abrupt step, fraught with the danger of losing one's way, a critical time of testing and ordeal. It is then that a person needs the help and guidance of all his people, the support of their massed spiritual strength. At these perilous occasions—birth, puberty, initiation, marriage, death—the whole clan or the whole village must mobilize all its forces of religious ritual and magical ceremony to keep the pilgrim firmly on the road. Such solemn practices at these times are so widespread among all peoples that the anthropologists have given them the special name of "rites of passage."

The first such rite for every Hopi is the one that helps him find his way into the upper world, makes a place for him in the world of nature and society, and sets his feet on "the Hopi road." So, when a Hopi is born, he may not see the sun for twenty days. A blanket hangs over the doorway to keep out the daylight while he follows the path of his race up from the underworld. Every fifth day his mother washes his head and her own, and rubs his body with ashes, for he has completed another of the four stages of four days each, and must be prepared for the next. From now on, for the rest of the child's life, every ceremonial preparation will include this hair-washing with suds made from the soapy root of the yucca. All this time, the mother will eat neither salt nor meat, for she too must be purified for the approaching birth rites. On the twentieth day, the baby is ready to start his eastward journey.

Now the birth rites are strictly a clan affair, naturally, and it might be supposed that they would be exclusively in the hands of the child's own clan. But as a matter of fact it is the father's clan that takes charge, as it always will whenever the child has another crucial passage to make on the road of life. It is as if the Hopis wanted always to remind him that he personally owes his existence and allegiance to two clans. The marriage of his parents has in fact been a joining of their two clans, and he owes special obligation to them both, as they do to him.

Before dawn on the twentieth day, then, the father's mother arrives at the darkened home of her daughter-in-law along with all her own daughters. She is not the child's grandmother, according to Hopi reckoning (for she is not of his clan), but she will be his godmother. She washes the heads of the child and his mother, she rubs him over with sacred white corn meal, and she gives him a name.

"May you live to be old," she says, "may you have good corn, may you keep well, and now I name you ———."

Each of the old woman's daughters, who have brought christening gifts of baskets of corn meal, also gives the child a different name. No one knows yet which of these names will become a favorite and stick. All his life the child will have a special relationship to the women of his father's clan who have named and christened him. They will be his "joking relatives," who will tease and spoil him and give him presents. They will call him "sweetheart," though he cannot marry among them any more than he can marry in his own clan. It is all quite different from his relations with his own clan relatives, especially his mother's brothers, who will discipline him and teach him his duties.

Meanwhile, the child's father has been keeping watch on a nearby roof, and now he calls down that the sun is about to rise above the horizon. The child is strapped into its cradleboard for the first time, and its godmother takes it outdoors to the mesa edge facing the rising sun. She sprinkles a line of corn meal to the east: it is the Hopi road. As the first shaft of light reaches the child and the women in their fresh gowns, the godmother raises him up as an offering to Father Sun. Thus the world accepts him, and as long as he stays on the road he will remain an important and necessary part of the world.

The first several months on the road he will be carried, trussed up in his cradleboard, his legs and back firmly bound to it so that he will grow up straight, his head resting against a firm hard cushion so that the back of his head will grow flattened in the Hopi ideal of male handsomeness. His mother carries the board wherever she goes on her round of daily tasks, and stands it up against the wall when she is home indoors. She takes the baby out only to bathe him or change his diapers, until he is old enough to begin crawling about on his own.

For the rest of his childhood, about eight years, he runs around freely, naked and happy, but watched over by his older sisters and brothers. They teach him to stay away from the mesa edge, the precipice that is their front yard. Almost as soon as he can walk, he is climbing up and down the mesa trail, beginning to develop the strong lungs and heart that must last him into old age for this daily exercise. Most of his time is spent in play, but he is also gradually learning to help at home and in the fields. He gets into mischief with the toy bow and arrows given him by his indulgent father, and is scolded for `` by his stern uncle. He is secure in the possession of many mothers in his own clan and spoiled by the many aunts in his father's clan.

Then, at eight, he is considered old enough for a first understanding of what it is to be a Hopi and is expected to make the passage into the second stage of his life. Eight may seem an early age to pass from childhood to youth and to be initiated into the mysteries of the adult world, but the Hopis do not like to treat their children as a separate group shut out from their parents' affairs. All ages, they feel, have their proper responsibilities, suited to their strength and understanding, in the common business of clan and village life.

The initiation they have devised for the little ones is no more difficult than is the first day of school among us, and it is made up of the same elements of solemnity, pain, and holiday excitement. But, for the boys especially, this is no longer a clan or women's affair. The whole village is concerned in this first preparation of future Hopis, and the rites of this passage are therefore in the hands of a men's religious society. And it is only fitting that the child's first initiation should take place in February, during the Powamu, the feast of germination and of young growing things.

It is also fitting that the first grown-up secrets revealed to the child should have to do with kachinas. Long before the first kachina dance of early spring, the mother of an eight-year-old will have asked some member of the Kachina Society to be his godfather. She will grind corn meal for the godfather for a week, and he will weave the boy a ceremonial sash and kilt. In February, when the kachinas are expected to return to the pueblo, heralding the spring, the children to be initiated are taken down into the kiva to wait.

Down the ladders come the kachinas, a fearsome sight, flailing whips made of yucca. While each godfather holds fast to his charge, the kachinas lash the children. This is the ordeal of pain, to make the initiates remember what they have passed through and what they are about to learn.

For now it is revealed to them that the kachinas they have always seen were really only their fellow villagers and neighbors dressed up in masks, that they only *represented* the real kachinas, who are present only in spirit. From now on, the initiated boys may come and go freely in the kivas and eventually themselves try out for parts in the kachina dances. Only they must never give away the secret to the uninitiated children; otherwise they will be whipped again.

The ordeal of pain, mild as it is, is also to tell the child that life can be serious and often hard, that it is full of responsibilities that cannot be evaded and hardships that must be borne. From now on, a boy's uncle becomes ever more exacting in requiring the respect and conduct that his nephew owes to his clan and fellow villagers. Greediness, laziness, self-indulgence, and thought-lessness are no longer excused or condoned.

A conscientious uncle will also worry about his nephew's growing up too soft, and will occasionally suggest that the boy take a winter plunge in the spring or in a snowbank. This will harden his flesh and cool his heart—that is, keep him from being quarrelsome or hotheaded, as we say. Or he may send the boy on a long run across the desert without water, to learn to do without, as the Hopis often must.

Above all, the children must be taught the great lesson of the clan—all for one and one for all—and that this means giving as well as receiving. The boy begins very early to help in the fields, at first by chasing crows and prairie dogs, later in the planting and harvest. He soon goes out for days, herding sheep or gathering wood or nuts, or even helps build a new house for a growing family. The little girl soon begins to grind a little corn, to fetch a little water from the spring, to take care of the younger babies.

Though the girls, too, have gone through the Powamu initiation and know the secret of the kachinas, they do not join in the kachina dances. On the other hand, since they are the future clan mothers, they go through an additional rite of passage when they reach adolescence. For this rite, which is naturally an affair of the clans alone, the girl goes, before dawn, to the household of her father's eldest sister, who was also usually her godmother for the whipping ceremony. She stays there four days, avoiding the sun (for she is about to be reborn), eating no salt or meat, and, from dawn to dark, grinding corn.

The girl grinds away as long and as busily as she can, her friends helping, white corn the first day, blue the second, red the third, and on the fourth day yellow corn in the morning and black in the afternoon. Grinding corn meal will be her chief and hardest task throughout her future life, as growing the corn will be her husband's, and she must now show that she is already an industrious woman, worthy of marriage and ready to run a household.

After four days of this backbreaking toil, she goes out on the

mesa edge and offers her corn meal to the rising sun, praying for strong arms to grind corn, strong legs to climb up and down the mesa path for water, and luxuriant hair for beauty. She returns to her father's sister's house for the women's feast to be held in her honor.

She appears at this feast as a new person, no longer a child. She has been given a new name. Her hair has been washed by her aunt and arranged in the style of the maidens, in big whorls that stand out beside her ears like butterfly wings. These are called "squash blossoms," and she is herself like a vigorously flowering squash plant, promising fruit and harvest. Later, when she has married, thus entering on the full stage of adulthood, she will undo the squash blossoms and wear her hair in two heavy coils hanging in front of her shoulders—representing the ripened squash itself.

The young men, too, are not yet ready for marriage and all the other responsibilities of adulthood until they have made still one more ceremonial passage. This one will take them beyond the women's world of the clan into the men's world of the tribe; it is the one that "makes a Hopi."

The grown-man initiation takes place in November, during the Wuwuchim, the last important ceremony of the Hopi year, after the harvests are in. This harvesting of the new crop of Hopis is conducted simultaneously by the four secret societies to one of which every Hopi man must belong. Since there must be enough youths approaching twenty to justify the simultaneous initiation rites in the four kivas, it is held only every four or five years.

The young man's godfather, the one who sponsored him in the Powamu whipping initiation, now brings him into his own society. Here, too, there is a kind of ordeal, to mark the passage with pain, but it is more symbolic than real. The young men are made to go through the wintry village, past the women, who pour jars of cold water over their naked backs. Thus the young men not only prove their hardihood, but also help magically to bring rain.

The initiates now learn the most sacred traditions of their tribe, and are given new names. What goes on in the kiva is so secret and solemn that the women and children must stay home and indoors during these rites. A line of corn meal is sprinkled across the path into the village, and guards are posted to keep out all strangers, in ancient times on pain of death.

The youths are now men and have presumably put aside all childish things. Nevertheless, at marriage they must once again put themselves in the hands of the clan, for marriage, like birth, gives the clan its significance. Nor should it be surprising that in such affairs the Hopis expect a certain amount of initiative from the woman, the future clan mother. A girl may propose to a young

man by sending him a basket of *piki*, the paper-thin corn wafers
of the Hopis, and he accepts by accepting and eating the food. If
she is seen combing his hair in public, that is an announcement
of their engagement, and means that their two families are already in the midst of negotiations and preparations.

For a Hopi, marriage is not a single simple ceremony, but a series
of them often spreading over a year. Two clans are about to enter
into a very special relationship, which must be marked by a great
exchange of gifts and services. Such serious matters are not as
quickly disposed of as the mere whims of two young people.
There must be all the solemnity and protocol that go with the
making of international treaties.

First, the bride makes a great deal of blue corn meal or corn
cakes, which she brings on a large tray to the groom's household.
There she settles down for a long visit. For two days she grinds
white corn. The third day she grinds blue corn, and the women
of her father's clan bring her baskets heaped with corn meal to
help her put on a big show. But on this day, too, the groom's joking aunts, *his* father's sisters, come to make things difficult for
her—taunting her for laziness, throwing mud at her, stealing the
wood for her fire, and in general making themselves obnoxious,
because she is "stealing away their sweetheart."

On the fourth day, she is up long before dawn, making piki.
Then the heads of the bride and groom are washed, and they go
out together to make an offering of corn meal to the rising sun.
They return to the groom's house for the first big wedding feast,
to which the whole village is invited.

But this is only the beginning. The boy's relatives now bring
her gifts of raw cotton, for which she gives them corn meal in
exchange. Then the men of the boy's clan take the cotton away to
the kivas, where they card and spin it into thread, and finally begin to weave her a trousseau—a large white cotton blanket-robe
for outer wear, a smaller white ceremonial robe wrapped up in

grass matting, a white fringed sash, a black dress for daily wear, a pair of white moccasins with bulky leggings that uses up a whole deerskin. All this takes weeks, and meanwhile the bride stays in her husband's house, grinding corn to feed the weavers and pay for the garments.

Finally, the wedding clothes are finished. The bride drapes the large white robe over her head and shoulders, puts on the buck-skin moccasins and leggings, and tucks the wrapped-up cere-monial robe under her arm. The wedding procession escorts her to her own home, together with gifts of food carried in pots and baskets. The bride's family must of course make a return gift of corn meal, which all the women have been grinding for days, for distribution to the groom's family.

That evening, the husband at last comes to his wife's house to live, and becomes a part of that household by hauling a load of wood for her the next morning. But for many days after, all her clan mothers and sisters will busily go on grinding corn until they have satisfied their sense of self-respect by making enough to pay for the wedding garments. Then it is their turn to give the final wedding feast.

At the next Home Dance in July, when the kachinas bid the people farewell for the coming six months, each bride of that year will once again put on her wedding garments and show them in public. And when her first-born child is offered to the sun by its father's mother, she will stand there praying, dressed in her cere-monial robe. It is the last time she will wear it in this life. Then she will store it away safely against the time when it will be used for her burial shroud. For it will retain enough power to waft her spirit down from the mesa and across the last passage to the west.

There is no ceremony to mark the passage into old age, though a ripe old age is always prayed for in all the other ceremonies, and fullness of years often brings special responsibilities. By living long enough a woman may become the clan mother or at least the head of a very large household, and a man may inherit the duties and responsibilities of chief priest of a society. But this last stage of life is the one that arrives least dramatically, most gradually, and all too often never comes at all. Besides, from old age the tribe hopes most for wisdom, and this is not invariably the gift of advancing years. So there is no initiation or special ceremony, though the life of the aged is a useful and honored one. To the last they will contribute whatever they are capable of to the work and activities of the clan, and to the last the clan will take care of them.

Death from old age is considered the most natural and proper way to die, for it means that the traveler on "the road" has truly completed his foreordained journey and is therefore fully prepared for the final passage. The spirit has reached its goal, pauses there like the sun at its solstice, and now turns westward for the return to the underworld. Though the Hopis do not fear the spirits of the departed, and indeed pray to them to return in the form of life-giving clouds, they are made profoundly uneasy by the fact of death itself, for they consider death to be contagious. So on the very same day that a man dies, he will be buried in a rude grave in the side of the mesa.

Again, it is not his own clan that performs these last rites. It is his father's clanswomen who wash his head for the last time as they washed it at his birth, initiation, and marriage. And it is his own son who buries him. Into the grave go his ornaments and food for the journey to the Sipapu. If it is a woman she is draped in the ceremonial wedding robe she has so carefully saved for this purpose. A mask of cotton batting is sewed to the clothes to cover the face of the dead, symbolizing the rain clouds which are never far from the Hopi mind and which the dead are about to become by becoming kachinas.

The corpse is buried in a sitting position, with the head sunk between the knees—exactly like the thousand-year-old mummies found in ancient pueblo ruins—and a prayer stick is inserted into the grave to allow the soul an exit. There is no tombstone or monument, for though nearly all American Indians venerate their departed ancestors, they do not remember or appeal to them by name. The dead live on but they are changed into something more powerful than man, and they must therefore have new names.

For three days, relatives visit the grave, leaving food and prayer sticks. On the fourth, the dead man's "breath body" is ready to undertake its journey. The trail back to the village is ceremonially closed by a line of corn meal. In the underworld, reborn among its ancestors, the spirit will continue to live a Hopi life, except that it will acquire all sorts of supernatural powers and there will be no lack of water. Perhaps it will graciously return now and then to Tusayan, as a kachina, bringing gifts or punishments for the children and rain for the people. The journey is ended.

8. A DAY OF PEACE

Out of the black desert night a powerful but beautiful voice seems to sing down from high above the sleeping village, piercing to the valley floor below:

"All people awake, open your eyes, arise,
  Become children of light, vigorous, active, sprightly.
  Hasten, Clouds, from the four world-quarters.
  Come, Snow, in plenty, that water may abound when summer appears.
  Come, Ice, and cover the fields that, after planting, they may yield
      abundantly.
  Let all hearts be glad.
  The Wuwuchim will assemble in four days;
  They will encircle the villages, dancing and singing.
  Let the women be ready to pour water upon them
  That moisture may come in plenty and all shall rejoice."

Three times the Crier Chief announces this November day's message, awakening men and nature, as he does every morning. He is the town's alarm clock, its calendar, almanac, and newspaper. All his messages are clothed in poetry, whether he is announcing a house-raising in which all are urged to help, or the annual rabbit hunt, or that it is time to clear the fields, or, as here, that an annual ceremony is about to begin.

By dawn, the villagers are all awake and stirring, but from the shadow of the valley below, the rising sun may not seem to reveal a village at all. The flat-topped houses, piled up pell-mell around the plaza, and made of the same red sandstone as the mesa itself, or of the local adobe clay, seem only to be the natural square battlements of the cliff wall. The streets between the groups of houses are nothing but the rock of the mesa itself, worn down by generations of sandaled feet. Soon, however, the plumes of smoke rising from the chimney pots reveal human dwellings and tell of women at work.

In these two- and three-story houses, the usual household has an apartment of two rather small rooms, each about twelve feet square. In former times the ground-floor rooms were used only for storage, the tenants climbing to their upper-floor apartments by ladders leaning against the walls. Now the ground floor is also used to live in. Of the two rooms in each apartment, the one in front, facing the plaza, with a blanket-hung doorway and a small window or two, is the family's living-sleeping-working room. With so much activity constantly going on in it, this small room is kept surprisingly neat and orderly. The floor is always well swept, and the walls are regularly replastered smooth with adobe and whitewashed with pipe clay. In the very old days even this room did not always have a doorway, entrance being by ladder through a square hatchway in the roof, like the entrance to the hold of a ship.

Considering the number of persons there may be in a Hopi household, it would obviously not be advisable to clutter up the living room with unnecessary furniture. The beds are sheepskins laid directly on the adobe or stone-flagged floor. In the morning they are hung up to air—along with blankets, clothing, and harness—over poles set in the walls or swinging from them, all making quite a pretty and neat display of the family's wealth. The family "at table" sits on mats or skins around the common pot resting on the floor, everyone in turn dipping his rolled-up piece of piki into the stew. Men and women sit differently—the women back on their heels in the kneeling position natural to them when they grind corn, the men with right foot firmly planted on the floor and the right knee raised, the left leg doubled under it, in the posture of readiness for springing up into instant emergency action. A low stone bench, however, is built into and across the back wall, where the family may sit and have work space for special tasks.

In every apartment, three stone-sided boxes are sunk into the floor. These are the *metates,* the family's flour mill. In each box there slants down a slab of stone. In the first, it has a fairly rough surface; in the second, it is less rough; in the last, it is almost smooth. The housewife kneels over the first metate, spreads a handful of dried kernels of corn over the grinding stone, and crushes them with a small hand stone by rubbing it up and down as if she were scrubbing clothes on a washboard. The coarsely crushed grain is then passed over the second metate, where it is ground finer. On the third metate it is finally reduced to a powdery flour ready for making batter.

It takes at least two hours out of a woman's day just to grind the corn for her family's daily meals. This is not counting the many additional hours she must put in at her metates almost every week for special occasions—for the corn meal used in every

ceremony or ritual, for the constant round of feasts and parties
following on births and marriages or to repay friends and relatives for helping with the harvest or a house-raising, or simply
for feeding unexpected visitors or as gifts to clan members in
difficulties. It has been calculated that one long-drawn-out wedding ceremony alone may require the grinding of a ton of corn
before it is over.

In such special cases, three women will work together at the
same set of metates, passing the meal from one to the other for
successively finer grinding, as if on a factory assembly line. They
will sing special grinding songs to lighten their labor and to
weave a magic spell so that the corn and the metates will cooperate in the work. (This, the Hopis say, is precisely what
birds are doing when they sing.) This eternal grinding, and the
fetching of water from the springs below, in jars strapped to
their backs, are the women's major and heaviest work.

Set into one corner of the room there may be a hooded fireplace, with a chimney made of a stack of bottomless clay pots. In
ancient times, the household fire had usually been made in a pit

in the center of the room, the smoke escaping as it could through the square entrance hatchway in the roof. It is generally believed that these chimneys were another gift of the Spaniards, who had themselves just learned the use of them from the Moors. But they look so natural in the Hopi buildings, so "pueblo," that many observers have felt they could not be such recent importations. In a way they may be right, for new excavations among Hopi ruins have shown at least the beginnings of corner chimneys among pre-Spanish pueblos. If the Hopis had already discovered the principle of the chimney for themselves, it may account for the ease with which they took over this Spanish gift.

Held up over the fireplace by short stone legs is a large smooth stone slab. It is a stone griddle, on which, when it has been heated by the fire, is poured a thin corn-meal batter mixed with a little wood ash. That is how the Hopis' bread is made, the piki that comes in fifteen varieties, differing in color, shape, and additional ingredients (such as roasted watermelon seeds). It is peeled off the griddle in cakes as thin as the paper of a hornet's nest, rolled into cylinders or folded into other patterns, and arranged on basket trays where it becomes as crisp as corn flakes. Other baking and cooking is mostly done outdoors.

This completes the furnishings and facilities of the front or living room. Sometimes the fireplace is to be found in the back room only, sometimes in both. This back or inner room—windowless, dark, and unventilated—is the storeroom, pantry, granary, and tool house. Here the ears of sun-dried corn are neatly stacked against the wall like cords of firewood, each color of corn in a separate bin. Here the squash, after being peeled, cut into long spirals, and dried in the sun, is hung in festoons. There are also shelled beans in bags and baskets, strings of dried meat, dried peaches and apricots, piñon nuts, berries, sunflower and watermelon seeds, and the dried leaves and fibers of yucca and other plants used for food, dyes, or basketry. All are safely preserved without salt or any other preservative than the sun and the extreme dryness of the climate.

Here, too, are kept the household pots and the simple tools and equipment of the Hopi family—the grass broom and hairbrush (which are two ends of the same tool), the stirring stick for cooking, the digging stick for gardening, the throwing stick for rabbit hunting.

It is a fixed rule with the thrifty Hopis always to keep at least one year's harvest in reserve, not to be touched until the next year's crop either is gathered or has definitely failed. Some of the corn in the storeroom is therefore two or even three years old, and must be taken out onto the flat roof terraces periodically for airing and sunning, to get rid of the occasional mold and the not infrequent insect pests, and to uncover the thieving field mice and other vermin. This brings us to the third and, in many ways, most important part of the family apartment.

Every home that is not on the ground floor includes a penthouse terrace, which is the flat roof of the apartment below. In the almost cloudless climate of this country, it is here, out in the open in front of the doorway, that the family spends most of its daylight hours at home and the members pursue their daily home tasks. Here the women do most of their cooking and mending, dry and air their corn and meat, and carry on the arts of basketry and pottery for which they are famous.

Outdoors will be found the beehive-shaped pit oven, with small openings in the sides of its dome of baked clay. It is made to retain heat long after the fire built inside has been consumed and the embers raked out, and so gives the slow heat required for the favorite stews and the endless varieties of baked and roasted corn-meal mush. The women begin heating the ovens before dawn, and by late morning, when the men return from the fields for their first real meal, there will be piping-hot jars of puddings and stews. The lack of variety in the ingredients of their diet—

the eternal corn basis—has encouraged such inventiveness in the cooks that most women pride themselves on the number and variety of their recipes.

Every Hopi woman is also a craftsman in one of the Hopi arts —basket making or pottery. There is a kind of specialization by villages, however. Of the three mesa spurs along which the pueblos are distributed, only one makes pottery, another does all the coiled basketry, and the third all the woven basketry.

The American Indian never developed the wheel, either for vehicles or for the potter's turntable. The Hopi woman builds up a pot by spiraling a long thin rope of clay, pressing the coils together with her fingers, and smoothing out the surface with a pebble as she goes on. Her work was evidently much prized among other pueblos even in prehistoric times, considering how far afield samples of it have been found. It was in fact a superior artistic product both in shape and in the designs painted on it.

Even more striking is the fact that the kilns for baking the clay are fired with coal, of which there seems to be a great deal under Black Mesa, often cropping out in the cliff wall. The ancient Hopis must have been among the earliest coal miners and coal users in the history of the world, having regularly used this fuel for firing pottery and even for heating kivas before it came into general use in Europe.

Basket making, as we have seen, was the older art, older even than the Pueblo culture. A typical Hopi product is the large shallow tray or *plaque* of coiled basketry, on which the Hopis stack the folded piki or heap the finely ground corn meal in colorful mounds. Coiled basketry is made by tightly wrapping strips of yucca leaf around a switch of dried grasses or willow shoots. This makes a strong, flexible rope, which is then spiraled on itself, the successive coils being held together by stitching. (Perhaps this is where the idea of coiled pottery came from.)

The women prepare the wrappings in advance by splitting dried yucca leaves with their teeth and fingernails, and dyeing them in bright yellows, greens, and reds. The continuous coil is wrapped little by little, so that the different colors will work out into the traditional patterns and designs as the basket grows and takes shape. A Hopi bride should have at least a dozen plaques just to give away to her husband's relatives with mounds of corn meal.

The other great household art for which the Hopis have always been famous is weaving, but this is not women's work. The Hopis are the only North American Indian tribe among whom it is the men who spin and weave. (Of course, there were not many who wove at all.) When the plundering Navahos came to this region, about the same time as the Spaniards, they learned and imitated the art of weaving from the Hopis, but quite "naturally" they handed it over to their women. From November to February,

when the men have no work to do in the fields, in almost every
Hopi living room a loom hangs from one of the beams near a
wall, and a colorful blanket may be seen slowly growing from the
floor to the ceiling.

The Hopi men still supply all the other Pueblo peoples on the
Rio Grande with white cotton ceremonial kilts, sashes, and robes
for their religious dances and rites. Every ceremonial godfather
still weaves a dancing kilt and sash for the godson whose initiation he is sponsoring, and all the men in a clan must be ready to
weave the white wedding robes for the brides of the young men
among them. Besides, the men used to weave the black cotton
dresses and the red cotton embroidered belts that were the daily
costume of their wives and daughters. After the Spaniards brought
the sheep, these ordinary "squaw dresses," worn with the left
shoulder bare, were made of wool.

The men's primitive looms, scarcely more than two horizontal
beams hanging from the ceiling, are also to be found in the kivas.
For these sacred chapels, these theaters of the people, are also
the men's club rooms, where they can go for a little peace and
quiet away from their families, a bit of gossip or story-telling, a
little uninterrupted meditation or concentration on the work in
hand. So they often hang their looms there and drop in for a
spell of weaving when they have the time and inclination, and at
the same time hear and learn the traditions recited and the songs
sung by the older men.

The kivas are the only other structures in the village besides
the family apartments. They must be underground, not an easy
requirement to fulfill on the stony top of the mesa. Often, therefore, advantage has been taken of some gap or ledge in the lip
of the mesa, the cavity being enlarged and squared off, and the
outer opening walled in, so that the kiva partly overhangs the
valley below. Unlike the very ancient circular kivas, these are
oblong, about twenty-five feet long, but entrance, as of old, is

still by a ladder through the square hatchway in the roof that also serves as a smoke hole. Thus a kiva entrance is easily recognized, with its square walls and roof built up above ground and its ladder sticking ten feet up in the air. Inside, besides the stone bench around the walls, and the fire pit, and the open space for sand paintings and dances, there is always the sipapu, a small hole in the floor leading to a buried square stone box, symbolizing the navel of the earth.

The Crier Chief's dawn announcements, besides being a calendar of ceremonies, are also like the help-wanted section of a newspaper or the bulletin board of an employment agency, so often do they "cry a work party," announcing that a neighbor needs help in harvesting or sheep shearing. But, of course, no pay is offered, only the expectation of a feast afterward. Sometimes there is not even that, as when, after proclaiming an approaching public festival, the crier reminds his listeners that the priest-chief whose ceremony this is must now retire to the kiva for fasting and prayer. If it is summer, the priest will not be able to tend to his fields. This is a signal for volunteers to organize a work party for him, a task gladly undertaken for the good of all.

Work parties are also cried for house building. When a household begins to feel cramped in its quarters, all the men and boys in it will haul up enough stone, clay, and timbers to build a new apartment, and then "advertise" through the village crier their need for help. The responding work party of men may spend a week putting up the walls and laying the roof beams. Then the women, who have all along been busy feeding the men, will form their own work party to finish the house, mixing adobe, plastering the walls inside and out with their hands, smoothing the walls and the floors, and whitewashing the rooms. Presumably, however, they must still take care of their own feeding and feast of repayment.

One other event that may be cried at dawn has all the excitement for the whole village that it gets from the announcement of a long-awaited important dance. This is the annual rabbit hunt, a truly communal affair with its own hereditary Rabbit Hunt Chief. Everyone turns out for this free-for-all, at least to help encircle and beat up the game. The hunters are provided with small throwing sticks, rather like boomerangs, with which they bring down every rabbit that is unlucky enough to be within the wide area chosen for the hunt.

Perhaps it is because hunting has never been too important to the Hopis' livelihood that they have a rather sportsmanlike attitude toward this game, preferring to pit their unaided strength, speed, and endurance against it, running it down on foot, bringing it down with their most primitive weapons. Perhaps also it is part of their attitude of respect for all animals that makes them avoid taking too unfair an advantage, as when they insist on capturing their eagles barehanded. Or is it all part of their typically thoughtful way of not upsetting the balance of nature? For holding this big hunt only once a year, without the use of shotguns, bows and arrows, or snares, could be a kind of insurance against the total extermination of the rabbits and the end of another village holiday.

For though the meat is entirely welcome, the rabbit hunt is pure social fun, and the Hopis love their games as much as they do their dances and group songs. They probably have more of these than any other Indian tribe. They are not known as the "Song Makers" for nothing and, in addition to the hundreds of ceremonial chants, they have innumerable work and play songs.

Their favorite games are athletic, including especially foot racing and a form of hockey in which the aim is not so much to beat the other team as to burst the big skin ball and spill its filling of seeds (again to encourage the crops to do likewise). The races, we have already seen, also have their sympathetic-

magic side, hurrying the rain clouds, speeding growth. The young men are remarkably fast and enduring long-distance runners over the broken waterless desert. They are the telegraphy of the tribe, carrying messages between the villages on different mesas or even to distant peoples. In the rain ceremonies, a runner will be sent to encircle every single field belonging to the village, no matter how remote, and to plant a prayer stick in each one.

There are many sit-down games, too, for the less athletic folk, but there is, as might be expected, practically no gambling, for that would mean personal competition of the worst sort, and losers as well as winners. It would be ka-hopi—uncooperative, quarrelsome, bad.

The daily life of the Hopis is full of hard work unlightened by the conveniences and amusements of the white man's civilization around them. Far from complaining, however, they consider theirs the *good* life. If it did not go against their grain to make invidious comparisons, they might even say the *better* life. They may be short on modern labor-saving devices, but somehow they manage to have more holidays and to find more time and leisure for their arts and simple recreations than do most city-dwellers. More important, they know that their deepest satisfactions flow from their religious ceremonial life, with which the white man has nothing to compare. They see clearly that their priestly dances are tied up with their daily life as primitive farmers, that both are parts of a single pattern and one cannot be given up without the other. This is why Hopi boys who do succumb to the lure of the white man's cities usually end by drifting back to the rugged life in their little villages.

It is also why the Hopis, of their own free choice, have deliberately rejected many of the civilized advantages available to them. Even the white man's "firewater," which made such quick cultural conquests among most other Indian tribes, has made almost no headway among the Hopis, who seem neither to need nor to want it. The same is true of the white man's other, seemingly less dubious, blessings. It is not due to the primitive man's fear of not being able to cope with their complications. The Hopis are far from being a stupid people; they are quite as capable as any other, not only of driving cars, for instance, but also of becoming good automobile mechanics. But they are also quite as good philosophers as their white neighbors. Before they will allow some big modern improvement to dig in among them, the whole village will carefully consider what will be its ultimate effect on the Hopi way of life. If there seems to be no real conflict, they will let it in. They do not like to experiment with such important matters, for they know that it is very difficult to get rid of a custom once it is firmly established in people's habits and people have come to depend on its benefits.

In recent years, for instance, it has been urged on the Hopis by their well-meaning white friends that life on the mesa could be made much easier for all if the water from the springs below were pumped up by electricity. Some Hopis have actually moved down to the valley floor to be nearer their fields and the springs and even to the white man's piped water, but they still acknowledge the government, such as it is, of the villages perched on the mesa edge. These village councils carefully considered the proposal, recognized its advantages, and turned it down. For, they said, who could assure them that this easy way of getting water merely by turning on a tap would not simply result in much sooner drying up the springs? Were not the white man's great cities themselves beginning to suffer from water shortages from just this lavish waste of it, even though built not in deserts but where water was as free as air? And would the pumps not make the Hopis dependent on outside capital to make them, and on fuel from the outside to run them? They were not prepared to take these risks of destroying their ancient self-sufficiency and with it their ability to protect their way of life.

Again, when it was pointed out to the Hopis by local business interests that if they allowed the coal, and possibly the oil, in their mesa to be mined and drilled, they might all become unbelievably wealthy by white men's standards. But, they answered, they were not in competition with the white man for his wealth. Would all these promised riches buy them insurance for continuing the Hopi way? Would they not rather close that way forever? Could there be any meaning or sincerity in dancing for the rain when they were no longer desert farmers who needed the rain to live? And what meaning could life have for a Hopi if he were no longer part of the forces that brought the life-giving rain to the parched desert and indeed to the world? The Hopis had seen what had happened to other Indians on whose lands oil was discovered, how they had become first rich, then lost. They preferred to keep their lands as farms and homes.

The Hopis have so far reacted to these problems and temptations like Hopis, that is to say, not out of mere blind habit (though

habit is behind this way of thinking) but from reasoned and deliberate choice. They have decided that it is better to accept the
physical hardships to which they are used rather than give up
the satisfactions that go with them. It is better, they feel, to
climb the mesa wall with heavy jars of water strapped to their
backs, to grow the corn in the ancient Hopi way, and to grind
it by hand on the metates, than to sacrifice the ceremonies and
traditions that give this heavy labor its meaning and are its
ample reward. They feel they do not have to chase after happiness and success along new ways, since they are already happy
and successful. They are, and want to remain, in balance with
the world about them.

HOPI

INDEX

Aeta, 33
agriculture, 34–35, 182–83, 197, 213,
    215–19, 223, 240–46
Americanization, of Indians, 239–40,
    243
Andaman Islanders, 33
angakoks, 69, 101, 112–13, 119, 121
Apaches, 234, 240
archaeology, 215, 218, 226–28
Arctic, 21, 65–67
art, 167–81, 258–59, 261–62, 272–73,
    291
Aztecs, 108, 214–15, 228

babies, 119–21, 124, 219, 274–76
Baffin Land, 100, 103–104, 106–107
bamboo, 41–46, 54, 174
bark cloth, 54–55, 139, 177–78, 205
Basket Makers, 215–21, 228, 233
basketry, 41, 46–47, 54, 177–78, 189,
    215, 246, 289–91
Bean Dance, Hopi, 264
beans, 219, 233, 245, 263, 288
bird hunting, *see* fowling
birdskins, 83, 179
birth rites, 273–75, 282
Black Mesa, 228–29, 232, 240–41, 251,
    285, 291
blowpipes, poison, 33, 44–45, 56
blubber, 77, 85, 95–96, 110, 115, 122
bow drill, 78, 85, 87
bows and arrows, 43–44, 56, 104–105,
    122, 156, 219–20, 265
bride capture, 118–19, 201
bride purchase, 50
Buffalo Dance, Hopi, 271
burial customs, 106–107, 216, 282–84
burros, 234, 243, 246
bush knives, 30, 42, 50
Butterfly Dance, Hopi, 271–72

caches, Eskimo, 92–93
cannibalism, 109, 153, 158, 165–66, 205

caribou, 103–106, 116, 122, 125
carving, 121, 161, 169–77, 197
caste, 142–43, 148–49, 150–51, 177
Chaco Canyon, 223–24
Chatham Islands, 136–37
Chenoi, 57–58
chiefs, Maori, 141–49, 153–54, 157–59,
    163–67, 170–79, 181 (*see also* priest-
    chiefs, Hopi)
childhood, 49, 83–84, 118–24, 178, 193–
    196, 265, 270–71, 275–78
chivalry, 152–54, 156–59, 163–65, 206
Cibola, Seven Cities of, 214, 229
clan mothers, 248–50, 252–53, 280, 282–
    283
clans, 222, 247–54, 274, 276, 278, 283
Cliff Dwellers, 221–25
clothing, 54–56, 60, 80–84, 122, 157,
    178–79, 215, 230, 292
coal, 291, 297
Colorado Plateau, 211–13, 222
Colorado River, 211–12, 228, 247
Columbus, Christopher, 102–103
Comanches, 234
combs, magic, 55–57
Continental Divide, 211–12
Cook, Captain James, 147, 161, 204–
    205
cooking, 52–54, 78, 115–17, 122, 175,
    186, 189–91, 286–90
corn, 216–19, 233, 240–46, 261, 264,
    266–67, 288–89
corn-meal offerings, 252, 261–62, 266–
    268, 270, 275, 277–81, 284, 286–87,
    291
Coronado, Francisco Vásquez de, 214–
    215, 225–26, 229
Cortez, Hernando, 104, 108
cotton, 215, 219–20
cradleboards, 219, 275–76
culture heroes, 107–108
cultures, 14–16, 19, 140, 170, 204–207,
    213–14, 226, 233–34

damar resin, 41–42, 52
dances, 60, 117, 155–56, 168, 177, 191, 196, 257–73, 296
David, King, 257, 272
democracy, 238, 255
digging sticks, 46, 182, 243–44, 289
dogs, 71, 77, 88, 91, 94–100, 109–10, 115, 118, 121, 139
dolls, 122, 265
Douglass, Andrew, 227
durians, 48–49, 57, 59
dyes, 176, 247, 291

eagles, 247, 255, 260–61, 294
ear ornaments, 179
Easter Island, 130–31, 133
education, 118, 121–23, 168–69, 192–200, 277–78
Egypt, 216, 240
eiderdown, 83, 92
El Paso, Texas, 214, 232
Erik the Red, 132
Eskimos, 21, 67ff., 165, 235

fear, 110–11, 146
feasts, 151, 177, 186–92, 194, 279, 281–282, 293
featherwork, 178–79
fern-tree root, 137, 139, 149, 182–83
fetishes, 252–53
firearms, 205–206
fire making, 52, 78, 87, 271
fireplaces, 287–89
firewater, 205–206, 296
fishing, 46, 184
fish spears, 46, 106
flax, 139, 177–78, 184
Fleet, the, 137–38, 144, 152, 160, 204–205, 207
Flute Dance, Hopi, 270
food sharing, 49, 93–94, 116, 122
food taboos, 47, 58, 105, 112, 116, 119, 122, 142, 146, 149–50, 157, 165–66, 174, 185, 198
foot races, 261, 264, 294–95
footwear, 83, 178, 215, 230, 282
forts, 139, 160–65, 220–21
fowling, 44, 46, 92, 106, 122, 124, 140, 184–86
foxskins, 83, 99
Frobisher, Martin, 67, 80, 97
frostbite, 82, 120

games, 117, 120–22, 177, 294–95
gifts, 50, 188, 281–82

Gila River, 222
glaciers, 103, 105, 109–10
gods, 56–58, 112–13, 134, 141, 168, 170, 174, 197, 251, 255, 260 (see also kachinas)
government, 38, 58, 111–12, 140, 142–145, 147, 150–51, 237–38, 250–51, 254, 257, 297
Grand Canyon, 211–12
Great Drought, 224, 227, 232
Great Spirit, 255
Greenland, 67ff., 134
Greenland Icecap, 72
Greenstone, 134, 156, 179

harpoons, 85–86, 88–90, 107, 121
harvesting, 183, 244, 270
Havasupai, 247
Hawaii, 130–31, 133, 138
headdresses, 55–56, 60, 82, 178–79, 230, 279–80
head flattening, 219, 276
Hiawatha, 108
Home Festival, Hopi, 243, 267–68, 282
Hopi way, 214, 226, 228–40, 242, 252, 273–84
horses, 234
hospitality, 115–18, 187–92, 194, 248, 266–67
Hotevila, 239, 243
houses, 51–54, 139, 167, 174–77 (see also igloos, pueblos)
huia bird, 179
hunting, 35, 40, 42–46, 49, 71, 80–81, 84–94, 104–107, 110–11, 122, 125, 217, 219, 233, 246, 255, 294

igloos, 73–80, 106, 124–25
Indonesia, 28–29, 130–31
initiation ceremonies, 199–200, 271, 276–80
Innuit, 67, 235 (see also Eskimos)
Io, 134
ipoh, poison, 43–45, 48
iron, 41–42, 52, 182, 205–206, 233
irrigation, 245–46

Java, 28
joking relatives, 275, 281

kachinas, 248, 267, 261–68, 277–78, 282–84
Karei, 56–59
kauri pines, 174

kayaks, 100, 103, 106–107, 122–24
kingship, 140–41, 144
kinship bands, Semang, 35–40
kivas, 220–21, 223–25, 252–54, 258, 260–71, 277, 280, 291–93
kiwis, 139, 179, 184
Kridlarssuark, 100–109
Kupe, 134–36, 138, 204

lamps, Eskimo, 77–79, 110
langsat tree, 43
Little Colorado River, 212, 224

magic, 101, 113, 264, 280, 286, 294 (*see also* witchcraft)
Malaya, 29–33
Malays, 32–33, 42, 45, 48, 54, 59
mana, 141–51, 154, 157, 164, 166–67, 181, 193, 197, 206–207, 236
mangosteens, 48, 57
Maoris, 129*ff.*, 236
marae, 177, 191, 194
Marquesas, 131, 133
marriage, 49–51, 118–19, 150, 165, 200–203, 271, 280–82, 292
Maui, 174
maupok, 88–89, 105
medicine, 55–57, 168, 252–53, 268
medicine men, 58 (*see also* angakoks; priests)
meeting houses, Maori, 175–77, 194, 197, 202
Melanesians, 130–31, 136
mere (Maori war club), 134, 154, 156–158, 179
mesas, 212, 221
Mesa Verde, 224
metates, 286
Mexican Revolution, 233
Mexico, 214–15, 217–18
Micronesia, 130–31
midnight sun, 123
Mikado, 148
missionaries, 214, 229–33, 246
moas, 139–40, 184
moko, 181
Moriori, 137, 152
mother-in-law taboo, 50, 56, 142
muru, 150–51, 202
music, 60–61, 117, 167–68, 270
myths, 57–59, 107–108, 117, 134, 140, 194, 197–98, 251–52, 268

Nanook, 82, 90–91
Navahos, 232, 234, 291

navigation, 132
Negritos, 33
New Zealand, discovery of, 131, 133–40, 147, 203–207
Ngatokorua, Chief, 158–59
nomads, 35–38, 51, 75, 124, 215, 228, 251
nose flutes, 60

Oceania, 130–31
old age, 38, 185, 194, 282–83
Oqé, 103
Oraibi, 228, 239
oratory, 154, 157, 167–69, 194
orchards, 233, 246
outriggers, 132, 170

Pacific Ocean, 129–31
Painted Desert, 212
Papagos, 247
Papaku, Chief, 201
parkas, 82
parrots, 179, 184
pas, 161–65
Peary, Commodore Robert E., 72, 108
Petrified Forest, 213
pigeons, 179, 185
piki, 258, 265, 281, 286, 288, 291
piñon, 213, 246
Ple, 57–58
poisons, 43–47, 55
polar bears, 82, 90–91, 105, 116, 118, 125
Polynesia, 130–33, 137
pottery, 219–20, 289–91
Powamu ceremony, Hopi, 263–66, 277–278, 280
prayer, 253, 256–61, 264
prayer sticks, 260–62, 266, 270–71, 284, 295
prestige, 140–41, 143, 153–54, 164, 167, 176, 188, 206, 236
priest-chiefs, Hopi, 237–38, 250–53, 259–60, 263–64, 267, 270, 283, 285, 293
priests, Maori, 148–49, 156, 158, 167–174, 185–86, 198–200
primogeniture, 143
property, 49, 93, 145, 165, 186, 242, 246, 249–50
Pueblo culture, ancient, 214–28
pueblo homes, 214–15, 219–22, 250, 285–89, 293
Pueblo Rebellion, 232
pukatea wood, 176

rabbit hunt, 255, 294
races, human, 13, 70
rafts, 46
rain forests, 27ff.
rangatira, 143–44, 149–50, 168, 201
rank, *see* caste
Rarotonga, 134–36
rats, 184
religions, *see* gods; myths; priests; rituals; spirit world
religious societies, Hopi, 251–55, 257–273, 277, 280
Rio Grande, 211, 222, 224–25, 231, 240, 247, 292
rituals, 149, 174, 186, 189, 197–98, 252–254, 256–73, 274–84, 296
Rocky Mountains, 212
Rongo, 168, 197
Ross, Captain John, 67–69, 73, 75, 80, 104

Sacheuse, 67–70
sacrifice, human, 156, 161, 170, 181
Sakai, 33, 44
Samoa, 131, 133, 167
sand paintings, 261, 263, 268, 271, 293
sandstorms, 212
San Francisco Mountains, 251, 263, 266–67
San Juan River, 212, 223–24, 227, 232, 240
Santa Fe, 228
schools, 133, 193, 196–200, 236–37, 239
sea ice, 73, 83, 99, 101, 105, 123
seals, 71, 85, 88–89, 105–106, 110, 112, 116, 122, 124
sealskin, 77–78, 82–83, 85, 107, 110
Sedna, 112–13
Semang, 27ff.
sewing, 81–82
shamans, *see angakoks;* medicine men
sheepherding, 233, 246
shipbuilding, 131–32, 138–39, 169–74
Shungopovi, 239, 252
sieges, 163–65
Simei, 57
Sipapu, 251, 260, 273, 283, 293
slaves, 144, 146, 150, 156, 159, 161, 166, 171, 182, 231
sledges, Eskimo, 69, 94–100, 121–22, 125
Smith Sound, 67, 70, 72
Snake Dance, Hopi, 252–53, 268–70
snowbeaters, 84

snow goggles, 89–90
snow houses, 75–77, 79, 122
snow knives, 76
solstice, 259–60, 262
songs, 60–61, 117, 119, 194, 272, 287, 292, 294
Soyala ceremony, Hopi, 259–63, 271
Spider Woman, 251
spirit world, 56–59, 69, 101, 103, 107–108, 111–13, 117, 119–20, 205, 217, 229, 251–52, 260, 268, 273–74, 283–284
sports, 195–96, 294
springs, sacred, 241–42, 246, 261–62, 266, 270
squash, 245, 288
stampedes, 105
Stone Age, 40–42
Sun, Father, 251, 259, 262, 275, 281
sweet potatoes, 133, 138–39, 182–83, 190–91
swimming, 195–96

table manners, 194, 286
taboos, 56–58 (*see also* food taboos; *tapu*)
Tahiti, 131–32, 134–37, 139, 152, 169, 204
Tane, 168, 170
Tangaroa, 168, 174
tapu, 142, 145–50, 156, 159, 165, 167, 174, 179, 181, 183–84, 186, 197–98, 200, 202
taro, 138–39
Tasman, Abel Janszoon, 203–204
tattooing, 55, 179–81, 197
throwing sticks, 231, 289, 294
tiponi, 252–53
tobacco, 42, 246, 261, 267
tohungas, 167–81, 193, 196–97, 207
Toi, 135–38, 204
Toltecs, 215, 218
toys, 121
trade, 39, 41–42, 230, 247
traps, 45–46, 54, 92, 124
tree climbing, 48
tree rings, 227
Tu, 168, 197
tupik (Eskimo skin tent), 75, 80, 92, 124–25
turkeys, 215, 219–20
Tusayan, 231
Tutamure, Chief, 187–83

Uerata, Chief, 164

upas tree, 43–45, 54–55
Utes, 221, 228, 232, 234
Utok, 88–89

ventilation, 74, 79–80

walruses, 71, 90, 105–107, 112, 116, 122–24, 133
war canoes, 170–74
warfare, 39, 139–40, 146, 151–66, 182, 195–98, 205–206, 217–18
weaving, 167, 178, 219–20, 234, 281–82, 291–92
Whakauruanga, Te, 159
whales, 71, 90, 103, 115
Whatonga, 135–36, 138

Whegu, Chief, 157
whips, Eskimo, 98, 110, 121–22
witchcraft, 171, 175, 189, 194, 198–200, 205, 236, 252, 256–57
women's work, 46, 52–54, 78, 81, 92, 106, 118–19, 121, 156, 166, 183, 186, 217, 270–71, 286–91, 293
wool, 233, 292
work parties, 237, 244, 246, 293
Wuwuchim ceremony, Hopi, 271, 280, 284

yams, 46–47, 139
yucca, 213, 246–47, 274, 277, 288, 291

Zuñi, 224, 229, 232, 247

Mason

each everybody 183
yar common land

musey hymn? 93
bryp bear club — grant cana
pubs — shellfish reave

Pueblo
men farm
13-7/100 flourigants
all our land
bees cattle sheep India 046
nat clan 248
nat local
non own
relig around 250
leg — rites each d
00 given land

prayer — dance if part 257
dance of life 258 — concentrate on
257 kachinas health
rain